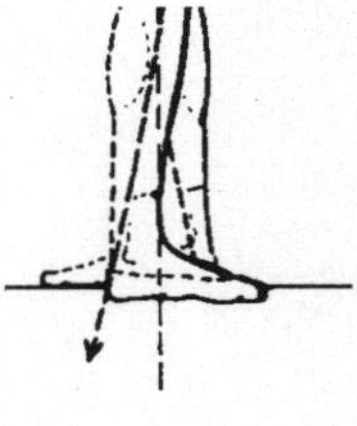

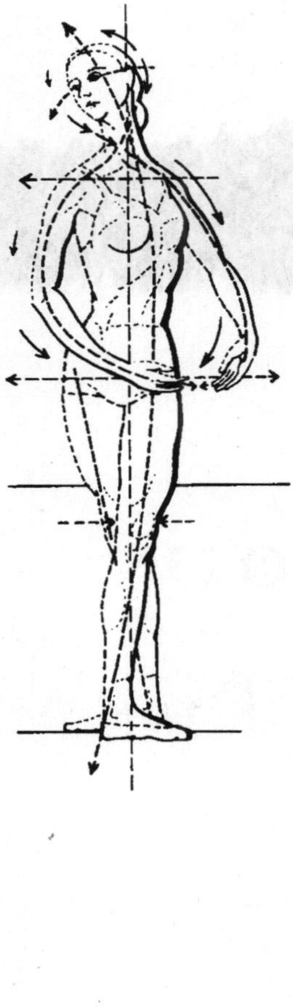

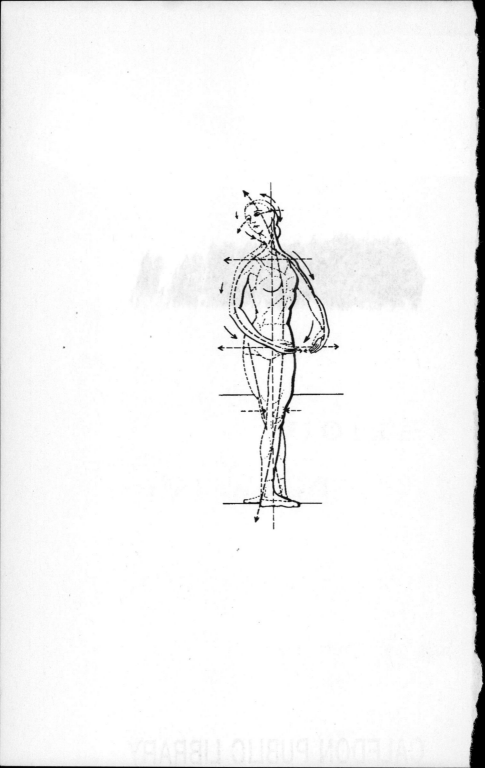

MARTHA SCHABAS

a Novel

VARIOUS POSITIONS

DOUBLEDAY CANADA

Library and Archives of Canada Cataloguing in Publication is available upon request

ISBN: 978-0-385-66876-7

This book is a work of fiction. Names, characters, places and incidents are products of the author's imagination or are used fictitiously. Any resemblance to actual events or locales or persons, living or dead, is entirely coincidental.

Book design: CS Richardson
Printed and bound in the USA

Published in Canada by Doubleday Canada,
a division of Random House of Canada Limited

Visit Random House of Canada Limited's website: www.randomhouse.ca

10 9 8 7 6 5 4 3 2 1

To my parents.

I STAND STILL AND PRETEND to be innocent. I allow my mouth to hang in a disbelieving O. I squeeze a hand into my pocket and find a jean stud with my thumb, push the nub of metal into my hip bone. The wind has whisked tears to the corners of my eyes, and the school blurs behind them until I blink. Everything is bright and sharp before it's ordinary again. I imagine I look ordinary too, just another body amidst the crowd that's gathering. But there's a thickness in my throat; it cinches as I swallow, and if someone spoke to me directly, I'm not sure I could make a sound.

Sixty looks over her shoulder at me. She's a few steps ahead and she's made fists inside her gloves. When she reaches for my hand, I'm grazed by empty fingers. She comes closer and drapes the bulk of herself on my back, rubs her head into my arm like a cat. Her dark hair falls in her eyes and she doesn't fix it. She gives me too much weight, the weight of real sadness, then shakes her head and sighs.

"This is crazy." Her lips stay near my ear.

"I know," I say.

We stare ahead together. A group of junior girls have clustered beneath the sign, and their heads dip down and up as they steer their bodies around it. Some wear winter hats but others have bare heads, and my eyes hook the pink crescent of a small girl's ear. I feel a twist of empathy for this bit of freezing flesh. With the studio entrance locked, it's unclear where we should go.

Something has distracted Sixty. She relieves me of her weight, her attention shifting sideways, and I trace the impulse of her movement to a couple of girls by the main steps. A winter sun bleaches their features, slings white light between the columns of the portico behind them. I can't make out their faces, but Sixty's perspective must have less glare. As she moves away, the panic rises.

"I have to tell you something."

She stops. The incline of her head asks its own gentle question. I let a big breath fill my ribs. But just as I feel the first word find its shape, the impossibility of saying it hits me harder.

"What?" she whispers.

The words are gone now, as though scattered by my pulse. The moment comes back to me in pieces—the shadow of his nose next to my nose, the grainy darkness of his cheek. I can feel the memory quiver down my legs, my underwear rolling to my knees, catching my ankles in a coil of nylon. And then I flick my underwear at him. I send it straight into his lap.

"Georgia?"

I just shake my head, as though I've miscalculated my thoughts, and send Sixty with my hand towards the other girls. She hesitates, but a steeliness on my face must convince her there's no point. I watch the swing of her arms as she walks away and wonder how I'll ever explain to anyone what I've done.

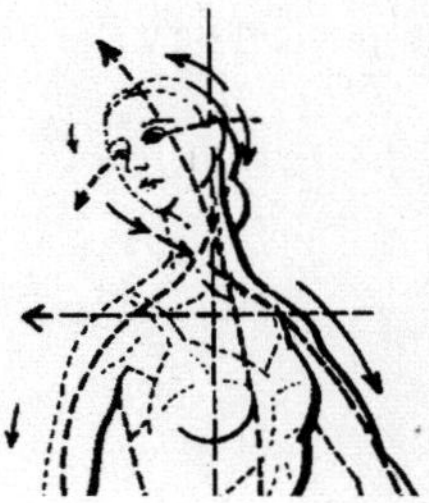

PART I

ONE.

I FOUND THE ENVELOPE IN a pile of letters on the hallway radiator. It was white, flat, ordinary as any envelope except for the strange look of my name across the front. I wasn't used to getting mail. There was a logo in the corner, the curving, antique script of the Royal Toronto Ballet Academy. I took the envelope up to my room. My fingers were stupid with adrenalin, and as I ripped off the top, I tore the letter too. I read the time and date of my audition aloud and recorded the information on the Gelsey Kirkland calendar above my desk, filling the March 27 box with tiny handwriting.

I observed what I'd written as though I didn't trust it, staring, squinting, trying to look at the ink askance. I muttered patchy sounds under my breath, little words like *yes* and *good*. March 27 needed to be distinguished from its meaningless neighbours, so I drew a green border around the date and added jagged diagonal strokes that tied like a knot in the middle of the square. I stepped backward, examined my work. It all looked a bit like the kind of flammability warning you'd find on a hairspray bottle. I worried this was a bad omen. Symbols of explosions might not lend themselves naturally to good luck. But maybe it could be a kind of reverse jinx, like whispering *merde* before going on stage, or grabbing your partner in the wings and screaming "Go to hell!" beneath the opening chords of the overture. That's what they did in Russia.

Above the March grid of the calendar was a black-and-white photo of Gelsey in rehearsal. She was standing with her back against a studio barre and bending at the waist to fiddle with the ribbon of her pointe shoe. Her oversized leg warmers crawled up to the middle of her thighs and she wore a leotard that reflected light like tinfoil. The material pinched at her chest in the shape of a tiny accordion. On either side of this accordion there should have been boobs, but there were no boobs; there was virtually nothing at all. Ha! It was a laugh in the face of everything.

I had been watching Gelsey on the Arts & Entertainment Network since my mom ordered specialty cable three months before. I had seen her in five different ballets and I loved her.

She didn't look wet and brainless like some other ballerinas, dancing across the stage as if they were lost in heavy fog. She attacked her steps as though she had something against them, pouncing ferociously from one to the next. These pounces were punctuated every few minutes by close-ups of Gelsey yearning into the camera. Sometimes her pale face would take up the entire frame and just hang there in a look of incurable distraction. Pain hammered deep around her crystalline eyes. A tenderness pillowed her lips. It was a beauty I had never seen before, too extreme for human beings. Somewhere along her vacuumed cheeks, inside the pout of her ruby mouth, Gelsey became less girl and more creature, so feminine she cancelled herself out.

I folded the letter back into the envelope and sat down on my desk chair. I would e-mail Isabel and tell her about my audition. I turned on my computer and waited for my e-mail account to load new messages. I had a separate folder for Isabel that I'd labelled SISTER. This wasn't really necessary, considering she was the only one who ever e-mailed me. The file name also wasn't technically accurate. But Isabel had told me it was tacky to always call her my half-sister in front of other people, and I wanted to make up for the mistake. I imagined scenarios where Isabel would happen to see the title of the e-mail folder. She'd be home at Christmas and we'd be hanging out in my room. She'd be telling me about the stuff she usually tells me about, her most recent semester at university, about after-dark activities and theories on gender and meaning. At some point I'd have to get up to pee.

Alone in my room, she'd glance at my computer screen, see the only folder in my e-mail account and smile to herself. When I came back into the room she'd poke me in the ribs and tell me how grown up I seemed.

My inbox loaded zero new messages. I clicked on the SISTER folder and scrolled through old messages instead. Isabel always filled in the subject lines, titling her e-mails things like "W'sup" and "Hola Infanta" and "Georgia on My Mind." I clicked on one e-mail with the subject line "Gelsey." It was from a few months ago, soon after I'd told her about my new idol. Isabel had written that she was "skeptical of a society so predicated on celebrity-worship." I had typed "predicated" into www.dictionary.com and written back that I wasn't trying to "derive, base, found, proclaim, assert, declare or affirm anything." Isabel hadn't been convinced. She'd done a little Googling and had written back that Gelsey was a cokehead who'd dated Pat Sajak in the eighties, and that her lips had been injected with an amount of collagen that Health Canada considered "unadvisable." When I hadn't believed her, she'd sent me *Dancing on My Grave*, Gelsey's tell-all autobiography, via priority post.

I looked at the bookshelf across my room. I could pick out the spine immediately, the font reflective like a speed sign on the highway, the rose wilting onto the word *Grave*. The spine looked worn, even from a distance, with a deep wrinkle scarred through its middle. I had read the book three times now and knew the quotations on the back cover by heart: "the dark side of fame," "a descent into drugs and madness," "a tortured quest for perfection." I loved Gelsey more with every read. Not only was she the most wonderful ballerina the world had ever seen, but she had suffered something horrifying and her face was brimming with poisonous chemicals.

Isabel had been e-mailing me approximately twice a week since she'd moved downtown for university. She lived in a three-storey house with six other girls, one working shower and no TV. Every time I visited I felt cold inside my kneecaps and smelled old beer and Pantene Pro-V. Still, I loved visiting her. My dad had only been once, and he called the house Moldova. *How are things in Moldova?* he'd ask when Isabel came home for dinner and he wasn't at the hospital. *Have you girls managed to get a land line yet?* Isabel's mouth would fatten into a smirk. *Moldova isn't so bad anyway*, she'd say. *It has a thriving viticulture industry. It's the crossroads of Latin and Slavic worlds.* My dad would lift his hands on either side of his body, palms facing Isabel as if she were a bandit with a gun. I would stand absolutely still, do my best to embody neutrality so that no one could accuse me of picking sides.

Right before she'd left for university, Isabel had taken me to the park for a talk. We sat on the swings and I followed her lead, digging my heels into the gravel beneath us, engraving hearts and then wiping them clean with my soles. The kid swinging next to me was pumping his legs hard, trying to propel his body towards rooftops, but Isabel was unmoving, so I would be too. I watched a tiny bulge in the middle of her neck and then another, as though she were swallowing her thoughts.

Half an hour went by and she still hadn't done any talking. Pins and needles fried the underside of my thighs. Finally she looked at me. The greyness of her eyes had deepened. They were the colour of the sidewalk after a thunderstorm.

"Things might be difficult when I leave, George. You'll have to be extra grown up."

"Sure."

"Just—" She paused, stabbed the rubber toe of her sneaker into the middle of a dusty heart so that a cloud of sand wafted up her ankle. "I know it's difficult when Dad's always—" She cut herself off and looked at the sky. "Just don't let it get to you. They're adults and it's not your problem. And call me if you need anything. Like anytime, whenever."

I nodded slowly, trying to put lots of meaning into it because I knew that's what she wanted to see. Isabel generally talked about my mom that way, ran circles around the problem without ever stopping to look it in the face. In her last year of high school, Isabel had stayed with us less and less, and this had distorted her perception of what was happening between my parents. Isabel never saw my mom's tiny provocations, the way she would stare out the window and announce the strangest things out of nowhere—that she missed smoking cigarettes in her old Ford Cortina, that she was curious about neo-punk. One time after dinner, I passed my mom the lasagna dish and she said she'd rather ram her head into the kitchen sink than wash it. Another time, when there was a segment on the radio about the fruit bat, she stepped out into the backyard and started to cry.

I swiped my finger on the trackpad to wake up the computer screen. I clicked on the Compose button and typed Isabel's e-mail into the address bar. I told her about my letter and asked how things were going at Moldova. I paused over the subject line. Then I brought my fingers back to the keyboard and typed *My Audition*. I sat back in my chair and looked at the title. I deleted *Audition* and wrote *Career*.

My parents weren't speaking at breakfast the next morning. Non-speaking mornings were identifiable by whether my mom got up to kiss me when I stepped into the kitchen, and she did today, bringing her hand to skate down the back of my hair, sighing as though there was something sad about the gesture. She had that cool look around her mouth too, a tightness that paralyzed the corners of her lips. She turned away and traced an unnecessarily wide semicircle to retake her place at the table, fiddling with the pearl at her collarbone. My dad sat perpendicular to her, hunched over a newspaper and a bowl of Cheerios. He shovelled the cereal into his mouth, slurping milk through all the tiny holes of oat on his tongue.

"There are English muffins." My mom's eyes were full of feeling. "In the fridge."

I'd planned on telling them about my audition, but a non-speaking morning made it impossible. I should have seen it coming. My dad had worked late every night that week and had been on-call most of the previous weekend. I pulled open the fridge door, smelled chilled plastic and immobile air, took the Baggie of muffins from the shelf. I tore my muffin along its pre-cut seams, slid both halves into the toaster. My mom's fingers fluttered from her coffee mug to her hair, played quick-fire scales on the table. She wanted my dad's attention but there was no way she would get it. My dad's mind was travelling inward, incubating new thoughts. When his practice was busy, he achieved heights of concentration of which few other doctors were capable. It's what made him the best in his field. Now he thumbed the corner of his paper, flipped the page without looking up. I could see just enough of his forehead to observe the process, one heavy wrinkle like an equator around his brain. I wished my mom would understand.

I took my muffin to the table. My mom wrenched her chair forward, made the linoleum squeak. I wouldn't meet her eyes. I feared the look they would have in that moment, tragic and on the brink of something I couldn't describe, a thousand times darker than tears. I needed to distract her.

"Could you pass the butter?"

She slid the dish towards me, got up to get a knife. Now I would stay calm because calmness was contagious. Then time would run its course. My dad's schedule would ease up by the end of the week. He'd come home with flowers or a bottle of wine, and things would go back to normal.

"Do you want jam?"

I shook my head. My mom walked over to the counter and poured what remained of the filter coffee into a travel mug. She twisted the lid on with a snap. Again her eyes jogged towards my dad. I wished she would watch me and learn. The trick was to hope for his attention silently, will it in a steady, invisible way.

When I was younger and there'd been no one to look after me, my dad sometimes took me to the hospital with him. He'd leave me in the nursing station, a see-through cubicle that bubbled onto the hallway, and tell me to wait. A nurse would usually give me some paper and whatever coloured pens she could dig up, but colouring was the last thing I wanted to do. The nursing station was beside the elevators, so I could see everyone come and go. I planted my elbows in front of me, bones sharp on the desk, made a hammock for my chin. I focused on the people in regular clothing. If they turned right, they were heading towards the neurology wing. If they turned left, they were my dad's patients. I tried to deduce who was who in the few moments before they turned. I searched their faces for signs of craziness. It wasn't obvious the way you'd expect. The ones with the strangest ailments, tremors that hijacked their hands, bandages choking their heads, usually turned towards the neurology clinic. The crazy ones looked normal. I remembered tired women in clothes that didn't fit quite right, not always the wrong size but somehow the wrong idea, a sweater that must have itched, a bag that dug marks in a shoulder. If these people seemed anything, I would call it pensive, or maybe just a little distracted. Most of the time they were girls.

I would watch them again on their way out of my dad's office, study their expressions for improvement. I was sure

I saw ease across eyebrows, as though a bad thought had been removed. This was my dad's accomplishment. Darkness captured his interest, things that grew mouldy in shadows. Loudness, flashiness, the prime time girlie stuff he rolled his eyes at—all that he couldn't stand. In the car ride home I would stare flatly through the windshield, let my eyes find the deadness of a patient's. I tried to evoke my own hospital feeling, the sad chime of the elevator, the bigness of life and death. If I concentrated enough, the feeling would emanate from every feature on my face and my dad would notice it, see a heaviness he understood.

"I'm off." My mom had her travel mug in one hand and her laptop case in the other. She had three kisses for me, forehead, cheek and cheek. Her hair swung towards me and the pearl did too, an opaque teardrop knocking the cleft of my chin. "Have a good day, sweetheart." One last glance shot towards my dad before she turned to leave the kitchen.

I left my dad at the table without a word so that I wouldn't disturb him the way my mom had. I brushed my teeth slowly in the upstairs bathroom, trying not to look in the mirror. I knew what kind of day it was and I didn't want my reflection to confirm this. But a mean urge wormed up the back of my neck. I lifted my head and squinted at the little person squinting back at me. It was a small day. I had them every couple of months, and they crept up without warning or explanation. It was hard to pinpoint the exact place where I seemed to shrink, but it was there, somewhere, like an invisible weather front pushing in from all sides. I placed my hands on either side of the medicine cabinet and leaned in towards the pale blob of my face. Yesterday it had been normal. Now it was unreasonable in its compactness, as if every feature had slipped a millimetre inward overnight.

I walked to school and stared at the traffic. It was cold and my breath made clouds in front of my nose. The street had been plowed about two hours earlier, before the city got out of bed, but I knew snowplows often missed black ice. I looked for older cars, the ones that wouldn't have anti-lock brakes. They were easy to pick out because they were painted dull colours that nobody liked anymore and had long, flat hoods that made me think of alligator snouts. I watched their rear tires and waited for the moment that they'd hit a dark patch of invisible ice. The brakes would lock, the wheels would spin and the car would swing onto the sidewalk and give me a concussion.

I got to school and walked along the parking lot to the first outdoor classroom, trying to crush the maximum number of salt crystals beneath my boots. The school was being renovated that winter and our classes had been transferred to a row of newly delivered portables. They were white rectangles, big metal shoeboxes that extended all the way to the school's back fence. I walked up the steps of the first one, the grade-eight math portable, kicking my boots on the final ledge to knock off snow and pebbles. The lighting was fluorescent, and I breathed in the familiar smell of something plastic and squeezable, a bit like a rubber duck. I took my usual desk in the middle and muttered hello to the kids around me.

I pulled my binder out of my knapsack and listened to their conversation. They were talking about a party they'd been to over the weekend. Julie Chang's party. I hadn't been invited, but that was okay because I would have had to miss a ballet class to go. They were discussing Chicken, the game where male hands wandered up female bodies until the owner of the body decided she'd had enough. I had never played Chicken before; the idea made my stomach feel like it was rotting. Everyone would be watching. I looked down at the small bumps that barely lifted my sweater. Inadequacy slithered up from my groin.

The lesson began and my eyes drifted from the blackboard to the window. It was snowing now; fat white flakes disappeared into the mud of the soccer field. What would I do if I were forced into a Chicken situation? What I needed was a plan. I sucked in my stomach so that my ribs puffed out. I sucked in even harder until it hurt. It would be a tricky position to maintain for more than five minutes, but it made my chest inflate with a buoyancy that might be mistaken for boobs. It did more than that too, taking me away from my body, lifting me out of the disgrace.

At four o'clock, I took the bus across Bayview Avenue towards the Wilson School of Ballet. The buildings shrank and lost their colour, becoming low concrete blocks on either side of the road. The final landmark was a church with grey bricks and a bulging chimney. You wouldn't know it was a church if it wasn't for the thousand pieces of broken gold glued to its far side in a big Jesus mosaic. The ballet school sat next to it, separated by a snowbank that, today, made the shape of a long, bumpy creature, maybe a humpback whale. I pulled open the door and walked into the foyer.

A group of older girls were stretching on my left. I loved the older girls, especially the ones with long hair. A few of them were going to make it as professionals, that's what all the parents said. I looked at their legs, long and muscled on the floor. I wanted to wrap my hands around them. A red-haired girl called out my name and waved. Her name was Emily and she liked me. Once, when I was leaving the studio, she'd tapped me on the shoulder. I felt her slender fingers on my bare skin. "You're soooo skinny," she said sweetly. Her friends agreed too. They shook their heads and smiled reprovingly. "Do you eat anything?" a second girl asked me. "She's so cute," a third one said. Another time, I found a chocolate bar taped to my locker. A Post-it Note was stuck to the wrapper. *Eat up!* it advised in permanent marker. *You need it.*

I waved back at Emily. A smile was wriggling up inside me, but I stopped it with my lip muscles so that I wouldn't look dumb. I went down the hallway to the change room. I pulled on my tights and leotard along with the other junior girls and coiled my hair into a bun. Then I walked towards the studio. As I approached the two steps of its entrance, Mrs. Kafarova glided into the doorway. She crossed her arms over her spandex bodysuit and peered at me beneath two turquoise eyelids.

"You hev your letter?" Mrs. Kafarova frowned. She normally frowned as she spoke, as if language itself was distasteful to her.

I nodded and told her the time and date of my audition. Her frown deepened. Auditioning for the Royal Toronto Ballet Academy had been her idea. She'd pulled me into her office a few weeks ago and stared at me menacingly from her swivel chair.

"Georgia, it iz time you were in proper akedemy."

I looked up at the posters on her wall. They were from the Soviet Union, and the images looked smeared, blue backgrounds that bled into the dancers as if the paper had been held under water.

"Yes, of course my school iz very good." She closed her eyes for a second, bowed her head, as though accepting applause for her school. "But you will hev future. And to hev riel future, you must hev riel training. Many hours, every day. And then every day, many hours, all again. Yes?"

I nodded solemnly. I knew I was experiencing the kind of moment that people talked about, one I'd remember for the rest of my life.

Now I stepped into the studio towards her. Mrs. Kafarova grabbed my arm and squeezed. She wore enough rings to handicap an average hand and they pushed against the underside of my wrist.

"You must hev good picture for zhe application. You must hev your hair perfect. You must make your lips pink." She stared hard into my eyes. "Promise me you will hev your lips pink."

I promised her I would. I joined the other girls at the barre.

"Please!" Mrs. Kafarova commanded the pianist with one dictatorial foot stamp.

Class started slowly, the first piano chords soft, bendable, as we eased our muscles back into familiar tensions. In the wall-length mirror beside me I saw fifteen bodies moving in unison, charging the air with silent effort. The chronically uncomfortable person who possessed me in ordinary life let go of her spindly arms and Tinkertoy legs. A volt buzzed up my spine and I grew between each vertebra. My small day was officially over.

"Girls!" Mrs. Kafarova stopped the pianist with another foot stamp. "Enough." She dismissed us with the back of her hand, walked away from the barre. "You stretch. We do centre."

As we pulled our legs around our bodies on the floor, Mrs. Kafarova tidied herself in the mirror. She smoothed two hands on either side of the yellow hair that contoured her head like a travel pillow. She reapplied lipstick on her skinny leather lips. She adjusted the sash on her black teaching frock and turned sideways to examine her profile, nodding at what looked back at her. I imagined she saw herself not in this reflection, but in the framed forty-year-old photos that hung in the school's main hall. There, in black and white, a fire-eyed blonde in a sequined tutu soared across the stage of the Mariinsky Theatre. Two white legs scissored the air, her back arched onto a tilting, crescent foot.

My mom helped me fill out the application form over the weekend. We sat at the kitchen table, and she watched as I entered my height and weight into the spaces provided, moving the pen slowly to keep my writing neat. When it was time to take the required photo of me in *tendu à la seconde*, I asked if I could use her lipstick.

"It's a picture of your body, sweetheart. No one's going to be able to tell whether you're wearing lipstick or not."

I nodded as though this was sensible. Then I asked her again in a slightly more desperate tone. She laughed and sighed. She produced a black, shiny pouch that whined when I scratched my fingernails along it. I unzipped the top and rummaged through the plastic capsules.

"Lipstick?" My dad had stepped into the doorway. He was wearing a tie and his plastic ID badge; he had just come back from the hospital. "I thought we were in the business of raising a feminist."

My mom didn't look up. "It's stage makeup."

He moved behind us, peered over our shoulders. I wanted to cover the application with my hands. I knew what he thought of ballet. It was even worse than what he thought of lipstick.

"Oh. Your *ballet* school application." He moved around the table to the fridge, where he pulled out the Brita water pitcher, poured himself a glass. "Ballet," he repeated, shaking his head. "God knows how I ended up with a ballet dancer for a daughter."

I wanted to laugh at this with him, be a really good sport. It burned, though, the disappointment in his voice. The worst part was that I understood it. Things like ballet tripped on his heels, slowed the world down from more meaningful pursuits. He took a big sip of water. I wished I had some brilliant argument that drew on history and philosophy to explain why ballet was okay.

"There are musicians on Mom's side," I said.

My dad gulped back the rest of his water, ruffled my hair with his hand. "Didn't you want to become a doctor?"

My mom looked up at him now. "She can still become a doctor, Larry."

"What are the academics like at this ballet school?"

"Excellent." My mom smirked. "They're excellent."

"Really?" My dad opened the dishwasher and fitted his glass into the upper tray. "Well, great, then." He pushed on the dishwasher door and it snapped shut. He walked out of the room.

My mom sat very still. I waited for her to say something. Finally she pushed her chair back and left the room too. In a minute I could hear their voices in the living room. I pulled all the lipsticks out of the case and uncapped them. The tubes made a forest of iridescent trunks, plastic, titanium and mother-of-pearl. I twisted the bottoms one by one. My mom's voice was louder now, shrill even, but I was going to focus on the lipstick. They looked funny together, like a flock of reddish creatures poking out of their shells. I chose a bright pink one with a sharp summit and a clean slope down one side. In the hallway mirror I pressed it firmly into my mouth. It was satisfying, the pull of the waxy edge on the skin of my lips, the sudden invasion of fuchsia.

My parents were quiet now. It always went like this. Fights melted into their opposites, as though somehow the two were related, maybe even different ends of the same thing. I tiptoed into the alcove of the dining room. My parents were sitting in the taupe armchair. My dad's back was to me and my mom sat sideways on his lap. I could see her foot dangling off one armrest. Her grey sock had a hole at the heel, and she was moving slowly through her instep, keeping her toes flexed. Her head dangled off the other side of the chair, as if she were leaning back to laugh. But then she moved her face towards the back cushion, where it met my dad's in a kiss. I stepped a little to the right so I could see them better. The kiss continued, their faces moving around in flattened figure-eights. My dad's hands went to my mom's bum. She made a sound, moved in closer. I looked away because I couldn't watch this part, the way she slipped her anger into something silky and attractive, like she was putting on a lacy nightgown.

We took the photos of me about an hour later. I attached them with a paper clip to the top right corner of the form. I tested the paper clip's snugness, shook the pages vigorously with my fingers pinched over the metal edge, slid the clip on and off several times. I was almost satisfied. But then I worried that the tests themselves had compromised the clip's tightness. I considered using a stapler, but thought that might disqualify me, sort of like using the wrong kind of pencil on a Scantron test. So I pulled a fresh paper clip from the small cardboard box, hyper-extended each side with a quick tug, and fitted the deformed clip over the assembled form.

TWO.

The day before the audition, Phil Dwyer was having a party and invited everyone in the class. It was a parent-supervised deal in the afternoon, pop, chips, pepperoni pizzas, maybe a rented movie in a basement with the lights dimmed just enough. I didn't want to go. I wanted to assemble and conserve every available molecule of energy for the next day. But my mom said this was a bad idea. I was putting too much pressure on myself, and it'd be better to relax and have a good time. Otherwise the pressure might backfire.

I didn't want the pressure to backfire. I went to the party, stood in the basement in the jean jacket I'd worn underneath my parka, took a paper plate from the collapsible bridge table, piled my plate high with Doritos. I chewed them attentively to keep myself busy, taking one mouse-size bite at a time.

"What's your problem?" It was Kareem Talwar. He was leaning past me to grab the blimp-shaped bottle of 7UP. He unscrewed it and poured some into his plastic cup, which was already half-filled with Coke.

I looked at his T-shirt. *Enema of the State* was scrawled in drippy letters across his chest, the font trickling onto an image of a nurse fitting her hand into a plastic glove. He took a giant swig of his pop cocktail, wiped his mouth with the back of his wrist and beamed at me.

"Tear yourself away from the chips, G. Come join the real party." He cocked his head towards an open doorway that led to another room.

I followed him, holding tight to my plate of chips, watching his skinny brown arms wag with each step of his Converse All-Stars. We passed through the doorway. A clump of kids were gathered in a circle and we levelled ourselves side by side onto the only available patch of carpet, dividing the oblong plot between our two bums.

"It's just stupid," Hannah McAdorey was saying, a hand flung on her hip. "I mean, it's not that I mind going again or anything, but isn't the whole point that different people get picked?"

"It's Spin the Bottle, reject," Phil Dwyer laughed. "The whole point is that the bottle does the picking."

"Yeah," Kareem said. "It's not a free-for-all or anything. It's not like . . . pick your tit."

There was a chorus of appreciation for this, not quite laughter but breathy chuckles. I turned towards Kareem. My face flushed with betrayal. I looked at the centre of the circle and saw a dented can of Dr. Pepper. I had to get out. I put my hand down on the carpet beside me and started to lift my bum. What would be my excuse?

"Pick your tit." Phil snapped his fingers. "Good one."

"Except it's a can." Elinor Leung smirked. "Tradition's already been, like"—she paused, chewed prodigiously on her lower lip—"massacred."

"But it is kinda stupid that Hannah just went," Sara Lowe said.

"Elinor went twice at Robin's party," Phil objected.

"How about new players have to go first?"

The suggestion came from Hannah, and everyone was suddenly quiet, considering. My heart started to pound. What would happen if I left? Everyone would laugh for hours, talk about it for weeks at school. My stomach was liquid with fear. I burrowed my fingers under my thighs, rocked from one hand to the other.

"Spin it, Georgia." I turned my head to Hannah. She was holding out the stepped-on can and smiling a toothless smile. "Spin it," she repeated.

The dread was everywhere now, spiralling up from my middle. I scanned the circle quickly, hoping someone might object on my behalf. But faces were smooth and impatient.

"Umm, like today might be an idea," Elinor sneered.

I took the can, felt the ruptured aluminum spikes on either side, pressed the pad of my thumb into the sharpest edge. What could I do? The pressure of tears was thickening behind my eyes. I bit down hard, pushed molar into molar, felt the strain radiate into my jaw. I placed the can back on the carpet and spun it.

"Hey, hey." Philip was nodding hard and nudging Kareem. "Looks like you're the man."

The top of the Dr. Pepper can was facing the little patch of carpet that Kareem and I were sharing. I looked at him. His eyes simulated shock and he sucked a long inhale for the benefit of his audience. I swallowed hard, ordered myself not to cry.

Kareem moved towards the centre of the circle. I followed his cue, letting instinct lead me in an awful, brain-dead way. We sat down on either side of the can, folded our legs beneath us. Kareem looked hard into my eyes and didn't hesitate. He placed a hand on my jean pocket.

"Chicken?" He dropped his voice low into his chest.

Hate congealed in my stomach; it felt like a hardball I could whip at his head. In a demented second, I imagined his face shattering into a million shards, like a Christmas ornament cracking on a tiled floor.

"Nope," I said quietly.

There was murmuring from the audience. Kareem ducked his head closer. Red dust stuck beyond the contours of his lips. I could smell ketchup. He placed his hand under my jean jacket and flat across my lowest rib. I could feel its clamminess through my cotton shirt.

"Chicken?" he asked a little more softly.

Sweat gathered on the small of my back. The next hand would be boob territory. I looked around at the circuit of faces again, caught Hannah squinting in her satisfied way. I could imagine what was coming, Kareem's palm over my sports bra and how he'd be able to feel my nipple underneath. The shame made me dizzy.

"I think . . ." I stood up and wiped my hands on the sides of my jeans. "I think I actually have to go."

Elinor looked at Hannah and both of them burst out laughing.

"No, I do. I forgot that I have this . . . thing."

"*Thing?*" said Phil Dwyer.

"A family thing."

I told myself to turn around and just walk back into the other room, where I'd left my parka, but for some reason I kept standing there. Maybe I needed to see if they believed me. Hannah's lips were up against Elinor's ear, and Elinor nodded.

"You should really go," Hannah said.

I turned around, looking down at the carpet to make sure I didn't step on Kareem's hand.

"You shouldn't get involved in games like this if you're too immature," Hannah continued. "It'll screw you up emotionally."

"Too late for that!" Phil said.

Everyone laughed, but Hannah kept going. "No, seriously, though. Have you been to the doctor, Georgia? You should probably get checked out."

Something slapped my chest. I took a step back so that I wouldn't fall over.

"Nothing to check out!"

It was Kareem's voice. I felt his fingers over my sports bra. Blood left my head and my knees went soft. The laughter got louder and I started to shrug his hand off, only to realize that he'd already taken it away. I could still hear everyone laughing as I went up the basement stairs.

I didn't realize I had forgotten my parka until I was jogging down the sidewalk. I had no idea where I was going, and the wind blew under my jean jacket and whipped up my back. The cold bore right to my spine and my shins, and I imagined myself skinned, a skeleton, my bone marrow turning into ice. I grabbed the sleeves of my jacket in my fists, yanked them down as far as they'd go. The sky curved in front of me, waxy and low, and I knew that everything would just swallow me unless I forced myself to be okay. I tried to think about something nice. Dancing. In ballet, I had control over my own maturity. I could work at things until I achieved them, train my muscles with microscopic commands until my body became what I wanted it to be. I closed my eyes and tried to focus on that feeling. Each step was no longer an ordinary step; it was a step taken by a dancer. I slowed down and watched my feet, tiny volts of beauty, take the sidewalk. If I concentrated on this without stopping, I'd make it home.

I woke up the next morning with a sad feeling all over my body. It clung to my skin with the silky desperation of a cocoon. It took me a moment to connect this feeling to a memory of the day before, the feeling of my heart evaporating as everyone laughed in my face. I got out of bed, splashed cold water on my cheeks. I had to stay focused.

I went downstairs to find my mom. The plan was to drive to the Academy at twelve-thirty. Sign-in began at one in the afternoon and the audition was at two, so this would give me ample time to change, warm up and steady my nerves.

But I knew the second I saw my mom that something was wrong. She was sitting in the chair closest to the sliding door to the backyard, an elbow on the table, her chin propped in her hand. It wasn't clear whether she was staring over her shoulder into the yard or at the wall perpendicular to it. Her pose had an edgy stillness, as though she were waiting for an unidentified noise to repeat itself. Her black hair draped onto her shoulders, fresh from bed and frizzed at ear level, where it had rubbed the pillow. Something about her skin was too white.

"Mom?" I whispered.

She turned to me slowly, her reverie broken, but broken smoothly. She must have heard me come in. Her eyes had a fragile look, a glassiness poised to crack. But they warmed as they took me in, and a smile coaxed the corners of her mouth. "How do you feel?"

It took me a second to remember the importance of the day. Her voice had a hollowness I didn't like.

"Fine." I sat down in the chair across from her. "Not nervous yet."

She smiled again, but it was a tired and recycled smile; it didn't involve her eyes. She rested her forehead in her hand and rubbed it, back and forth, with her fingers. She did this slowly, thoughtfully, as if the repetition of the rub was troubling but necessary. I was afraid to ask her if she was okay.

"Where's Dad?" I said instead.

"At the hospital. He had to leave early." She looked back at the spot out the window.

"Are you okay, Mom?"

She made a snickering sound, a rush of air exhaled through her nose. "Of course I'm okay." She looked me straight in the eye to convince me. "I just have a headache, that's all, sweetie. A really tight, front-of-the-head thing." She rested two fingers on each temple and applied pressure, pulling the skin upward so that her eyes narrowed and lengthened. "I didn't sleep well," she confessed quietly.

"Why don't you just go back to bed?"

"Mm." She shook her head lightly. "I've made coffee."

I glanced over at the full pot of drip coffee on the counter and registered what I'd been smelling, a coarse tang spread thick on the air. Even though I wasn't a coffee drinker, I understood the sacredness of the freshly brewed.

"Go back to bed, Mom."

"We have to leave in a few hours."

"I'll wake you up." I shrugged like it was no big deal. My dad had encouraged me to do this sort of thing, to reassure my mom when she got like this.

She looked out again into the backyard. Our little lawn was muddy and unkempt, my old wooden swing set rotted from years of rain. The single orange seat had that eerie, deserted look of child abduction. "No." Her voice was airy, distant. "No, I won't be able to sleep."

But she was able to sleep, and at noon, when I popped my head into her room, her breathing was deep and regular, almost a snore but teetering on the edge of something more ladylike, an impassioned exhale. I took a step towards her, stopped. I wished she'd wake up without me. There was a logic to people's actions, a very simple kind of truth. I closed her door quietly and went to my bedroom. I lifted my phone from its cradle and dialled Isabel's number.

It rang three times. Someone answered, but a beat went by before there was a person. Instead I heard crinkling, a body moving through sheets.

"Hello?"

It was a guy, which didn't make sense because all of Isabel's roommates were girls, and the suddenness of this, a voice with the rumble of an engine, made my heart beat hard. I asked for Isabel anyway, and strangely the voice muttered a yes, told me to hold on. Now there was the squeak of a mattress, footsteps, breath. A door opened, a rush of water, voices beneath.

"Hello?"

"Isabel?"

"George, is that you? I'm halfway out of the shower. Give me a sec."

The water stopped. I tried to make sense of the picture I couldn't see: Isabel naked, the voice of a man.

"Hey." She was back. "What's up?"

"Who was that?" I asked.

"That?" There was a pause, the sound of shuffling. "That was Pete. My boyfriend."

There was an apology in her inflection. This was the first I'd heard of a boyfriend.

"Isabel?"

"Yeah, G?"

"I need your help."

Isabel and Pete were on my doorstep by twelve-thirty. Isabel had borrowed her mom's car, a wide sedan the colour of roasted chicken, and we drove south through the city. The family homes and boutique restaurants of Mount Pleasant Road became the motels and subsidized housing of Jarvis Street. Isabel put on some thin-voiced indie band and rolled her window down. Pete shook his head to the music as he drove. He was very tall and very narrow, his body tapering from the waist up to culminate in a pointy head. I imagined them naked together in the shower, two pale forms against all the textured plastic. I always thought people looked funny with wet hair, shorter and sort of like seals. And if Pete and Isabel kissed with their mouths open they'd get hot water down their throats. I hated that feeling, the nostril spasm, the burn at the bridge of your nose. I looked at Pete's face in the rear-view mirror. He had thin eyes and little lips, lips that had been on my sister. He didn't hold the steering wheel like a responsible driver; he sort of tapped it like it was always in his way. There were freckles around his knuckles, clusters of orange accidents. They gave the illusion of softness, but Pete's hands weren't soft, not entirely. These were the hands that had groped Isabel, maybe pinned her against the bathroom wall so he could touch her the way Kareem had touched me. Except Pete's touch was private, real. It stemmed from something buried inside him that had nothing to do with showing off to his friends. The idea made me shudder. I pulled on my seat belt, let it snap against the bones of my chest.

I listened to Pete's voice for signs of his private self. He was talking about a guy they both knew from Montreal who was starting up a magazine that, Pete explained, intended on having zero mandate.

"It's just not that subversive anymore, you know?" His voice was deep and he karate-chopped the steering wheel for emphasis. "It's just derivative *Seinfeld*. The magazine about nothing? I mean, who's going to buy into that now?"

"Okay," Isabel conceded, "but I mean it still actually has a mandate. Even if the marketing ploy is to make it seem mandate-less. That's just another lever, right? It's still very much after a certain readership. A certain reading"—she paused, rubbed a finger on her lower-lip—"you know, demographic."

Isabel sounded happy. Her voice curved gracefully through her ideas and she kept looking at her boyfriend. She must have looked at him a hundred times.

There were papers on the seat beside me, a stack of them. A skin-coloured folder sat on top of the pile and on it was a Post-it Note, *Pilar Navarro* written in blue ink. Isabel's mom.

"Your mom didn't mind that you took her car?" I asked.

Isabel turned around. "I told her what it was for."

I looked down at my lap, felt my cheeks redden. I thought about Pilar sometimes. I felt like I knew her, even though I hadn't seen her since I was a kid. She was so real to me, though, the giant woman who'd come to our house to pick up Isabel. In my clearest memory, she was standing beside my dad in the vestibule. She wasn't quite as tall as him, but their bodies left the same impression of geometry. Her shoulders didn't decline with the gentleness of my mother's; they jutted out in flat horizontals. What was most amazing was her strength, oversized hands that I was sure could fix major appliances, lift all the recycling even when the bin was full. I imagined her kitchen, the dark blue tiles that Isabel walked on in bare feet so that she could admire the butterfly tattoo below her baby toe. Unlike my mom, who made sandwiches for dinner or ordered in Thai food, Pilar could cook. She prepared heavy foods from where she was born, near the Mediterranean, pies made of egg and potatoes, seafood fried into rice. I pictured myself sitting with them at the table, not as a guest but as someone ordinary, permanent. Pilar would ask me questions about life and school, and I would confide in her without worrying that it would make her more depressed. Sometimes I pretended that there was a room upstairs in Pilar's house for me too. I knew her house was older than ours, built in the nineteenth century, and I imagined following her up the steps, other people's memories creaking through the hardwood. The feeling I'd have would be like falling asleep while it stormed outside, sheets of rain pelting the window as I curled into warmth.

"Guess you must be pretty nervous, huh?" Pete's eyes met mine in the rear-view mirror.

Isabel placed a hand over the gear shift and onto his beat-up jeans. "Don't stress her out." She looked over her shoulder at me. "I think this is great, George. It's great that you're doing this. Don't let Dad discourage you. Dad is a jerk."

"I'm not nervous," I said.

It was true. There was something about the day that already felt beyond the sway of my influence. The need to be accepted into the Academy had crept up on me so slowly, so steadily, that it had accumulated determination and desperation in equal measures. The day would be a brilliant success. It had to be.

The Academy looked like a temple from ancient Greece. It seemed completely out of place in Toronto. The exterior made me think of planets too stark to support life forms, moonstone smooth enough to rub my cheek on. Five pillars grew out of the porch, propping up the ceiling like big toothpicks. We followed black arrows down a staircase and through a labyrinth of hallways, until the corridor opened into a high central space. I looked up at a row of skylights, down at dozens of girls. A woman gave me a number—fifty-nine—to pin to the front and back of my bodysuit. Isabel sent Pete off to have a cigarette and took me to the change room. I took off my clothes, and she pinned the numbers to me, front and back, sliding her hand inside the leotard so as not to poke my skin.

We followed another set of printed arrows up a staircase to a studio. On the door was a sign that read JUNIOR DIVISION WARM-UP—AUDITIONEES ONLY.

"Well." Isabel grabbed my arm again and squeezed it. "I'll be cheering silently. Meet you in that big room after, okay?"

The studio was full of girls, all of them wearing pretty much the same thing, pastel tights with a hint of pinkness and black bodysuits without sleeves. Their legs were over the barres or in splits on the floor, chests rolled out between them flat as rugs. Some girls lay on their backs and yanked their heels towards their shoulders. No one spoke; instead, everyone pursued an imaginary solitude, as though invisible walls curved throughout the room.

Only one girl broke this rule. She had her elbows propped up on the barre, her back leaning against it. She looked around the room, her eyes stopping full on one girl, then jumping to the next. Her gaze was full of muscle, without a hint of shame. She was tall, or at least tall by my standards, and thin, but not in my shapeless way. There was breadth to her thinness, a strength. She had black Cleopatra hair slicked into an unusually high bun and a nose that was so long it almost grazed the bud of her lip.

"What?" She was staring at me.

Everyone looked over. Blood poured in from the tops of my ears. This was probably the first thing that'd been said in the room, and the sound of a voice was jarring. I cocked my head towards the bit of empty barre beside her, tried to make it seem like I'd been searching for some space to park myself. She shrugged as I walked over. The other girls went back to their stretches.

But now, closer, I wanted to look at the girl more. It's not that she was so beautiful or anything. I instinctively compared her sharp, oval face to Isabel's delicate beauty, a trial I subjected every pretty girl to, knowing that she would come up short. But this girl had an authority about her, a careless way of occupying space that was either impressively grown up or thoughtlessly childish. Her eyes slanted up away from her nose. They were that unusual kind of hazel that seems more orange than brown, like two polished pennies.

"Fifty-nine, huh?" she asked. The number 60 was pinned beneath her rib cage. She had breasts. They were small and pressed tidily into her bodysuit.

"That means you better be either really good"—she pressed her lips together, popped them at herself in the mirror—"or really shitty."

"Why?" I tried to sound uninterested.

She sighed and unfurled a leg up onto the barre. The leg was long and perfectly sinewed, strong along the inner thigh, where ballerinas should have muscle, and streamlined along the exterior, where they shouldn't. She stretched her chest onto her leg and reached for her foot. It was a perfect ballet foot with a high, convex arch, an instep that could almost fold in two.

"If you're really shitty, then I'll just look extra good beside you. And if you're really good . . ." She paused and met my eye in the mirror. "Well, that's even better." She smiled slowly, her mouth wide. "They'll spend the whole time looking over at the two of us."

A woman stepped into the studio and told us to line up in numeric order. I looked around me, meeting the eyes of other girls looking around too. I felt a tug on my hand.

"We're at the back," Number Sixty said, pulling me towards the barre. Her hand felt bigger than mine. "Which is perfect for standing out."

I stood in front of her as the other girls lined up. When the line started to move into the hallway, she yanked me towards her.

"Don't fuck up," she whispered.

Studio A was large and yellow with sunlight. The room was split in half, one side reserved for the audience on fold-out chairs, the other set up for dancing. We walked up the side of the studio, past the audience. Six movable barres were lined horizontally across the dancing area. Behind that was a long table at which sat five adults. They leaned into the table and held their faces towards us at curious angles. This was the faculty. I registered them with a jet of nerves in the pit of my stomach.

The woman explained that we'd be taken in front of the panel in groups of five. They'd look at us from every perspective, front, back and both sides, and then we'd be asked to bend over and touch our toes.

"If you can place your palm flat on the floor that's even better." She raised her eyebrows, made peaks sharp as tents. "Then I'll direct you to a barre. Once everyone's at a barre, the class will begin."

The first five girls were led forward. I watched their bums as they walked away, the syncopated strides of their legs. I wondered who would be able to lay their hands flat on the floor and who wouldn't. They were positioned at even intervals in front of the table, one girl to one faculty member. I watched the teachers' faces. They were wired with curiosity. I looked at the girls' heads, the row of tiny shoulders, and wondered how it felt standing there, being stared at. The teachers made notes on their notepads.

When it was my turn, I walked forward, keeping my neck long and my gaze just above eye level. I could feel Sixty behind me and I knew she was doing something similar, trying to walk the way a dancer should. I was placed in front of the second-last teacher, the only man. My pulse quickened. I'd never had a male ballet teacher before. I knew they weren't unheard of, but still. It seemed suspicious. Maybe he was gay. I pressed my thighs into first position and tried to see out of the corner of my eye. Isabel could always tell if a guy was gay. She said her methods weren't foolproof but right maybe 85 percent of the time.

When it was time to touch our toes, I lowered my chest to my shins, my back level as a table. I placed my hands flat on the floor. Then, to intensify the stretch, I turned my hands around so that my wrists pointed forward. I put them down on either side of my feet and curled deep into my legs. In Mrs. Kafarova's class, I was the only girl who could do this. My nose stuck between my ankle bones.

A voice told us to roll up. I unwound through each vertebra, rolled my shoulders back. We were instructed to take our places at the last barre on the right. I turned to follow Sixty, and as I did, I glanced over my shoulder at the panel. The man was looking at me. On his face was a look of supreme insight, like he knew something about me that I didn't even know myself. It made me feel naked, but even stranger was the realization that I liked the feeling. I looked back at Sixty and the blush descended, hot as a sunburn.

The final exercise was a waltz from the far end of the studio, connecting a series of *piqué* turns into suspended balances on pointe. The steps had a fairy-tale flavour, soft elbows and featherweight hands, like the bones in our bodies were hollow. We gathered in the corner of the room to begin, trying to maintain our numerical order. The first two girls started to spin before stepping straight into difficult positions. I looked at the man to gauge his reaction. He'd moved forward in his chair now and was tapping a finger on the side of his chin. He had broad shoulders and black eyebrows.

I felt a warmth on my neck. Sixty leaned in towards me.

"You can do doubles, right?" Her voice was a hiss.

I stared into her eyes, two spirals of mischief.

"Yeah."

If Sixty was turning doubles, I needed to turn doubles beside her. I had never done this before. Sixty was moving in front of me, lifting her arms into the preparatory position. I felt a shakiness around my knees. The two girls in front of us were turning now. I wrenched my left foot into the starting position. Our phrase of introductory music began.

We started to turn. Sometimes when I'm dancing, I feel like my eyes are closed even though they're not. My body takes over and it's like I don't need to see, like I've lost control and have tons of it at the same time. Every movement harbours a secret fall, and it's the danger that makes it beautiful. Isabel told me that she had smoked pot once, and that it made her limbs feel balletic. It made me think that dancing might be like doing drugs, breathing gentle poisons into your muscles. I stepped into the last set of turns. My weight stayed centred over my supporting leg and I whipped my head around to build momentum. My eyes found a groove in the wall at the far end of the studio. The turns came faster. I was almost at the end now, just a few steps away from the panel. I stabbed my pointe shoe into the floor for a double turn and something slid. My ankle wobbled the wrong way. My hand went out to take the fall, and there was a thud on the back of my wrist and then another one on my hip bone. I was on the floor.

Pain knotted inside my ankle and shuttled along my side but I got up anyway, as though I could disguise what had happened by moving quickly. I could feel the redness on my cheeks. The teacher at the end of the panel, a woman with silver hair, was moving towards me.

"Are you okay?" She looked down at my ankle.

I nodded. I would not cry. I rotated my ankle once in each direction to show her. She looked up into my eyes again, her face unsmiling.

"Doubles were not a good idea. That ankle will need some ice." The teacher walked back to the panel.

I joined the other girls, my cheeks still searing. They were gathered against the wall, waiting to be told what to do next. Sixty was at the end and I stopped beside her. I was scared to meet her eye but I forced myself to do so anyway. I thought she'd be smirking but instead her expression was soft.

"Don't worry," she whispered, and she brought her hand up to my shoulder, pressed her fingers into my skin.

The man stood up from the table. He cleared his throat.

"Good afternoon, ladies. First of all, I want to thank you for your hard work today. Auditioning can be"—he paused and rubbed the back of his neck—"well, it can be a rather distressing experience, and I think your industry and courage shouldn't go unmentioned." He spoke slowly, as though tasting each word in his mouth. His accent was crisp, almost English, but it had a fullness too, a tone coming deep from his torso. "Unfortunately the entry competition to the Royal Toronto Ballet Academy is on par with the entry competition to the ballet world itself, which is to say"—he paused, looked down at his feet—"uniformly fierce. So although we'll be able to accept only a very select few of you this afternoon, I hope this doesn't diminish the pleasure you derive from your dancing and I encourage you to continue your studies at the amateur level." He frowned. "We're going to take five minutes now. Then we'll be back with our decision. To avoid any unnecessary commotion, it's probably best if the dancers remain on this side of the room and friends and family stay on the other."

The other teachers collected their notes and stood up. The man took a step away from the table and let his colleagues file out ahead of him. As they passed the line of us against the wall, I let my body slouch into the barre. The man took up the rear, and as he got closer to me, I looked down at my feet. I wanted him to pass, for the moment to be over. He got closer and closer, and then he stopped. His eyes went to Sixty, then volleyed back to me. A smile dangled, favoured his left cheek.

"How's your ankle?" he asked.

"Okay."

He rubbed the back of his neck and chuckled. "You two are lucky that I like risk takers."

He turned and walked away. His shirt creased as he moved his arms, one side, then the other, like the crease itself was moving.

"Roderick Allen," Sixty whispered.

"What?"

"The artistic principal."

"Oh."

"Oh." She rolled her eyes at me. "He's famous."

After a few minutes, Roderick Allen stepped back into the room. He was holding a piece of paper and he walked to the centre of the studio.

"We've made our decision." His eyes scanned the audience for a moment, dropped back to the sheet. "Number forty-two, Miss Molly Davies. Number fifty-nine, Miss Georgia Slade. And number sixty, Miss Laura Feinstein. Could those three ladies please make their way to the main office."

Sixty extended her arm out in front of me, her elbow locked, as though she needed to hold me back. She flashed hot eyes at me. In the audience I saw Isabel. She had got up from her seat, and even from a distance, I could see her excitement, all her weight on the tips of her toes. Her hands were clasped in front of her and there was a giant smile on her face. She gave me a big thumbs-up. I smiled at her, but my smile hid a confusion of freshly churned feeling. Sixty grabbed my hand. She folded her fingers into mine, the way lovers hold hands, and we walked across the studio.

THREE.

My mom came into my room that night. I was sitting on my bed with a bag of frozen peas on my ankle and two pillows beneath my foot. I had taken the calendar of Gelsey off my wall so that I could flip through the photographs up close.

"Congratulations." Her voice was soft.

She was in her pyjamas, the same pyjamas she'd worn earlier, although an undone cardigan ballooned over her torso. It was beige, the tone inconsistent like oatmeal, and I figured it belonged to my dad. I wondered if she'd gotten dressed at all that day. She'd fixed her hair, though. A ponytail rested on one shoulder.

"How do you feel?" She sat on the edge of my bed.

"Good," I said.

She looked down at the bag of peas. I waited for her to ask about my injury, but she just tugged on the serrated edge of plastic, centred the bag over my ankle. She placed her hand on my other foot. I was wearing a thermal sock, but I could still feel her hand. There was a warmth to it, an instant familiarity.

"Sweetheart, I feel like a real jerk for not taking you there today." She was leaning over my foot and her ponytail obscured her eyes. "Really," she continued softly. "I should've been there."

"It's okay," I lied.

"Yeah," she sighed. "I know it's okay. I mean, your dad wasn't there either." She lifted her head and looked up at me. "But still." She pulled herself up so that she was lying beside me, her head in her hand. "I wish I had been there. I'm so proud of you."

I looked into her eyes. I loved my mom's eyes, so dark you could barely make out her pupils.

"I do take some credit for this. I did take you to your first ballet." She placed her hand on my knee and rattled it affectionately. "You remember?"

Of course I remembered. It was a memory I had replayed many times. I was about five years old. Isabel was going to an art gallery with her mom that same afternoon, and I remember thinking that there was something very reasonable about this, Isabel with her mom, me with mine.

"You were so mature for your age. So articulate. People used to stop me and tell me so."

We had driven downtown in the Mazda hatchback she had then. She was wearing a long skirt in an earthy nineties colour—orange, burgundy, something that could've fallen off a tree. It clung low on her hips and flowed out below the knee. With her rippling black hair, she looked like an autumnal mermaid. I remembered her being an awful driver even then, the kind who thinks it's safest to go twenty in a forty zone and who always manages to be mid-daydream, eyes fixed nostalgically on a billboard or a tree, when the light turns green.

She explained what we were going to see, telling me it was perfectly okay if I didn't like it, stressing how important it was to dislike generally. *Don't be afraid to hate things, Georgia. I think we might learn the most from the stuff we can't stand.* We were crossing the street just then; in fact I distinctly remember us jaywalking. I squeezed her hand as we made it safely to the traffic island. Yonge Street extended north in a blur of lights, parkas and car exhaust. I felt safe beside her, my dark and beautiful mother. But I also sensed there was something reciprocal about that safety. I was like the third prong on a wall plug, grounding a dazzling but precarious surge.

"You hated the first act," my mom chuckled. "There was something specific that you objected to. God, what was it?"

"The cheese prop."

"That's right." Her laugh was full now. "The cheese."

There had been huge wedges of cheese that life-sized mice nibbled on. The mice kept bringing the cheese to their mouths, supposedly to eat it, but every time they took it away again, the cheese stayed exactly the same size.

"But the second act. Something clicked. I remember turning to check on you and your little mouth was just hanging open." She reached up to pinch my chin.

"Mom," I moaned, dodging her touch.

She was right, though, and I remembered exactly what had changed my opinion. The Sugar Plum Fairy. She took centre stage and my concentration sharpened. Her neck was miles long, so that her head seemed to drift regally above the rest of the world, her shoulders like small, delicate reminders that she was real, earthborn. Her skin was all white ice against the pink satin of her tutu and I loved the fragility of her body. It looked like it could blow away. The Prince lifted her high above his head, and her legs sliced outward, downward, upward, sculpting the darkness into unnameable shapes. There was something too good about it, too beautiful, such unjustifiable precision in an otherwise lazy December afternoon. I placed my hands on my thighs, right above the knees, and I squeezed them through my textured tights. I willed them to grow into better legs, ballet legs, legs made for a more gorgeous world.

There was a thud on my comforter. My mom had dropped her hand from her head to the bed. Now she pinched the cover away from the duvet and rubbed it between her thumb and finger.

"I had the worst day," she whispered.

"Why?"

I watched her chest rise as she breathed in. She let the air out on a giant sigh, hitting a tremulous key at the high back end of her throat.

"Things might change between your dad and me."

There was a cold clang inside me. I waited for her to continue. She let go of the comforter and smoothed the empty hillock she'd created with her palm. Her hand moved tenderly, in one direction.

"I don't want to upset you, sweetie. And I definitely don't want to get you in the middle of it. I just"—she paused—"I want you to be ready."

The cold got worse. I could feel it clattering up my spine.

"Okay?" she whispered.

I didn't answer. The cold moved into my head. Was she being serious or only looking for a reaction? My dad accused her of doing that sometimes. He'd say, *Let's tone down the histrionics, Lena. Only a small audience tonight.* Now it was my responsibility to say something similar, to do my best to calm her down.

"Mom?"

"Yeah?"

I could feel the hurdle in front of me. I needed a few words and just the right ones.

"Dad's just busy," I began slowly. "It doesn't have anything to do with you."

I watched her absorb this, the tiny flinch beneath her eye.

"I know it's hard for you, when he works so much. But, no offence"—I brought my hand to her forehead, stroked her hair—"I think you take it way too personally. It doesn't mean he doesn't care."

This was the bulk of it, so simple when you spelled it out. Again I waited for her reaction. She lay still for another moment, unchanged, as though she hadn't heard me. Had I insulted her? I could feel my heart in my chest. Then she did what I never would have expected. She started to laugh.

"Your dad isn't busy with work, Georgia. Wouldn't that just be great?" She shook her head. "There's stuff you don't understand, sweetie. The shit stuff," she added under her breath.

Her expression made me uncomfortable; a bitterness tightened the skin around her eyes, made them crinkle like paper.

"What do you mean?"

There was a sound from the doorway. My dad was standing there.

"Oh god," he chuckled. "Who died now?"

His plastic ID card swung on his neck. He had just come back from the hospital.

My mom lifted her head with a jolt. She looked at him flatly, didn't move.

"Hello?" my dad said.

"Hi, Dad." It came out as a whisper.

I wasn't sure if he had heard me because he was looking at my mom. There was a shakiness to his expression, an anger or a fear. My mom hoisted her body off the bed, stomped towards the doorway. As she passed him, he reached for her hand and missed it. He put more of his body into the next attempt and caught her wrist. She yanked it away immediately. They stayed there, their faces just centimetres apart. I thought he was going to try to kiss her on the mouth—it looked like he was about to—but after a moment she took a step back and walked out of the room.

I expected my dad to follow, but he stayed where he was, staring at the corner of the door frame as though a part of her had stuck there. Finally he looked down at me and sighed.

"She had a bad day, huh?"

"Yeah."

"How bad?"

"She couldn't take me to the audition."

His head started to move, shook slowly back and forth like the air around him resisted. "I don't know what to say, Georgia. God knows what is going on with your mom these days."

I reached down to take the bag of peas off my ankle. It made a raw sound, the shards of ice displacing.

"What did you do to yourself?"

I brought my hand to my ankle. It had a reptilian dampness, felt like something other than skin. "Fell."

"Does it hurt?" He sat on the edge of my bed and lifted my foot by the heel. Slowly he turned my ankle one way, then the other. I focused all my attention forward, sent him secret messages in my head. *Ask me about my audition. Ask whether I got in.* The hospital badge dangled from his neck like a jewel. *Dr. Lawrence Slade.* The laminate peeled from the top corner, and in the photo his forehead was a splotch of flash, but his eyes were absolute power. I reminded myself that he'd had a busy day full of dozens of patients. Expecting his attention would be acting like my mom.

"It's no big deal," I told him.

He touched the bone lightly and felt the skin with the back of his hand. "You should probably stay off it for a day."

"Thanks, Dad."

He walked towards the door, shut it behind him.

I counted to five slowly in my head. Their voices started. My dad's came first, a low rumble of sound. With the door closed there were no words, just the essence of his frustration. I waited for the treble to kick in, the soprano ring of my mom's fury, the screaming match to follow. But when her voice came it was tiny, a thousand miles away.

I took a pillow and wrapped my arms around it. My mom's mind had taken a turn for the worse, and it was best that I didn't deny it. She had homed in on something specific now and was feeding it all kinds of distorted junk. *The shit stuff.* What did she mean by that? I couldn't guess the details of this new delusion, but the core of it was mangled, I had heard it in her laugh. I squeezed the pillow into me. I didn't want to acknowledge what I was looking at, but it was there, a solid demarcation, the yellow line on a busy road. She was crossing the divide between what was normal and what, no matter how you tried to soften it, was strange, dark, wrong.

I looked down at the photo of Gelsey on the April page. She was so beautiful. I traced my finger up the shimmery greyness of her pointe shoe, let it rest in the accordion pinch of her leotard. This would be me now, a real dancer. It meant something significant. I was conscious of their voices again. My mom was screaming and the sound carried down the hallway, filled all the dead space in my room. I moved my finger along Gelsey's sinewy leg. Ballet school meant I would never be touched by someone like Kareem again. It also meant I would never need to scream like my mom.

FOUR.

I COUNTED THE DAYS UNTIL I'd start at the Academy, but counting them made them slow down, so I hid my calendar at the back of my desk drawer and tried to lose track. But my mind counted anyway, even more carefully than before. I became conscious not just of days, but of half days, quarter days, the inescapable tick of my watch. One morning, I woke up with the feeling that I'd spent the whole night staring at the red robot lines of my radio alarm. I got out of bed and took the calendar from my desk drawer, pinned it back to the corkboard. I drew red X's through all the days I'd missed.

The house was quiet that morning and I figured no one

was home, my dad working at the hospital and my mom teaching at the university. I liked summer weekdays when I could stay in my pyjamas until lunchtime, eat cornflakes from the box while practising *pirouettes* on the kitchen floor. I put on my ballet slippers and stopped to answer the phone. A woman asked for my mom and I offered to take a message.

"Do you have any idea where she is?" the woman asked. "I'm calling from the college and she hasn't shown up for her lecture."

I walked down the hallway, covering the receiver with my hand. My mom's door was just a little ajar and I kicked it open with my foot. The lights were off, and the air inside was warm and maybe a little musky. I stepped onto the grassy rug at the foot of my parents' bed and made out her form beneath the giant duvet.

"Mom," I whispered.

Her breathing grew more and more audible until it became a groan. She turned onto her side.

"The college is on the phone for you. Mom?"

She stayed quiet for a moment and then she mumbled something.

"I can't hear you," I said.

"My assistant is teaching today. Tell them to read the goddamn schedule."

I looked down at the receiver in my hand. The last thing I wanted to do was speak to this woman again. What if she told me that my mom was mistaken? I had a feeling that she might be, or that, even worse, she was lying.

"Do you want me to say that, Mom?"

This time her sigh was full of frustration. She pushed herself off the pillow and reached out her hand. Her face looked bloated with sleep. I passed her the phone and listened to her tell the woman that her T.A. was supposed to be there, and that she was fed up with the department's incompetence. She jabbed the hang-up button with her thumb and hoisted her body out of bed, moved languidly to the stool of her vanity table. She rested her chin in her palm and stared at her reflection. The mirror was the shape of a big egg and the table was covered with glass jars and perfume atomizers that she'd collected while travelling before I was born. She opened the top drawer and pulled out a small package. I couldn't see what it was until she lifted her fingers to her lips and put a cigarette in her mouth. She pulled a lighter out of the same drawer and lit it.

"What are you doing?" I asked.

She blew a ribbon of smoke at the mirror and smiled at me. "Don't tell your dad."

I had never seen her smoke in my life. It was difficult to make sense of, like seeing a puppy with a vest or an old person without teeth. I felt like I should tell her to stop but I worried she'd get angry, so I just walked over to the bed and watched her. She watched herself too, eyes fixed on her mirror-eyes as she sucked the smoke in, parted her lips to blow it away.

"Am I losing it, George?"

"Losing what, Mom?"

"You know." She ran her hand through her hair. "My looks."

I was relieved that she hadn't meant her mind. But the reference to her looks was almost worse. I hated when she talked about them that way, like looks were a collection of bobby pins that you misplaced one by one until you didn't have any left.

"Looks aren't important, Mom."

"Is that right?" She seemed to find this funny. "Who told you that? Your dad?"

The mention of my dad made her laugh more, but the laughter sounded sour now and a sadness flashed in her eyes. She ground her cigarette into the green-glass ashtray that she'd always told me was just for show, then got off the stool and ruffled my hair. "I better get to the university."

When she'd left the house, I went back into her room to see what she'd done with the cigarette butt. She'd left the door closed and a pale cloud corkscrewed in the light, the smell of smoke still heavy. The butt was just where she'd extinguished it, in the middle of the ashtray. Seeing it made me stomp my foot. What if my dad came home early and found it? I looked over her array of perfumes and chose a clear bottle with a golden seashell head. I sprayed it all over the room until I thought I would gag on the wet jasmine air. Then I took the cigarette butt and flushed it down the toilet.

I finally drew the last red X on my calendar. The air shifted that evening too. From my bedroom window, I could smell the change, delicate and a little charred, as if what had built up on the barbecue grill all summer had finally burned into the atmosphere. I packed my knapsack with everything I'd been told to bring for my first day at the Academy: two pairs of pink tights, one black leotard, leather ballet slippers. We'd be fitted for pointe shoes by a specialist at the school. I lay on my bed and focused on the swirls of the drywall ceiling until they took on the significance of the night, one plaster rift becoming my old life, another the new. I must have dozed off because I had dreams that wrenched me from sleep and found me staring at the radio alarm again.

Still, I felt rested in the morning. There was a crispness in my head and a place for everything, thoughts and feelings tucked where they belonged. My parents had left early, so I had the kitchen to myself, didn't have to worry about whether they were talking to each other. A bowl of cereal had been laid out for me, even a small plate of sliced cantaloupe and wedges of pear. Beside it was a note torn from my mom's day planner. She'd sketched a map for me in pencil, an elegant scribble of street names and arrows that traced a route from our front door all the way to my new school. Even though I'd rehearsed this journey a hundred times on Google Maps, I held the paper in my hand on the subway, let it soften beneath my thumb. I felt an amazing forward momentum all the way to my stop. I had passed by Wellesley Station before but had never got off there. The turquoise tiles lining the station would have looked normal in a bathroom. I followed the crowd up the escalator and stepped out into the street.

I walked quickly down Church Street, passing storefronts I'd never seen before—a Yogen Früz with a peeling sign like a homemade banner, a video-rental shop that claimed to be open all the time—and knew that soon enough they'd be ordinary, things I'd look at and not register. When I turned the corner, I could see the edge of the Academy right away. It was bigger than I remembered it and whiter too, the sun hitting the steps at a blunt morning angle, lighting the pillars as if they were on a stage.

We were taken to a classroom on the second floor. Sixty found me almost immediately, pulled me around to the desk where she'd already left her things. She was wearing a short dress that cinched at the waist and looked grown up enough for Isabel. The skirt billowed away from her body, so that when she walked I could see far up the backs of her thighs. She was tanned, even up there. Her hair was loose, almost black and with an aura of frizz, like it was full of chlorine or salt water. I asked her if she'd been away for the summer.

"Away from where?"

"Toronto."

She stuck her lower lip out and blew a stream of air onto her forehead. "Of course."

I sat at the desk next to hers and watched the rest of the class come in. My class. It was hard to focus on one person for very long. Just as I was taken by a blonde girl with a ribbon of moles below her collarbone, a black girl was on her heels, her hair a cloud of tiny coils. I tried to absorb the feel instead of the details, the general wash of motion the way you'd examine the sky. I saw long hair and bare legs, knapsacks and shoulder bags trailing. A rebel giggle erupted from the centre, like the trill of a piccolo in a symphony. The feeling I had was private but radiant. I looked around the room at all the faces. Girls. And not just that, but *dancers*. Each of us here for the same thing.

A teacher led us through the school towards the theatre. The halls seemed older than I had imagined and shabbier—no hardwood or marble or bay windows. The floors looked like they must be linoleum and were that funny colour between yellow and beige. I peered into classrooms with the same perforated ceilings as my old school, the same Formica desks with attachable chairs. But it felt different here, better, as though the inanities of math and science were okay because they were part of a bigger purpose.

We stepped into the theatre. It was exactly what I hadn't been expecting too, no curves or bobbles or ceilings made of glass, just pure geometry, the stage a giant rectangle, the boxes freckled with rows of squares. I followed Sixty down an aisle near the front, sat beside her. The cushions were thick and covered in material that reminded me of carpet. I focused on the stage. Maybe its simplicity made it better. It was empty except for a few bits of white rehearsal tape; the longest was the length of my arm and ran in a sharp diagonal. Whatever ballet it had been used for had probably only just opened. I saw flashes of different heroines: suicidal Giselle in her death-white tutu, Spanish Dulcinea with her fan of damask lace.

A woman stepped onto the stage. She kept her face towards us as she walked, legs gliding under a pin-straight back. She was a dancer, or at least she used to be. Her hair was short, and beneath it was a long and fatless face, cheeks that didn't sag but didn't seem there at all. I looked at Sixty to gauge her reaction.

The woman introduced herself. Beatrice Turnbull. Sixty nodded. It was the name she'd been expecting. Beatrice Turnbull said she was the executive director of the Academy and used meaningful words to stress the enormity of the day. Our achievement was momentous. We were joining a historic student body, a tradition of excellence and prestige. Her voice was soft and it drew my attention to her neck, long and marked by tendons that settled into her collar like the roots of a tree.

"She was famous." Sixty's face was at my ear. I could smell artificial strawberries. "In the seventies, I think."

Beatrice Turnbull looked famous, with her all-bone face that made me think of ice, giant swaths of it like glaciers. She said we were to collect our schedules in the lobby and would reconvene for our inaugural technique class after lunch.

"Roderick Allen will be teaching you. I'm sure you all remember him from the audition, and if not, not to worry; you will know him very well soon enough."

Sixty grinned at me, baring front teeth with little ridges. The other girls reacted similarly, turning to their neighbours, everyone whispering. It drew my attention away from the noise and to the only girl who wasn't talking. She was a seat away from everyone else, her chin pointed up towards the stage, eyes frozen on Beatrice Turnbull. She was a nerd; I knew right away from her T-shirt, peach-coloured and shapeless, not tight enough to show her boobs. She seemed wrapped up in her own thoughts, the way you'd expect from a nerd. She watched the stage thoughtfully, as though something was happening up there, an invisible ballet that only she could see.

I followed Sixty and the other girls up the stairs of the auditorium, back through the hallway and into the school. We heard piano music from two directions, notes that collided together into a dreamy clutter of melody. I noticed two boys now, standing side by side in the middle of the clump of us. I tried to get a good look at them but couldn't without being obvious. Our schedules were pinned to the bulletin board in the main lobby, our names printed in the top left corner of each. I pulled mine down, rubbed my finger over the piercing left by the thumbtack, joined Sixty and some other kids on the bench. We had school from Monday through Saturday. Weekday mornings started with two hours of technique class, followed by an hour of either pointe, modern, character dance or pilates. Academics were in the afternoon, only two classes each day, and the early evening was reserved for repertoire and rehearsals. Saturdays began with something called body-conditioning. Sixty said that she'd had it at her last school, and that it involved a lot of bending and rolling with giant rubber bands. This was followed by two hours of *pas de deux*, and the afternoons were set aside for rehearsal.

"Come." Sixty weaved her fingers through mine. "I'll show you my room."

We turned left from the lobby, went down a hall I hadn't seen yet. The ceiling was lower here and it led to a stairway at the far end. We took the steps two at a time. Her flip-flops snapped with each hoist, marked our pace like a metronome. Again I saw up her skirt, saw more than she probably realized, looked down at the steps and back up at her thighs. I let my index finger drag on the wall behind me while I listened to her, traced the painted grooves between the fat, porous bricks. She had moved in two nights before and she already knew most things about everyone.

"That's Veronica Orr's room." She held the door open to the landing and I squeezed in as it tottered on its hinge. She pointed to the first door in the hall. An erasable board was stuck to its front, two names committed glassily to its surface, bright blue on skating-rink white. The handwriting was different—*Veronica* lowercase and organized, *Anushka* a bloated cursive, the final *a* looping off to make a heart.

"Veronica's the blonde girl. The one with— " She brought her finger to her chest, traced a row of invisible moles. "She's really pretty, but she might be a snob. I haven't met Anushka yet. She's from Los Angeles and she missed her flight or something."

We continued down the hallway. Each door had the same erasable board, two personalities married on it with a plus sign. I read all the different names while Sixty explained. There were seventeen in our class altogether, fifteen girls and two boys. Thirteen lived in residence and were mostly from different parts of Canada, small towns that Sixty couldn't remember to repeat.

"But Sonya Grenwaldt's from New York."

We looked up at *Sonya + Limor*. *Sonya* rolled downward, five squished letters aiming for level ground. *Limor* ate space voluptuously, gaps between each letter big enough for two.

"And Limor's from the south."

"Like Mississippi?"

"No." Sixty looked solemnly at her feet. "Somewhere underneath Hamilton."

We continued down the hallway until she stopped in front of the final erasable marriage. *Laura + Chantal*. Sixty's handwriting was bubbly and complicated, Chantal's vertical and neat.

"What's your roommate like?" I asked.

Sixty made a face. "Nerdy."

Sixty turned her key in the lock and we stepped inside. There was a bunk bed on the left, a desk on the right and a large window on the wall between. Both bunks were made. The top could have belonged to a princess, a purple comforter with the sheen of an amethyst, a mosaic of round pillows at one end. The bottom was the complete opposite, an old hospital-green blanket pulled to the corners, one starched pillow at the top. I turned to the desk. A corkboard was mounted above it with a black line marked down the middle. One side was bare except for a small black-and-white image of a dancer's feet thumbtacked to the centre. The other side was covered with overlapping photos: Sixty in a bikini on a white rocky beach; Sixty in toque and mitts in front of the Eiffel Tower; Sixty sitting atop a camel, a scarf wrapped Grace Kelly–style over her head, her arms arced high in a perfect fifth *port de bras*. She looked happy in each of them, but always in a quirky, theatrical way, her eyes opened to cartoon proportions or her lips pursed in a supermodel pout.

"My dad's a banker," she explained, passing me an opened bag of Cheetos that she'd pulled from under the bed. She sat on the lower bunk and I did too. "We moved constantly."

I accepted a Cheeto and tried not to seem too impressed.

"It's made me chronically restless." She tossed a cheese curl into the air, caught it like a dolphin in her mouth. Then she laughed. "What an annoying thing to say, huh? 'Chronically restless.' I hate people who talk like that. But it's true. I've lived in sixteen different cities. But at least maybe I'll have a boyfriend now." She shaped her hair into a ponytail, draped it over her shoulder. "Do you have a boyfriend?"

I shook my head, ran my finger along the ridge of the Cheetos bag. "Not right now."

"Have you done stuff, though?"

"Stuff?"

"With a guy?"

"Yeah."

I heard the squeak at the top of my voice. Her eyes were steady, impossible to read. She lifted her leg, stabbed the end of her flip-flop into the floor and said, "All the girls in Monte Carlo had done it."

"Really?"

"It's different in Europe. Nothing's a big deal." She sighed and threw her body backward onto the mattress. "Which is, like, bad and good, you know?"

"Yeah."

"I mean, it's better than complete repression. Like my roommate."

"What's wrong with your roommate?"

Sixty motioned towards the desk and again I looked at the severed dancer's feet floating in a sea of cork.

"She's *really* serious about ballet."

I nodded as though I understood what she was implying, but I couldn't help but think the image was beautiful. It was just newspaper or something, but the feet looked suspended out of nowhere, and even though the picture wasn't sharp, you could feel the muscles of it. The dancer appeared to hover over a step, one foot extended in front of the other one, and staring at this idea of motion made me think she'd moved a hundred times.

There was a sound from the hallway, a key tinkering in a lock, and a girl stepped into the room. She had a round face and brown hair that folded into her head at chin level. I looked at her T-shirt, oversized and peach, and recognized her as the girl who'd sat alone in the theatre. She watched us for a moment. Finally she said hello.

"Hi," I said.

"We were just going for lunch," Sixty said. "Do you want to come?"

Chantal moved passed us without answering, placed her keys down carefully on her side of the desk. She was wearing jeans that weren't cool; they rested too high on her waist and were a funny pale blue. The pockets looked disproportionately miniature on her bum, and it was kind of a big bum, I noticed, for a dancer.

"Thank you, but I need to prepare for class."

Sixty shot a look at me. "Prepare what?"

"I just need to get organized. Roderick Allen is teaching." Chantal had a strange way of talking, not what she said but the way she said it, her voice a rush of childish breath.

"He's teaching *all* of our technique classes, you know?" Sixty said. "Plus he's supposed to be totally nuts."

I looked at Chantal. But she was massaging the arch of her foot, apparently not listening.

"Veronica told me what the grade eleven girls told her," Sixty continued. "They call him the Rodomizer."

It was a weird word, I thought, with an ominous grumble, like a motor ready to hurtle.

"The Rodomizer," she repeated with the same clever severity, grinning at Chantal. "It's a mix of *Roderick* and *sodomize*." Air hissed through the grate of her teeth. "Roderick's approach to training dancers is like bending them over and doing them up the ass."

I barked an uncomfortable laugh.

"No, it's true. They say his approach to teaching is like systematized humiliation. And do you know why?"

I shook my head.

"Do you know why?" Sixty asked Chantal.

Chantal shook her head.

"Because he hates women," Sixty pronounced. "Ballet is his revenge."

"Revenge?"

She nodded.

"For what?" Chantal asked.

Sixty shrugged. "I don't know the details." She turned to me, twisted a lock of hair on her finger. "But I'm sure it's something horrible."

I followed her towards the door, paused. My attention went back to the corkboard, the feet that moved without moving. I wanted to ask Chantal who they belonged to, but I didn't want Sixty to hear me.

"Bye," I said.

Chantal looked up. Her eyes were soupy, the kind that never focus on anything, thrive off their own secret. It made her look a little cross-eyed, but there was something pretty about it too.

"Bye," she whispered.

Roderick Allen stood in the centre of Studio A, tall and fixed, like the spiked leg of a drawing compass, his eyes tracing the circumference of dancers in the room. His hair dashed away from his forehead, leaving two gothic points of skin. My lungs felt slippery with nerves but I tried to breathe normally. I wanted to look just right. I had my back to the barre but was careful not to lean against it. I felt it was important to stand up straight. Sixty was next to me, and Veronica, blonde and square-shouldered, was on my left. My other new classmates curved around the room.

Roderick considered us slowly, his feet still. There seemed to be amusement hidden somewhere in his expression, but it wasn't on his lips and I couldn't pin it down. He nodded at the pianist, a nod that seemed to mean more stop than go. I looked at the funny recession of his hairline. I thought of what Sixty had just told me, that he hated women, that ballet was revenge. I searched his face for evidence. I wasn't sure what I was looking for but I thought I might know when I found it.

Suddenly, Roderick jerked his arm out and lifted his sleeve to look at his watch. He smiled now, widely. It crinkled the corners of his eyes.

"Sorry to keep you all in suspense. I just like to take a little time on the first day of school to find my bearings." He had a resonant voice, warm and deep, but shaped into careful consonants. "And I'd say that's a good starting point for all of you, taking some time to find your bearings, because you're going to find that the demands placed on you here are . . . well, different. And different in the most exceptional way." He looked around, made sure he had everyone's attention. "I'm going to throw something at you. Just a thought. A phrase." He paused again, frowning. "*Reading between the lines.* What does that mean to everyone?"

I looked to my right, towards Sixty. She was looking towards the rest of the class. No one said anything.

"*Reading between the lines*," Roderick repeated. "Tell me what that implies." He crossed an arm over his chest and propped the other elbow on top of it. He held his face in his hand, his middle finger curving beneath his nose like a moustache. He started to walk along the perimeter of the room, taking one slow step at a time.

"You probably all have similar stories. Similar stories with minor variations. You love ballet more than anything. You've been dancing since you were five years old. You were the star of your regional school." He turned his head and flashed a few teeth at the girls he was passing. "Not to insult anyone with a glib generalization."

The girls blushed and one of them giggled.

"Now you've been accepted into the program of your dreams and you've arrived with a variety of preconceived ideas. And here's where your stories diverge." He stopped abruptly and uncrossed his arms. "Because no two of you will have come with the same assumptions. But you will all have your assumptions, and they're the first thing we have to address."

He started to walk again, looking down at his feet. There was a rhythm to his behaviour, as though this speech was a phrase of music and he was waiting for the instrumental part to end.

"Some of you are going to be tempted, tempted right from the very beginning, to behave in a *certain* way." He lifted an eyebrow, held it there. "If I can leave you with one thing this afternoon, one suggestion, it's this: if you feel yourself tempted to behave in a *certain* way, you should take a moment, and stop yourself."

I looked around the room. Fifteen girls and two boys. I got a good glimpse of the boys now, both smaller than any at my old school. They had tidy haircuts and gentle faces.

"One of the first things that will happen is your consultation. Each of you will be having a one-on-one meeting with me. We'll start scheduling them as early as tomorrow." He hooked an arm behind his neck and rubbed it. "Don't be intimidated by how that sounds. You're going to hear some difficult things from both me and the rest of the faculty over the course of your four years here—it's a policy we're really committed to. And that will start with this first consultation. I'll be talking you through your weak points as a dancer, and I won't be mincing my words. We can save that luxury for amateur hour. Understood?"

I nodded quickly. I itched to know how my classmates were reacting, but I needed to appear focused. I had known that studying at the Academy would present a host of tests and challenges, and this was the first. I could take it. It was crucial that my expression reveal this, in case Roderick could see it.

"And we'll be discussing more than just your physicality at the consultation. Be prepared for that." He paused. "Ballet is physical, yes. Ultimately it's a physical medium. And some ballet schools are happy to leave it at that. They train physically proficient dancers. Graceful athletes, I like to say. But that isn't what we're doing here at the Academy. We're here to train artists, and this demands something else." Again he scanned the barre, swallowing us with eyes. "So if you aren't interested in becoming an artist, please"—he lifted his hand and held it out towards the door—"get out of my studio because you're wasting everyone's time."

The change in his expression was immediate. It wasn't anger. It was more like a shock of blankness, a TV screen turned to snow. An embarrassment flooded up from my chest. I didn't understand it, but I had to look away. There was an enormous silence in the room. After a moment Roderick cleared his throat. He told us to face the barre and began to count us through the first exercise.

I couldn't concentrate throughout the class. I moved my arms and legs in the appropriate configurations, but my attention wasn't inside my body like it should've been. It was on Roderick. Unlike all the ballet teachers I'd had before, he didn't circle the inside of the studio while we danced, poking bent knees and keeping the rhythm with his foot. He stood in the very far corner, almost completely behind the piano. He leaned his body into the crook between the walls, holding his face so that his fingers covered most of it. I tried not to look at him but it was impossible. His reaction felt so important. We were doing what he'd told us to do, but still, there he was, slinking as far away from us as possible. I couldn't see his mouth but I was sure there was something strange along his eyes, something almost sneering. *This is it,* I thought; *this is the Rodomization.* I bent forward in a deep *port de bras devant* and felt a tingle all over my body.

FIVE.

I WATCHED THE OTHER GIRLS in the change room the next morning. Sixty chose a locker next to mine, and Veronica was beside her. They took off their tank tops and skirts and stayed naked for much longer than necessary. There were no windows in the change room, just long tubes of yellow light that dangled beneath exposed piping. Veronica had blue underwear with white elasticized trim. It cut a blunt line below her hip bones and she had moles there too, hooking beneath her belly button in the shape of a bass cleft. I tried not to look even though I wanted to, but then my eyes were on Sixty instead, tanned everywhere except for a tube around her boobs and the white ghost of her bikini bottom.

"You should really use a higher SPF." Veronica sat on the bench now, gathered her tights into scrunches and placed a foot inside. "Tanning will age you prematurely."

Molly Davies laughed. She was the black girl with a cloud of curly hair. She only had her tights on and she reached up for something on the top shelf of her locker. The seams curved over both her bum cheeks, dropped straight down the middle of her legs.

"Gorgeous." Veronica smacked her lips at the magnetic mirror inside her locker door. In her hand was an uncapped lipstick, rolled up to reveal a ruby bullet of wax.

"Gorgeous for who?" Molly leaned over her shoulder. "Nathaniel or Jonathan?"

Everyone laughed. Nathaniel and Jonathan, the two boys in our class, looked like mannequins for kids' clothes and weren't the kind of boys whom anyone normal would date.

"We're going to need alternative options." Veronica shut her locker with a clang. "I'll make it my mission."

Molly tossed her ballet slipper like a Frisbee, aimed straight for Veronica's gut. "Nympho," she said.

"Pretty much," said Veronica.

At ten minutes to nine we left the change room as a class and made our way to Studio A. I felt slightly deadened by the conversation about boys. It hadn't been what I'd expected. We were supposed to be focused on the task at hand, preparing quietly and seriously for our second technique class. But I forgot about it as soon as I saw Roderick. He had the same air of lazy interrogation, eyeing us up and down as we walked into the studio. It sent a throb up my body, the challenge of it. He leaned against the piano. His striped dress shirt was rolled neatly above his forearms, and he pulled on the end of his chin as we arranged ourselves at the barres. I yearned for invisibility. I would watch him stare at the girls, observe exactly where his eyes went, figure out what went on in his mind.

We completed the first exercise. "That was awful." Roderick shook his head. "Terrible." He turned his body towards the piano, as though too repulsed to look our way.

My head dropped to my feet. I wasn't individually responsible for this assessment, but I felt the shame of it intensely.

But when Roderick turned around again he was smiling. "Disgusting. Do it again."

I adjusted my leotard strap. Molly, in front of me, did too. Something about his nastiness was irresistible. It was like when someone teases you, and you're charmed against your will. We repeated the exercise. I channelled pure power into my muscles, could picture the energy, hot and white. I had never wanted to be so perfect before. When we finished, Roderick pushed himself off the piano and walked slowly across the studio floor. I could see only the side of his face, but I was desperate to read his expression. Was he pleased with our work this time?

"Let's do centre."

We moved away from the barres to begin the centre portion of the class. Roderick didn't demonstrate the exercises.

Instead he talked us through them, occasionally lifting a hand to symbolize a jump or a turn. We were divided into three groups to perform the exercises. This meant I could watch two-thirds of the class dancing, and I did, greedily. Veronica was in the first group. She was an athletic dancer with high jumps and quick turns. Her footwork was what teachers called *clean*. She moved with an edginess that made her body seem two-dimensional, cut from paper and easy to fold. Molly danced beside her. Her legs were long and bendy, and her arms undulated as if they had no bones. When she paused in a *développé à la seconde*, I measured the distance between her head and foot. She was more flexible than I was, not by much, but by just enough for it to bother me. Sixty was in this group too. Her legs pierced the floor like spikes.

My attention went back to Roderick. Did he prefer the fluidity of Molly's body, the strength in Sixty's balances or Veronica's speedy turns? A perfect *pirouette* was wasted if he hadn't turned his head to see it. Veronica stepped into a *first arabesque*, stole a glance at him as she rolled through her foot. Molly did this too, sneaking a peek towards the mirror as she aligned herself for a sequence of turns. The girls spun around one another, vying for his interest.

When it was my turn, I felt a thirst right in my gut. I needed to have him watch me. I pushed myself through the steps, my mind storming with instructions: *pull up, turn out, lift from beneath your arm*. I caught a glimpse of Chantal in the mirror. She was beside me and I saw immediately how good she was, even though she was chubbier than everyone.

Her flexibility was second nature, but she had muscles too, the strength to hold her legs high and propel her body upward. She moved through everything ethereally, a quality that rarely co-existed with such steady athleticism. I forced myself to look away. A low panic flapped in my chest. We finished the exercise and I looked at Roderick. He was leaning against the mirror now, eyes on Chantal. His expression was unsettled, as though he hadn't quite made sense of things. But the approval in his eyes was clear.

"Don't forget"—he pushed his body off the glass, took a step towards us—"that I'm not interested in good *students*. I'm interested in good *dancers*. If you don't understand the difference instinctively, then it's something you'll need to figure out." He scanned our faces one last time and started to walk out of the room. "Let me just suggest that a *student* brings her emotions into the studio. Her feelings are hurt when she receives a harsh correction or embarrasses herself by falling out of a turn. A *dancer* is never hurt or embarrassed." He paused. "I want you to think about that."

We whispered about this as soon as we'd left the studio. Veronica said the girls in grade eleven had told her that Roderick hated wimps.

"Last year, a girl started crying in pointe class and she was expelled a few days later."

"That's terrible," Sixty said.

"Sounds like bullshit," said Molly.

Veronica shook her head solemnly. "I'm sure there were other reasons. But the crying was the last straw."

We moved as a group into the lobby, where the air felt cool after the studio's humidity. I had never cried in Mrs. Kafarova's class but the idea of expulsion freaked me out. I couldn't fathom the sadness of it, being forced to leave the Academy after working for so long to get in. I followed Sixty towards the bulletin board to check the master schedule for any changes. Veronica stood in front of us and pointed to something tacked on to the cork. It was an envelope with Molly's name on it. People started whispering. Molly weaved her way to the board, reached up and took it down. She ripped it open and took out the letter, read it with a look of stern composure.

"My consultation," she said, folding the paper back along its seam.

The meeting was scheduled for the second half of lunch. The girls made sympathetic sounds that I knew were mixed with envy. Molly assured everyone that she didn't mind being first, and Veronica wrapped an arm over her shoulder, ushered her through the crowd.

The cafeteria was a small room on the other side of the basement. The walls were a pale blue, the colour of newborn-boy stuff. It emphasized the air's dampness; dips on the surface looked wet to the touch. There were only four round tables, room for seven or eight at each, which meant there were two separate lunch periods and we overlapped with a different grade each day. Today we ate with the grade twelve class.

They were already there when we walked in, seven of them ringed loosely around the table beneath the only window.

"There used to be fourteen," Veronica said as we unstuck orange trays from a plastic tower, rolled them onto the metal tracks.

"What happened?" I asked.

Veronica reached into the refrigerated compartment for a Tetra Pak of apple juice, placed it on her tray. "If you piss Roderick off, it's pretty much curtains."

I accepted a plate of spaghetti and followed Veronica and Sixty to the nearest table, inhaled a spicy steam of tomato and starch. I looked at the grade twelve class as I walked. There were three boys and four girls. They were hardly talking to one another and I wondered if that was normal. Two of the girls had finished eating and didn't seem to be doing much. One see-sawed her fork, pressing down on the end where it overhung her plate, letting the tines crash into the ceramic. The other had her head in her hand, was staring out the window.

Sixty sat next to Veronica and I sat next to Sixty. Chantal, Anushka and Sonya came over to our table and sat down too. Chantal sat right across from me, her tray stacked with spaghetti and all the extras: fruit, yogourt, a granola bar and salad. She wore a different pair of bad shorts, plaid and cotton, something a kid would have worn. Her T-shirt was baggy again too, and I looked at the soft arms that extended from the sleeves, not quite fat but chubby and formless. I knew I wouldn't like them if they were mine. Strangely, her face was full of shape. Her lips formed a perfect rosebud, dipping to make the cleft of a heart, and her nostrils were wide and shadowed, as big as kidney beans. It wasn't unattractive. The largeness of her features pulled you in.

I heard a giggle and turned towards it. Veronica had her wrist pressed into her mouth, pretending to choke her laughter. She pointed at Chantal's plate.

"Do you always eat like that?"

"Like what?" asked Chantal.

"There's enough on your plate for all of us."

Chantal looked down at her tray and I could see her whole face go funny. I thought she wasn't going to say anything, but then she whispered, "Fuck you."

Veronica turned to Sixty and then to me. Her lips parted in shock and she exhaled loudly. "It was just an observation. Excuse *me*."

I kept my focus on my spaghetti because I didn't want to get involved. Veronica whispered something to Sixty and I heard Sixty mutter something in agreement. When Veronica had finished her lunch, she asked Sixty and me to come with her to meet Molly. "I told her I'd meet her in the change room after her consultation. We should make sure she's okay."

I locked eyes with Sixty across the table and I knew she was telling me that she wanted to go. She and Veronica got up and started walking to the exit, so I didn't really have a choice but to get up and go too. I looked at the top of Chantal's head as I passed. I wanted to say something nice to her, but I couldn't think of anything in time.

Molly was already in the change room when we got there. She was standing in front of the full-length mirror by the entrance to the showers, watching herself as she pulled up onto *relevé* and rolled back to first position. She'd taken her tights off, and her bare legs were dark and glossy.

"How did it go?" Veronica asked her.

Molly stopped what she was doing and looked at us in the mirror. She didn't say anything and bit the corner of her lip as though she was trying to hold something inside. She moved to the padded bench in the middle of the room and plopped her body down.

"What happened?" Veronica asked.

Molly shook her head slowly. I'd thought she'd be too mature and sarcastic to get upset, but I saw now that I was wrong. Her eyes were going glassy. Veronica sat down beside her and threw her arms around her neck.

"You didn't cry, did you?"

"No."

"Did you look like you were going to cry?"

A tear dripped down Molly's cheek and she wiped it with her finger. "I don't know. I don't think so."

"Did you look upset whatsoever?"

Molly shrugged and smoothed her hands over her hair.

"Did you?" Veronica repeated.

"I don't know."

"You can't do that!" Veronica slapped the side of the bench and stood up. "Oh, man!" She shook her head at the ceiling and started pacing around the room. "No matter what he says, you can't show any emotion. Didn't you hear what he said in class?" She turned to Sixty and me. Then she reached out for our hands and pulled us onto the bench so that the four of us formed a huddle. "You have to take whatever he says without flinching, no matter how bad it is. Promise."

We all said that we promised and Sixty squeezed my hand. Her eyes were bright and serious, and I could see how much she loved the moment. Veronica and Molly went out to buy iced coffees at the Coffee Time around the corner, and Sixty and I rebandaged our blisters from pointe class.

"I think I can do that," she said.

"What?"

"Let him say anything to me without reacting. Look." She sat up a little straighter and let the smile drop from her lips. Her mouth gaped open like it had been frozen at the dentist and her eyes lost focus.

"You look like you're high on drugs," I said.

She seemed disappointed for a second and then she burst out laughing. I started laughing too, which made her laugh harder and a sound came out of her nose. She grabbed my arm, as if to brace from further nose sounds, and we both fell back on the bench.

"How about this?" I pushed myself up and tried to remember the face I'd made as a kid when I wanted to look like my dad's patients. I thought of the blankness in the eyes of the women he treated, the empty way they moved down the hallway, as though nothing would ever have meaning for them.

"Oh my god," Sixty whispered. "You look like you're dying."

I turned to her, silent for a moment, and then we both started laughing all over again.

"Hey," she said when we'd regained control of ourselves, "can I have dinner at your house sometime?"

I faked an itch on my ankle and noticed my palms had gone clammy. I wanted to tell her that we didn't have real dinners. My mom barely cooked and my dad was generally home late.

"Yeah," I said instead. "When?"

"It doesn't matter. You decide."

I was about to say that it'd be best to wait a month or so, but she kept talking. "I could come tomorrow?" Her eyes were very still.

I worried about this dinner as soon as I'd agreed to it. I hadn't brought a friend home since elementary school. I imagined my parents at the dinner table together, my mom howling for attention, my dad doing his best to just eat. I hoped for his sake that he wouldn't be home. My dad didn't deal well with girls. When Isabel was sixteen, she called him a misogynist because she'd brought a friend home and my dad had walked right past the friend without saying hello. The next time Isabel brought a friend home, my dad did say hello, but Isabel claimed it wasn't a nice hello, cool and aggravated, as if the girl were in his way. I tried to explain to Isabel that his aloofness was only a defence mechanism because he was surrounded by crazy patients all day, but she said that was no excuse. Later I heard laughter from Isabel's bedroom and felt two things at once: the desire to be laughing with her and shame at desiring what my dad disliked, the silliness that insulted his home.

There was little point in warning my mom that Sixty was coming for dinner. She'd say *oh sure, no problemo* and then forget the conversation immediately. But I would need to prepare Sixty for my family, tell her as little as possible, but enough. I waited the whole next day until we were on the subway.

"My dad probably won't be home tonight. He's on call all the time."

Sixty swung her leg under the seat, then kicked it back up again with a jolt to her knee. "What kind of doctor is he?"

"A psychiatrist."

"And he needs to be on call?"

"Yeah."

"That's strange."

"Why?"

"You just wouldn't think there'd be so many emergencies."

I had never really thought of this before. I imagined my dad in the long hallway of the psychiatry wing that I'd visited as a kid, pacing up and down like a prison guard. He needed to be there because he was in charge, the only expert with genuine authority. If there weren't any emergencies, maybe he'd retreat to his corner office and put a dent in the paperwork on his desk. He kept detailed reports on every patient, wrote all his insights and diagnoses down too. Other doctors were lazy with their records, but my dad did things right and his tower of files grew, made a skyscraper in the corner of his office between the window and his ficus plant.

"He just has a lot of work." I paused. "And my mom can be funny."

"Funny how?"

I shrugged. "She's emotional."

"What does that mean?"

I looked at my hands, smoothed them over my lap. "She just has a lot of feelings."

Standing on the front stoop, I fitted my key slowly into the lock. A gentle entrance would set the right tone. I took Sixty's jean jacket and hung it in the hallway closet. Then I cocked my head towards the living room, indicated she should follow. Sixty pulled on the end of her T-shirt, looked down to make sure it was clean. I tried to see her through my mom's eyes, her black hair, frizzy in a good way, her small running shorts that cut high on her thighs. I couldn't remember the last time my mom had met a friend of mine. I had no idea what she'd think.

My mom was sitting on the rug in the living room, one knee up. Her hair was in a ponytail and she wore her glasses, black squares that drew a heavy line between her eyebrows. Books were stacked around her body in low piles, like squat clumps of stone. She had a hardcover against her thigh, was writing something inside it.

"Hi," I said.

She looked up at me, shut the book with a jerk. She hoisted herself up on her hand and got rid of it quickly, adding it to the pile on her left. It was an old book, a burgundy cover that looked leathery, no image on the front. I strained to make out the title, saw a blur of engraved gold.

"What are you doing?"

"Organizing." Her hand went to her forehead, swiped away a strand of hair.

"I brought my friend Laura home for dinner. I hope that's okay."

My mom looked past me as though only seeing Sixty now. Her gaze just stuck there, distractedly, her mind slipping somewhere else.

"Mom?"

"Oh, it's fine." She tried to smile a bit. "There'll be five of us, then. Your dad is home tonight. And Pilar is dropping Isabel off."

There was ice in the way she'd said *Pilar*, a twitch of the usual spite. I hoped that Sixty hadn't heard it.

"Go ask your father what he wants to do for dinner."

Sixty followed me through the next alcove and past the dining room. I swallowed this mixture of good and bad news. Isabel would improve the evening by a thousand times, but my dad might make things difficult. He would be mad at me for bringing a friend home. He wouldn't say anything but I would feel it, the dark pit at the centre of his mood.

He was sitting at the kitchen table. His BlackBerry, keys and some change were spread out in front of him as though he'd emptied his pockets before he sat down.

"Hi, Dad."

"Hi, Georgia."

"This is my friend Laura. She's staying for dinner."

He registered this with something between a smile and

a frown, his lips stretching horizontally, not sure which way to curve. I looked at Sixty. She was exactly the kind of girl my dad would like least. She was too pretty and her voice was high and loud, full of cheerful flourishes and extra words. I looked at her short shorts and felt ashamed. She was smart, but he would never think so. My dad liked the kind of smart that stapled people to the floor, made them solid and unsilly, smiling only at appropriate times.

"Hello, Laura."

"Hi." She rolled her foot onto the edge of her sneaker. "Thanks for having me."

He didn't answer, picked up his BlackBerry and swept his thumb over the keys.

"Mom wants to know what we're doing for dinner."

"Okay." He didn't look up at me. "Thanks for the message."

I led Sixty up to my room. I was expecting a lot of questions, but she just walked slowly up the staircase, looking at the art reproductions framed along the wall. Maybe things didn't seem that weird yet. My mom hadn't raised her voice, hadn't been all that mean to my dad. Sixty paused on the last painting. It belonged to Isabel, a gift from her mother. A completely naked woman reclined over a background of oily shadows. Her body looked soft and pale and her globular breasts stayed very upright despite the fact that she was lying down. The woman's arms were crossed behind her head, and what Isabel loved most about the painting was her hairdo. She had a helmet of brown curls that hung over her forehead and down to her chin. Isabel said the woman looked like the guitarist from Def Leppard, even though the painting was two hundred years old.

"It's by Goya," I said.

"Oh." Sixty wiped her finger along the bottom edge of the frame as though the gold finish might come off on her skin.

We walked into my room. I'd kept my door closed all day and it had the stuffy smell of sleep. Luckily it was pretty tidy, with maybe only four or five pieces of clothing crumpled on the floor. Again, I expected her to start asking questions about my family, but she just stepped over the jeans I'd worn yesterday and moved to my desk. She leaned in towards the calendar of Gelsey. The September page had her in a long tutu, stepping into a deep *arabesque*, her calf a dark inch from the back of her head. Sixty walked by my bookshelf, trailing a finger over a few spines. She glanced at the Pre-Raphaelite print of Ophelia drowning that Isabel had given me for my fourteenth birthday. Then something caught her eye, the picture frames on my dresser. She moved towards them and lifted one. It was of my mom holding me as a baby. It was summer and I must have been only a few months old, just a crescent of blanket in her arms. My mom inclined her head to one side so that her dark hair swung completely over one shoulder, and she wore a pale dress with thin straps that tied into bows. Her skin had a lustre to it, darkened by the sun. She was looking straight into the camera, smiling goofily at the photographer.

"Your mom's hot."

I shrugged. "Thanks."

"She's really young, huh?"

"There?"

"No." Sixty replaced the photo on the dresser. "Now."

"She's almost forty."

"She looks younger than that." She went over to my bed and bounced backward onto the mattress. "How old is your dad?"

"Older."

"Yeah. No kidding." She placed a pillow behind her back and leaned against it. "How did that happen?"

"What?"

"Your dad scoring someone so hot and young?" She liked the question. I read the pleasure it gave her, the burst of novelty in her eyes.

I moved towards her, sat on the edge of the bed. "It was just—" I stopped, not knowing how to answer her.

"How did they even meet?"

"At the university."

"Doing what?"

I moved my body around so I was sitting beside her. "My dad teaches at the medical school. And my mom was doing her PhD. I don't know the actual story."

"So he was a teacher and she was a student?"

"No!" I rocked my shoulder into hers, sent her body towards the bedside table.

"But your dad was a professor and your mom was going to school. That's teacher–student. It's totally illegal."

Her grin was huge. She was trying to be funny, but even the sound of it, those two words pressed in beside each other—teacher–student—made me feel gross.

"It's not like that. You get paid to do a PhD. And they were in different departments."

Sixty shrugged. "Who's Pilar?"

"Isabel's mom."

"When did your dad and her get divorced?"

"Before I was born."

"How long before?"

"I don't know."

Her eyes narrowed. "Was it a few years?"

I was sick to death of the questions. "It must have been."

She looked at me strangely. Her mouth opened to say something, but she stopped herself and sat back against the pillow, a slow contentment washing across her features instead. I felt a dull worry in my stomach, not in the middle part where emotions got violent, but up in the triangle between my ribs. My family had given the worst impression. I wasn't sure what it was but it needed to be fixed.

"Pilar and my dad woke up one morning and realized there was no more passion. My mom said it was the perfect divorce."

"Wow."

I watched her expression carefully and I didn't like it. "There's no bitterness or anything," I continued. "They've even had coffee together, Pilar and my mom."

"Really?"

This part wasn't true. I don't know why I said it. My mom did her best to avoid Pilar. She sometimes called her things like "that self-entitled bitch" or "that bad habit your father kicked" and then apologized right away with a crooked laugh, pretended she'd only been joking. When Isabel was young and Pilar came to the house to get her, my mom was always tinkering with something in the basement or, if it was summer, out in the backyard pretending that she liked to garden. I could picture the whole scenario like an old movie where the characters wore out-of-date clothing. My dad answered the door and I wrapped my arms through the spokes of the iron banister as though it was more a matter of being stuck there than any real desire to stay. And there was Pilar, tall and solid, her skin the colour of a manila envelope.

"Pillars," Isabel once corrected me, "hold up the ceiling. My mom's name is Pi-LAR. It's Spanish. It's beautiful. It's totally different."

I stared at this woman as she waited in the vestibule for Isabel. I remember wanting desperately for her to look at me, but she never did. She had a strange face, hard and tight, with none of the feminine softness I worshipped in my mom. I squinted at her folds and edges. Was she ugly or pretty? I could never figure it out, but knew she must be very much one or very much the other. I shimmied my rib cage from side to side, tried to hoist myself up on the banister, did all the stupid things kids do to get attention. But I never managed to get hers.

"It's really unusual that they get along," Sixty said.

"Is it?"

She flipped to face me. "My mom remarried three years ago. My dad can't even say the guy's name. I saw him try once, *Robert*, and it was like he'd filled his mouth with lemon juice." She puckered her lips to demonstrate. "He says divorcing my mom is the biggest tragedy of his forty-six years on the planet."

"Oh." I looked down at my lap. "My family's not like that."

"I'm really close with my dad, though," she added. "We talk on the phone all the time." She bounced onto her stomach, kicked up a bare foot. "I guess you don't talk to your dad much. With him always on call."

"No. Not much."

"Does it bug your mom?"

"What do you mean?"

"You said she was really emotional."

"Oh." I turned my head, bit the corner of my lip. "That's just her personality. It's completely unrelated."

Isabel called Sixty and me down for dinner. I felt immense relief at the sound of her voice, warm and normal, carrying up the stairs. Isabel would make my family seem okay. I led Sixty out of my bedroom.

"Isabel's twenty-two. She speaks Spanish and French perfectly. She just started her master's."

"That's cool."

"It's a part of English Literature called Critical Theory. It's pretty complicated."

Isabel was standing at the foot of the stairs, gripping the banister as she leaned away from it, so that her body curved like a bow. I introduced her to Sixty and watched them shake hands. Isabel looked as nice as I had hoped she would. She was wearing a short dress the colour of a camel with little black buttons down its front. We started along the hallway but she hooked her arm around me from behind, pulled me towards her.

"How's everything?" she whispered.

"Fine."

"You like your new school?"

"Yeah. It's good."

"And has Dad been around? Have things been okay?"

I looked at Sixty's back as she moved down the hallway, a couple of feet in front. I didn't want her to hear. "Yeah. Fine."

"Good." She squeezed me in closer. "Remember to *call* me, G. Anytime."

Isabel stepped in front of Sixty and we followed her into the dining room. I heard the two gold bangles clang on her wrist. The table was set, someone had even laid a tablecloth, and my dad was sitting at the head, BlackBerry still in hand. I pointed to the chair where Sixty should sit and took the one beside her. I wasn't sure whether I wanted my dad to look up and acknowledge us, or if it was best as is. There was a bottle of wine in front of him, a waiter-style corkscrew at its side. Isabel picked it up and had the wine uncorked in three swift motions. She filled my dad's glass first, twisting sharply at the end to clear the rim of drips, then moved around the table to where Sixty and I had sat down.

"Would you girls like a drop?"

I pushed my water glass forward even though I didn't normally drink wine.

"Thank you," Sixty said, pushing hers forward too.

My mom came in from the kitchen carrying a giant bowl, two ochre ribbons painted on the ceramic.

"Pesto pasta." She placed the bowl on the table. It made a thud through the tablecloth.

Isabel and I locked eyes. Her cheeks lifted to stifle the smile that leapt to her lips and she raised her hand, covered her mouth thoughtfully. Pesto was my mom's protest meal when she was forced to cook without notice. She kept bushels of basil in the freezer, separated into meal-portioned Ziploc bags.

My mom wiped her forehead. "I made a salad too."

"I'll get it." Isabel stood up and left the room.

My mom sat down. She took a sip of wine and paused, brought the glass to her lips again and gulped. Isabel came back holding a wooden bowl, a well of romaine lettuce, sunflower seeds sprinkled on top. We passed the bowls around and started to eat. The pesto tasted like it always did, which was a good taste, a nutty taste, alternately velvety and rocky on my tongue. My mom bought Parmesan cheese in big geological chunks from St. Lawrence Market and it melted into the sauce, made lumps of salty oldness. I wrapped the linguine around the fork and tried not to be bothered by how quiet it was. When I focused carefully from the middle of my ear, I could hear Sixty chewing beside me, a wet kissy noise inside her cheeks. I looked up at my mom. She was staring at her plate without blinking. I hated when she didn't blink.

"This is really good," Sixty said. "Thanks again for having me."

My mom lifted her head, perplexed a bit, called back to the world despite herself. "Oh, it's nothing. Sorry it's all been a little improvised."

"So." My dad replaced his wineglass on the table, rubbed the stem between thumb and finger. "What did you want to talk about, Isabel?"

"Oh." Isabel looked from my dad to my mom. "I just . . . I have a little news."

"News?" My dad's chin retreated, turtle-like, towards his neck. "What is it?"

"It's not such a big deal or anything. I'm having a paper published in an academic journal."

"Wow." My mom leaned forward, her voice stretching through the word. "That's fantastic. Which journal?"

"*The Journal of Popular Culture*. It's based out of Michigan State University. I didn't know anything about it, but my mom sent my essay in and, yeah, I guess they liked it."

"That's great, Isabel." My mom glanced at my dad. "Really impressive. It's early in your career to be publishing already."

I turned to Sixty, wondered if she was impressed too.

"What do you think, Dad?" Isabel asked.

His forehead rippled in three thick folds. "I think it's excellent. You should publish as much as possible."

"Yeah, well. I guess I'll try now."

"So what's the topic?"

"It's called *The Abject on MTV*."

My dad made a show of turning his ear towards her, as though he hadn't heard. "Come again?"

"*The Abject on MTV*."

He rubbed the side of his face. "I think you'll have to expound on that."

"It takes Julia Kristeva's notion of abjection and applies it to portrayals of young women in all those really popular reality-TV shows. You know, the ones that are half-scripted and have twenty-year-olds lounging around in bathing suits?"

"Like *The Hills*?" Sixty asked.

"Exactly."

My dad stabbed a piece of lettuce. "Interesting."

I recognized the tone and I knew Isabel did too, a sound knotted with disapproval.

"So explain this to me," he continued. "This . . . sorry, what was the term again?"

"Abjection?"

"*Abjection*. Yes." He took a sip of wine. "What exactly does that mean?"

Isabel wet her lips. "Kristeva is a literary theorist who writes a lot about the body and how, historically, the body is associated with the female and then written off as weak, immoral, dirty. She thinks that in a patriarchal society, a person has to *abject* the female body—you know, turn *against* it—in order to achieve selfhood. It's kind of like Freud's Oedipal thing, but earlier, because we all come from a female body, so that body is the first threat to a person's independence in a patriarchal world. But if you're a woman, it gets really complicated because . . . well, you're basically rejecting yourself."

My dad narrowed his eyes, turned his head a few degrees. "Okay."

"So in my paper, I guess I deal with the issue of complicity. Why are these women on TV complicit with their own objectification? And I look to Kristeva's theory for possible answers."

Isabel moved her hands when she talked, not a lot, but in a delicate way, almost balletic, enhancing her ideas with little flutters of her wrist. I would never be able to talk this way, but I loved listening to her. The problem was my dad's reaction. He saw invisible things, tiny wrinkles in her argument. I was amazed by his ability to locate them, run his fingers along the seams of her ideas and dig out the strings, instantly split them open. It was miserable for Isabel, though. The impact of my dad's action would seize hold of her, shake off all the poise I admired. A heat would rush her cheeks and her mannerisms would go a little clownish.

"Cool." My dad turned his attention to his pasta.

"Well, what do you think?"

"This gender theory stuff is all pretty much beyond me, Isabel. I don't think I'm a qualified critic."

"It's not *gender* theory." Isabel's eyes flashed to my mom. "It's just an idea. An interpretive idea. And I mean it's, like, an extrapolation of Freud, Dad. It's right up your alley."

"I'm a neuro-psychiatrist, Isabel. I don't do psychoanalysis."

"I think it's a very clever application," my mom said. "I look forward to reading your paper, Isabel."

"Thanks, Lena." Isabel reached for the bottle of wine, refilled her glass.

"Me too." I said it quietly. Maybe my dad wouldn't hear. I often found myself stuck in these quandaries, captivated by the melodies of Isabel's ideas and then forced to reconsider once my dad had intervened. It went quiet around the table again. I hoped this was the end. The salad travelled from my mom to Sixty to me. I didn't want any more but I took some, bought time as I clamped down on leaf after leaf. The longer my dad waited, the better. Maybe he'd forget what he'd been saying and the air would be cleared for something new. I passed the bowl to my dad. He took it without looking at me.

"So when will this journal be out?"

"Not till Christmas. But Mom's colleague is chairing a conference and she wants me to present it then."

My dad's expression changed. "What sort of conference?"

"A regular conference. A few grad students and faculty from other schools. Her colleague's been researching post-modern representations of the body, so Mom figured that my paper would fit right in."

"Well, that's . . ." My dad glanced around the table. "This paper of yours must be something. Your mother's standards are high."

Isabel shrugged.

"Well, we'll go." He opened his hands, grinned at my mom across the table. "We'll all go. When is it?"

"It's the first week of November. The Saturday."

"Great."

"Aren't you in Boston that weekend, Larry?" my mom asked.

"Oh, right." He paused. "Well, I'll move a few things around. I think I can reschedule."

"I thought you were speaking at the American Medical Association."

"No." My dad hesitated. "That's not till the end of the month."

"You told me you were in Boston that weekend." My mom's voice stuck to the sides of her throat. Sixty was staring at her now, and this just about killed me.

"You've got your dates wrong, Lena."

"It's really not a big deal," Isabel said. "Really, no one needs to come."

"Of course we'll come. It's your first academic honour."

My mom stood up. Her arms hung at her sides, stupid and unmoving. "What the fuck were you planning on doing that weekend if Boston was just a lie?"

The room went still as we stared at her. I had no idea what to do, and in my head I heard *oh god oh god oh god*. She looked shocked by her own outburst, and in a moment she had knocked back her chair so that she could step away from the table. She walked out of the room.

It was worse than anything I'd imagined. She'd never done anything like it before, at least not in front of a guest, and the word *fuck* rang in my ears. Normal moms didn't talk that way. What would Sixty think? She was working on a piece of lettuce, cutting it meticulously into quarters. I did this too, focused on the eating, even though it felt like my stomach might collapse. I forced my fork into a clump of noodles, twisted from the stem. Isabel placed her napkin on the table and stood up.

"I'll be right back." She walked out, following my mom.

I wouldn't look at my dad. I brought a perfect coil of linguine to my mouth and chewed through it silently. I prayed he'd say something to make the situation seem more ordinary. He would feel it and tell a joke, do something poised and adult, smooth out the catastrophe as best he could. I tightened every muscle in my body and willed it to happen. He lifted his wineglass and drained it in one gulp. Then he got up and left the room too.

Isabel took a taxi home and dropped Sixty off at her residence on the way. I waited for my parents to go to bed, crept down the staircase to the living room. My mom had put the books back on the shelf and I searched for the burgundy one I'd seen her writing in, the flash of gold emblazoned on its spine. I found it on the second-to-bottom shelf, *Tess of the D'Urbervilles* by Thomas Hardy. The yellowing pages smelled of firewood and postage stamps. I flipped to the title page. There was my mom's name in the top right-hand corner,

Lena Omsky, in her tall, clear hand. I ran my finger over the ink as though it might be fresh enough to smudge. I opened more books, chose the older ones in hardback, things I knew she liked. There was her name again and again. Was she worried someone would steal them? It seemed like such a weird fear, and the fact that she indulged it made me angry. This was just how she saw the world, as though her body was more delicate than other bodies and invisible winds conspired to knock it down. I imagined her at the head of the dinner table again, the terrible look in her eye as she stood up and said *fuck* in front of Sixty. She never cared if she embarrassed me, never cared about much but the tiny drama of the moment and how it might make her feel. I was getting so mad that I could have taken all her books and thrown them against the wall. But instead I was careful to straighten each one and put them all back on the bookshelf until the room was just as I had found it.

I lay down on the carpet and watched the slick black window, where streetlights blurred to make gold stars. Isabel would be home by now and I pictured her on the stool in her kitchen, one bare foot propped on the water-stained wall, and the noises that her house was flush with, warbling pop music from someone's bedroom, the murmur of a reality show on someone's computer. She'd call her mom and tell her about her day and Pilar would be sitting in her living room, ready to offer advice. I tried to imagine Pilar's face in a close-up. I wanted to see what she looked like, not her features but the appearance of her compassion, how it revealed itself on her face. Something about it seemed heartbreaking, the hugeness of a good mother's love, and imagining it I felt the clamp in my chest that I get at the saddest part of a movie, a squeezing that reaches all the way up my throat.

SIX.

A FEW DAYS LATER, WE were waiting for Roderick to come in and start our pointe class. I sat beneath the barre in Studio A and examined my feet. I had just tied on my new pointe shoes. They were Freed's of London, fitted by the school's specialist the day before. The shoe's vamp made a stiff tomb around the top of my foot, so that my toes felt impenetrable, ready to be thwacked into the floor. The ribbons were in perfect contrast, delicate and soft, such a pale pink that they were barely pink at all. If I rocked my legs slowly to the right, the sun from the window mottled the satin like gasoline on the surface of a puddle. I pointed my toes and felt a new strength scuttle down my calves and into my ankles, ricochet off the arches of both feet.

The girls beside me were talking.

"Do you know the one with blonde hair and big teeth? She's in grade ten," Veronica said. "She's really skinny."

"Not as skinny at the French girl," Molly said.

"Yeah, but that doesn't look good. She's weird skinny. It's not spaced out the right way."

"The blonde girl's just as skinny," Anushka said.

Veronica was shaking her head. "Okay, maybe if you put them both on a scale, but the French girl's shoulders are too high or something. It makes her look stiff."

"I like that girl Alana in grade twelve," Anushka said. "She has the perfect body."

"Yeah," Molly said. "Pretty amazing."

"Yeah," Veronica agreed. "It's good for ballet but she still has other options. I mean, if she decides to do something else with her life she'll still be really hot."

"I bet Roderick likes her body," Molly said.

The girls looked at each other, moved inward as they giggled.

"Do you think he notices?" Anushka asked.

"Of *course* he notices. He still has a dick." Veronica had her chest on the floor, her legs splayed in middle splits. "And"—she pulled her body forward with her hands so that her legs bent like a frog's—"I heard that something happened between him and a student once."

"What?"

"I don't know exactly."

Anushka moved in closer. "Like *sex*?"

"It's possible."

"Who told you?" Molly asked.

"No one actually told me. I just heard the rumour."

The girls drew nearer to Veronica as though pulled instinctively. Veronica was silent now but the idea was there. Sex. I could tell that the girls wanted to ask more, but it was like they couldn't find the right questions. Veronica flipped onto her back, so that her body imitated the curve of a canoe. She rolled a shoulder back, arm stretched to the ceiling.

"I mean, I have no idea if it's true."

There was a noise in the doorway. Roderick stepped into the studio, walked quickly across the room.

"Ladies." He placed his briefcase on the piano and smiled. "Where do I get off being so late?" His eyes went to the clock on the wall. It was fifteen minutes after the scheduled start of class. He whispered something to the pianist, then turned back to face us. "I need a volunteer."

I caught my breath. His entrance had happened so quickly and now he was looking over the group of us, waiting for someone to raise her hand.

"No? Not one brave soul among you?" He undid the cuffs of his shirt and moved to the centre of the room. Then he rolled up his sleeves, folding instead of scrunching. "If you could all come together a little." He moved his hands towards each other. "Form an audience."

I got up and moved with the others in the direction he had indicated. My leotard crept up my bum. I pulled on the elasticized bottom, forced it lower on my hip as I sat back down. Roderick was making a strange face, squinting on the top, smiling on the bottom, as though he was pleased and displeased at the same time.

"We can wait here all day if you'd prefer. Les Grands Ballets Canadiens will be busy training the stars of tomorrow, but I'm happy to whittle away the time doing nothing."

There was a sound in front of me. Molly stood up.

"Ah." Roderick pressed his lips together, nodded. "Good."

I looked up the long seams of Molly's tights. The left one went crooked right below the swell of her bum cheek.

"Thank you, Molly. Please come and stand up here."

She walked around the other girls so that she was standing beside Roderick. She looked at him, waited for more instructions. There were no emotions on her face and I knew she was trying to do as Veronica had advised us.

"I just want you to stand here. Pick a position that's comfortable to stand in, like first position or *cou-de-pied*."

Molly nodded. Roderick moved around us. I turned my head to see him lean his body into the corner at the far end of the room. Molly took a few steps backward, making more space between herself and the audience, and moved her right foot behind her ankle into *cou-de-pied*.

"Good. That's fine, Molly. Now just stay up there and relax. Imagine you're on stage, waiting to dance your segment."

Molly inhaled and made the final adjustments to her

position. Her expression was still absolute nothingness and it impressed me. I wasn't sure that I'd be able to stay so neutral for so long.

"In the meantime," Roderick continued, "we're going to watch you. Because that's what audiences do."

There was a little murmuring around me.

"Is that clear, ladies? I want you to watch Molly as though she's a dancer who's caught your eye in the *corps de ballet*."

Sixty was sitting beside me and I could feel her eyes veer my way, but I didn't look at her. I looked up at Molly and tried to do as Roderick had said. What would I think of Molly if I just happened to see her on stage? The first thing I'd notice was her height; she was probably the tallest fourteen-year-old I knew. She was very skinny too, but it was a skinniness that looked natural, like there was just too much of her for any amount of food to fill. She had a small face, high cheeks round as plums. Her mass of hair was slicked tight to her scalp, black as underground oil. I scanned the length of her legs. Pink tights on brown skin made an ashy colour. I could tell her feet were powerful; they were big and the one in *cou-de-pied* showed off a protuberant arch.

"How tall are you, Molly?" Roderick asked from behind us.

"Five–nine."

Roderick paused. "Hmm. And still growing?"

"Um, I don't know."

"How tall are your parents?"

"My mom's just five–six."

"And your dad?"

She looked down at her feet for a moment. "Pretty tall, I guess."

There was a pause. "Can you go up on pointe for us, Molly?"

She was about to say something but Roderick beat her to it.

"Just *relevé* into fifth position. I don't care what you do with your arms."

I thought I saw a new tightness around Molly's mouth. She placed her *cou-de-pied* down on the floor and *pliéd* in fifth position. Then she snapped her feet together so that she was standing on pointe, one leg crossed snugly over the other. The impression was powerful. Her body became an endless pike of muscle.

"I have news for you, Molly." Roderick had pushed himself out of his corner and was walking slowly up the side of the audience. "You're not five–nine anymore."

She lost her balance a little and had to move her front foot. "Okay."

"You're about six foot two now, which is a good five inches taller than the average male dancer."

Molly kept her eyes fixed.

Roderick crossed his arms over his chest and turned his body towards us.

"So actually, we can't imagine Molly as a dancer who's caught our eye in the *corps*, because Molly will never get a job in the corps. Or at least not the corps of any reputable classical company. She's just too tall."

I looked at Molly. Would she be able to stay in control of her feelings? She tottered to the left again and had to move her foot to keep her balance.

"You can roll down now."

She did as she was told but I saw the first flicker of defeat in her eyes.

"Now don't look glum." Roderick was moving towards her. "It's not as though you were any shorter when we accepted you last spring." He was just a foot or two away from her now and he stopped. "Some of the best ballerinas of all time have been as tall as you. Suzanne Farrell. Sylvie Guillem. And their height wasn't a disadvantage to them. No. It wasn't a disadvantage at all. It made them magnificent." He crossed in front of Molly and stopped at her side. "So that's your challenge. That's your work cut out for you. Your height means that you have to be better than good; you have to be the best. Do you think you can be the best?"

"Um"—she pinched the strap of her bodysuit, looked at the floor—"I don't know."

A meanness smeared Roderick's expression. "Well, that's a problem." He crossed his arms over his chest. "To tell you the truth, I'm not sure I know either."

I watched Molly process this.

"But we'll find out. When the company directors come to watch you dance at the end of senior year, they have to pick you out and say, 'I want that girl as a soloist.' They may look at someone else and say, 'Hmm, she's talented, let's take her on as an apprentice and see how it works out.' But you, no way. They need to be able to hire you on the spot and drop you straight into their toughest repertoire. There isn't likely to be more than one male dancer over six–two in that company, and you've got to prove that you're worthy of him." Roderick shook his head. "Okay, Molly. Go sit down."

She looked surprised for a moment, as though she'd misheard him, but then she rejoined us, lowered her body to the floor. Roderick just stood there. A piece of hair dipped over his forehead and he swung it away without using his hand.

"The point of that wasn't to pick on Molly. It was an example for all of you. We could take the time to go through that process with everyone, and we will, one on one. You all have your individual challenges, and it's crucial that you know what they are from the outset so that you can monitor them from here on in. Because otherwise"—he lifted his hands in the air, shrugged—"what are we doing here?"

He turned around and took a few steps with his back to us.

"All right, ladies. Everyone at the barre."

He talked us through the first exercise. He nodded at the pianist and the music began, languid, drippy notes running into the notes beside them. We bent our knees, made diamonds of negative space, lifted heels into ankles. The end brought a suspension, *soutenu* in fifth. I lifted my arms.

"Stop."

The music stopped. My arms found my sides and we turned as a group to face Roderick. He was marching across the studio to the barre, heading to where Veronica stood. I saw a tiny flash of fear on her face.

Roderick motioned towards her. "You go back to that last position."

Veronica hesitated for a half second, then put her hand back on the barre. She lifted the other arm, resumed the *soutenu* in fifth. Her focus shot forward, deliberately unflinching. She was still as a statue; her pale hair caught the light.

Roderick turned to the rest of us. "What is *that*?" He pointed at her hand. "Those fingers," Roderick continued. "Yikes."

I looked at her fingers. Technically they were in the right position, her middle finger dropping to her thumb, the index finger isolated and lifted. But I saw what Roderick was talking about. They looked wooden, complicated, like a severed set of antlers. She must have been double-jointed, because her thumb even curved the wrong way.

"Jesus, that's going to keep me up at night." He turned away from her, fluttered his hand over his shoulder the way a king dismisses a servant. "Put that thing away."

Veronica lowered her heels to the ground, let her arm drop to her side. She suddenly looked very young, not fourteen but more like seven, a kid lost at a crowded mall.

"Where the hell did you learn that?" Roderick was pinching the bridge of his nose, shaking his head.

"I don't know," she answered quietly.

"No, tell me. Where did you train?"

"The local school in St. Catharines."

"Called?"

"The Niagara School of Ballet."

"The Niagara School of Ballet," he repeated slowly. "Wow." He brought his hand to his stomach. "That just about killed my lunch."

Veronica stood very still, stony across her shoulders.

Roderick talked us quickly through the next exercise, then went back to his usual corner behind the piano, slinked his body between the two walls. His eyes pulled into two narrow sneers and there was a tilt in the line of his lips, like he was just a breath away from laughter. Why did he want to laugh at us? It was as though, without knowing it, we had collectively done something ridiculous. I could see Veronica on the opposite barre. She was biting the inside of her cheeks and her eyes had the tender look of someone who's just taken off her glasses. I figured she was doing everything to keep her feelings from boiling up onto her face.

When Roderick dismissed us, we walked as a group back to the change room, lifting our heads only to swig back water or wipe perspiration from our brows. No one spoke and the distant warble of piano chords sounded as sad as funeral music. Sixty found my side and we drifted together without looking at each other. When we got to the change room, Veronica and Molly dropped their T-shirts and reusable water bottles and hugged.

"You were so good," Molly said after a moment. "You didn't even flinch."

"You too," said Veronica. "You were totally deadpan."

"I thought I was going to hyperventilate."

"You couldn't tell," Veronica assured her. "I couldn't even see you breathe."

Anushka and Sonya moved in towards the girls and took turns hugging both of them. Anushka whispered that she was so *sorry* and Sonya said she'd heard that it was a good sign to get picked on first. Sixty looked at me, her expression steady with compassion, and moved in to hug them as well. Molly was crying now and Veronica handed her a box of Kleenex from the bottom of her locker. I tried to join the group of them, moved over as much as I could so that I was in the general hub of activity, but I didn't know what to say or how to initiate a hug without looking stupid.

"What are you staring at?"

It was Veronica's voice and my heart stopped. I looked up and saw that she was talking not to me but to Chantal, who was standing alone in front of her locker. Chantal looked completely pissed off by the question. She shrugged a shoulder and turned towards her locker.

"That is *really* inconsiderate." Veronica glared at Chantal's back.

The other girls turned around.

"What did she do?" Molly asked.

"She was just standing there looking"—Veronica shook her head as though the whole thing was too infuriating—"weird." She turned to her own locker and started pulling out the hairpins from her bun until a loosened ponytail swung across her back. She yanked out her elastic and her blonde hair went everywhere. "Let's do something fun! Let's go to Coffee Time."

"Yes!" said Molly

"Coffee Time?" Anushka asked.

"All the guys from Eastern Collegiate hang out there. Come!"

Veronica explained that she and Molly had seen a group of guys smoking and drinking coffee in the parking lot adjacent to the shop. They'd been too far away to judge how hot the boys were, but Veronica was sure they looked promising, had shaggy hair and tapered pants, boys who could have sung indie music. The three of them started to get ready, pulling lots of extra clothes out of their lockers so that they could try on each other's things. A pile of pointe shoes and dirty tights accumulated on the floor, and the girls laughed as they threw their heads upside down to fluff up their hair. Veronica found a spandex leotard in the clump of discards, the back a giant V that would dip down to your last vertebra. She stepped into it, smothered her boobs with her hands.

"You look amazing," Anushka said.

Sixty and I got dressed too. She didn't say anything but I could feel the hope lining all her movements. The last thing I wanted to do was meet boys, but I wanted Sixty to be invited for her sake. Chantal left the change room without saying bye to anyone, and Veronica, Molly and Anushka burst out laughing before she'd even closed the door. I thought about Roderick as he smirked at Molly's tallness, ridiculed Veronica's hand. The spandex bodysuit cut into her skin now, gave her bum a double bulge. I looked at it and remembered the exact tone of Roderick's disgust. Was it a coincidence that he picked on the girls who talked about boys all the time? Maybe he could sense it in ballet class, a girl who wasn't just dancing but was conscious of her boobs in her bodysuit, who imagined male eyes sizing up her legs. What if Roderick could smell it on them, like a kind of sex smell? Maybe it leaked from their limbs, left a stickiness in the studio air. And there was a danger in this, the sex inside our bodies. It could so easily ruin ballet.

I thought about this steadily throughout math and science. When we were back in the change room before repertoire class, I didn't want to be there, didn't want to hear any more gossip about Coffee Time or boys. I moved faster than everyone, pulled my tights on in such a rush that I tugged a run right beneath the waistband. It helped that my bun was already made, only needed an extra puff of hairspray. I took the blue bottle of Finesse from Sixty's locker, shielded my eyes with my hands. I slipped out the door and went straight to Studio B. The pianist wasn't even there yet. I took the best spot at the barre, the corner where the mirrors collided, so that I could see my front and side at the same time. I scrutinized my torso. I had little boobs now. I looked at the door, made sure no one was approaching and ran my hand over them. I lifted the straps of my leotard so that the cotton pulled over my chest, tucked everything into place. I wouldn't think about them. Instead I sucked my stomach in and dropped from my rib cage, lifted my arms into a perfect fifth *port de bras*.

There was a cough from the doorway.

"Hello." Roderick stepped into the studio. "Please, keep practising. I just need to grab a DVD."

He walked over to the TV stand behind the piano. I turned back to the mirror, tentatively lifted my arm. My pulse was fast and everywhere. I heard him shuffle through things and then stop.

"This is great, this extra initiative." He was watching me in the mirror, arms crossed over his chest.

"Oh, I just . . ." I paused. I was so nervous. I could feel the muscles in my cheeks. "I wanted to practise my placement."

"I can see that." He walked back across the wood towards the door. "Practice is essential." He looked me up and down, paused. "Why don't we schedule your consultation for tomorrow, Georgia? Let's do it after lunch."

He walked out. I turned back to the mirror and stared into my own eyes. They burned with the thrill of what had just happened. This was good, all of it, Roderick wandering in and seeing me alone at work. I was swallowing this little taste of success when there was another sound in the doorway. Sixty rushed over. She'd been looking for me, asked why I had come in so early. Silently, I dug my toes into the floor, kneaded knuckle into wood.

"Well, I wanted to tell you"—she moved closer so that we were wedged inside the corner—"Veronica said Coffee Time was awesome and that they're gonna go again later in the week. She wants us to come."

"Oh." I moved away from her, lifted my leg onto the barre to stretch. "Great."

SEVEN.

I ATE MY LUNCH QUICKLY the next day and went back to the change room to prepare for my consultation. I didn't tell anyone where I was going, not even Sixty—kept it to myself like a precious stone at the pit of my pocket. A few grade ten girls stepped out as I held the swinging door open by its metal handle. One said hi to me, lifted a hand with fingers stuck tightly together, more a salute than a wave. She asked me what was being served in the cafeteria and it took me a second to remember the flavour that was still in my mouth, the tofu stir-fry I had just eaten. I walked around to the mirror by the toilets and waited for sounds. I heard nothing, which was just what I wanted, time to prepare for my consultation alone. I had chosen my outfit carefully that morning, dark blue jeans that were loose at the knees, a white T-shirt that hung from my shoulders like a garbage bag. I leaned into the mirror, squinted at my little face, eyes and nose trying to balance over the pale thread of my mouth. I smoothed the crown of my head with my hand and adjusted a hairpin that had crept out of place.

In my head was an image of Roderick in class the day before and the sound of him too, the nasty things he had said to Veronica. Then there was his laughter, that meanness that had flashed from his eyes when we obeyed his demands and performed the exercises as instructed. I had to show him that whatever he objected to in Veronica and Molly did not exist in me. I fiddled with the edge of my T-shirt, fanned it in the air to propel it away from my body. Roderick wouldn't find it in me, the hidden thing that he disliked. There would be no sex in me anywhere. It couldn't nestle in the pretty curve of the small of my back or sneak up my thighs to the place where my bum started. I had to be a dancer and not a girl. I swallowed hard and muscled my lips into a frown. Could I speak while maintaining this level of severity? I pressed molar into molar, made an intimidating sound from the back of my throat.

A toilet flushed. Veronica banged open a stall door.

"Are you okay?" She stood there, glaring at me.

I repeated the sound with a little more phlegm, turned it into a kind of stunted cough.

"Yeah." I pointed to my throat. "Just had this itch."

She nodded slowly and raised her eyebrows, moved to the mirror. Her expression was steely everywhere, an alloy of suspicion. She pulled her glitter gloss from her back pocket and squeezed it all over her mouth.

"Sixty said you're coming on Friday." She held my eye in the mirror. It sounded like a question or maybe a challenge. "Meet us on the steps at five."

"Okay."

I waited for her to move but she didn't. Finally she sighed loudly and held out the lip gloss towards me. Something in my manner had made her think I wanted some, or maybe she always thought people wanted what she had.

"I don't have a cold or anything," she said.

I accepted the lip gloss. It was tinted a plum colour, smelled like grape juice and plastic. I brought it nearer to my mouth, tried to think of an excuse not to use it. Shiny lips were the last thing I needed now. I could picture the face Roderick would make, his eyes dipping beneath my nose to clock my eager painted mouth, then that all-knowing sneer. I coughed again, slid the tube over the counter to Veronica.

"I shouldn't." I pointed at my throat. "My cough."

She shrugged, stuffed it back in her pocket.

"See you Friday." Her eyes hit me once more in the mirror before she kicked the door open with her foot, caught it with her hand as it swung back on its hinge and walked out.

I knocked on the door to Roderick's office and he told me to come in. I pressed down on the handle. The clamminess of my hand gave me a good grip on the metal. He was sitting at his desk, writing something, and as I stepped inside I realized he wasn't alone. Two shoulders hunched in the chair facing him. They were wrapped in the kind of ballet sweater that you usually see only in ballet movies; it was a grandmotherly lilac and tied into a bow. Chantal. I waited to be told what to do. Roderick paused on a word, weighed the fountain pen in his hand and continued writing. I expected Chantal to turn around to see who I was, but she didn't move.

I looked around the office. There was a framed photo of a ballerina above the desk but otherwise the walls were bare.

"Just give me a second, Georgia. Chantal's just on her way out."

Chantal, accordingly, pushed herself out of her chair and made her way towards the door. She walked with her chin lifted, focused on something far away. Her expression reminded me of the martyrs on the Christian playing cards that Isabel's grandmother had sent her from Spain. Her face was pale but illuminated, the rosebud of her lip almost quivering. She met my eye as she passed, not a warning but a look of trust, as though we were running a relay and she was passing the baton.

Roderick was still writing. He wore a barely pink collared shirt, undone a button lower than necessary, revealing honeyed man-skin, maybe the remnants of a suntan. I imagined him getting dressed in the morning, which was a strange concept in itself. Clothing didn't magically bind to his body; he went shopping, removed labels, folded things away. I imagined him standing halfway inside an open closet, selecting this particular shirt from several very similar ones, doing up the buttons in front of a wide bathroom mirror and deciding to leave the last one undone. Did he admire his reflection? Did he narrow his eyes and smile slyly?

He rested the pen on his desk and looked up at me. "How are you?" His eyes took me in steadily. I whisked a strand of invisible hair from my forehead, tried to steady myself with a breath.

"Fine, thank you."

"It's all a little overwhelming at first." He paused. "Are you finding it overwhelming?"

I shook my head. My cheeks were hot under his stare. It was important that I not blush, because blushing was girlie. My eyes searched for something to latch onto and found the photograph of the dancer above his desk. A ballerina in a white tutu was featured from the thigh up, so that you could just see the disc of tulle at her hips. The photo was obviously from *Swan Lake*. The dancer wore what looked like a headpiece of cotton balls and her hands drooped in front of her body like a dying bird.

"Beautiful, isn't it?" Roderick said.

The woman's pose was pristine Marius Petipa, the original choreographer of all the major Tchaikovsky ballets. Her arms were delicate lines of curving muscle, neither frozen nor moving but suspended somehow perfectly between. But her face was something else. It would be unfair to call her ugly; still it was impossible not to notice the roughness of her features. Her nose was large and its slope interrupted by a bulge of bone midway, knobbly as an elbow. The rest of her face was narrow, tapering to a pointy chin.

Roderick laughed. "Eva Hermann was exquisite on stage. You should have seen her. The kind of presence that actually felt electric. Really, you'd swear she plugged herself into a socket. She just"—he shook his head as he looked up at the photo—"she commanded your attention. Wouldn't take no for an answer. I love that about ballet, how it transcends all of our conventional expectations." He looked back down at me. "Especially when it comes to beauty."

"Mm," I said. "Yeah."

"But in this day and age, ballet is a pretty strange discipline to pursue. That's what's so remarkable about it. We're constantly coming up against our own obsolescence. Makes it essential that we know exactly what we're doing, right?" He leaned in towards me. His eyes were dark and bright at the same time. "So what is it you're doing, Georgia? Why must you become a dancer?"

It was like I'd swallowed something whole and could feel it lodged in the wrong part of my throat. "I . . . why must I?"

"Yes. You agree that we have to be able to define the value of what we do. So tell me"—he extended a hand in a diplomatic gesture—"why is ballet something you have to do?"

"I . . ." I looked down at my lap, smoothed my hands over the dark denim. I needed something insightful. I opened my mouth to say something about art and meaning, but my tongue felt leaden.

Roderick sat back in his chair. "Yes?"

"I . . . I guess . . . it's kind of hard to put into words."

Roderick lifted a hand, palm forward, like I was traffic that had to be stopped. "And that's just it, isn't it?" He chuckled. "That's the very strange paradox of it all. We have to be able to articulate what we're doing in order to fend off the detractors, the people who say ballet is archaic, conservative." He rolled his eyes, shook his head. "And yet ballet is dependent on its ineffability. If we could explain it, if we could summarize it in a paragraph . . . well, it wouldn't be art then, would it?"

"No," I said. "Not at all."

"I *explained it when I danced it*." He shrugged his shoulders and wistfully shook his head.

I had heard this quotation before, I was sure of it. I just couldn't remember the source. I combed my brain for names, for dates, for anything that would sound smart.

"Margot Fonteyn." Roderick raised a single eyebrow. "In 1957. The Sadler's Wells Ballet. Some critic asked for a comment on her performance and, boy, did she put him in his place." He looked over my head for a minute as if this scene were playing out above me. "Are you a quote person?"

"Oh, yeah," I lied. "Completely."

"Me too." He leaned an elbow on his desk and seemed to consider me more carefully. "I'm actually a little obsessed with them."

In my head, I saw the July page of my Gelsey Kirkland calendar. It was early in her career, when she was still with the New York City Ballet. The photo was from Balanchine's *Apollo*, and Gelsey wore the crisp, white frock associated with the ballet, more tennis than tutu. Her arms were splayed akimbo and her back curved in a giant arc, ribs open to the ceiling. There was a quotation beneath it.

I spoke slowly, remembering it word by word. "*In my ballets, women come first. Men are consorts.*"

"Woah." He sat back in his chair, his face alive with new thought. "Someone knows her Balanchine."

Again a blush rose from my chest. I gripped the muscles in my neck to stifle it.

"Balanchine," he repeated, smiling. "Quite the man, I'd say. *The ballet is a purely female thing; it is a woman, a garden of beautiful flowers, and man is the gardener.* Now that's a choreographer I can respect." He made a funny face, flaring his nostrils and holding my gaze hard. I laughed faintly and he seemed to enjoy that. "But these days people are so quick to write off that kind of thing as objectification. Personally, I think it's crazy." He sighed. "So let me get this straight—you recite Balanchine and you practise between classes? Not bad for a grade nine student."

I stared downward, as though what he was saying was unpleasant.

"That kind of dedication is vital. It's something I really respect."

My body felt light. *Respect*. I tried to control the rush of pleasure.

"But be careful." He folded a hand over his chin so that his index finger tapped his nose. "Do you remember what

I said in class the other day? About being more than a good student?" He paused. "Do you know what I mean by that?"

I nodded.

"Good. Because what we're doing here is so much more complex than ticking the right boxes. You need to approach the training with an availability that involves less thinking and more . . . trusting." He paused again, considered me carefully. "Do you think you can do that?"

"Yes," I said firmly. "Yes, I can."

My relief was enormous, intoxicating. It followed me all through afternoon academics and accompanied me on the subway ride home. Not only had Roderick been nice to me, not only had I impressed him with my knowledge of quotations, but he had expressed his respect. *Respect*. I let the fullness of the word hit me as I climbed the stairs to my bedroom. I had never considered the possibility of earning the high opinion of a grown-up man. What would my dad say if he knew? I pictured the surprise loosening his jaw, the way he'd lift his eyebrows and turn away from me, take a moment to believe his own ears. A wicked thrill shot up my spine.

I walked down the hallway. My parents' bedroom door was open and my mom stood in front of the closet, the mirrored doors pushed to the left to reveal my dad's side, suit jackets in gloomy colours and two rows of dress shoes beneath. Before I had a chance to say hello, she burrowed in between the hangers and her head disappeared inside a blazer. For a moment I watched her pull it down, stuff her hands inside the outer pockets and then skim the interior lining. Then I kept walking to my bedroom. I didn't know what she was doing but it gave me a feeling I couldn't stand, like watching someone trip on an escalator when you're a thousand steps above. It made my temples pound and I rubbed my thumbs against them and sat down at my desk. I didn't have time to worry about my mom now.

I typed RODERICK ALLEN into the Google bubble on the top left corner of my computer screen. I didn't know what I was looking for but I knew I was looking for something: information, clues. Why had Roderick become a choreographer and what did he really think of dancers? Did he hate women, as Sixty had told me on the first day of school, or did he notice their bodies, like Veronica had said? Was there some complicated history that could make both things true at the same time? The monitor hesitated for a moment, then loaded 1,730,000 hits. I scanned the first page; they were mostly from the Academy. I double-clicked on the top one and was redirected to the faculty bios. Roderick's was first. I read it slowly and repeated aloud the various European cities he'd worked in: *Paris, Stuttgart, Bratislava*. What was I doing in 1996 when Roderick was awarded the Prix Pavlova in St. Petersburg? I was in senior kindergarten.

I moved on to the next page. Here there were hits from the companies where he'd worked as a choreographer. There were links to newspaper articles too, reviews of his original ballets and announcements of new appointments. I clicked on one from France's *Le Monde*. It was an article about the premiere of a commissioned piece for Ballet Marseille and at the top was a photograph from the opening-night gala. Roderick wore a tuxedo and stood next to a dark-haired woman in a strapless dress. Her eyes flashed with a feeling I recognized, the exhilaration of having been on stage. I read the caption and confirmed what I'd suspected; she was the leading ballerina. I moved in towards the screen, studied Roderick's position. How did he feel about this woman? One hand held a champagne flute, the other hand disappeared behind the dancer's lithe, silky waist.

My bedroom door creaked open.

"George?"

I sat up a little, startled, looked over my shoulder. My mom came into the room. I hit the backspace key once, twice, without thinking, turned to meet her eye. She was wearing the oversized T-shirt she sometimes slept in. The cotton was so worn it looked gossamer in places, stretched softly into evaporated patches. She belly-flopped lightly onto my bed.

"Who's that?" She motioned to the computer screen.

It had rebooted to the headshot of Roderick next to his bio.

"My teacher. Well, the head of the school."

"Oh." My mom swivelled her legs around so that she sat on the edge of the bed and leaned towards the computer. "He's very handsome."

I examined the photo, felt my mom next to me doing the same. It was mainly of Roderick's head and shoulders but his knees folded into the frame as if he was sitting on the floor. His torso was a shadow, a black shirt enveloped by an even blacker jacket. A bare forearm crossed over his knee. There was something soft about his gaze, but something urgent at the same time.

"How old is he?" my mom asked.

"I don't know. Your age."

"No. He's older than me." She leaned in closer. I could smell her jasmine body cream. I looked down at her bare legs, the pear-shaped beauty mark above her left knee. "What are the dates in his bio?"

"Huh?"

"Does it say when he finished his first degree or joined his first company or something?"

"Oh." I looked back at the text. "He graduated from the English National Ballet School in 1979."

"Is he married?"

"I don't know."

She nodded again. Then she went quiet, seemed lost in thought. "Do you like him?" she finally asked.

"What do you mean?"

"Is he a good teacher? Do you learn a lot in his classes?"

"Yeah." I squirmed in my chair a little. "He's really famous. Well, pretty famous."

"Does he flirt with you girls?"

"Mom."

"No, I'm curious." She laughed. "I'm just curious about how it works in ballet school. Is he stern with you girls? He looks . . . so charming."

"It's not like that." I spoke quickly and turned my head away. I didn't want her to see me go red. "It's just normal."

"Does he touch you when he gives corrections?"

"*Mom*."

"I just thought that, I don't know, maybe the male teachers stopped putting their hands on you once you reached a certain age."

"Nobody thinks that way." I sank lower in my chair, frustration curdling inside me.

"Oh." She got up, moved behind my chair. She lifted a piece of my hair, stroked it softly with the pads of her fingers. This irritated my scalp in a tiny, gentle way. "Your friend Laura is very pretty."

I watched the screen.

"She seems a little older than you, doesn't she? A little more grown up." She leaned over, hooked an arm around me. "Does he like her?"

"Who?"

"Your teacher." She read off the screen. "Roderick Allen."

I shrugged, tried to push off her hug.

"Men are always men, sweetie. Even when they're teachers." The phrase had a heaviness to it, not sad but exhausted, like she'd been lugging it around for years. "Just take a look at your father."

I bit my lip because I wanted to scream. "That's not true."

"It doesn't matter how many degrees they have or how principled they are about other things. They're really all the same in the end. It's probably just biology."

I swivelled in my chair to look at her and recognized the danger in her eyes, like a glass teetering on the edge of a table. If she was trying to say something, I wished she'd just spit it out. "Do you mean that they're all perverted?"

The question woke her up. She took a step away from me, tripped over a pair of my pointe shoes that I'd left on the carpet and laughed.

"No, George. I'm exaggerating. You're absolutely right."

"So what do you mean?"

She couldn't stop laughing now, and this was more annoying than anything she'd said, her ability to jump from one extreme to another and make everything feel meaningless along the way.

"Don't stay up too late." She kissed me on the forehead and shut my door as she left.

EIGHT.

I COULDN'T GET THE PHRASE out of my head. *Men are always men.* Why had my mom even bothered to say it when she instantly retracted her words? It was probably a game like all her other games, but I needed to be sure. So I watched for it, wondered whether it might reveal itself in the ordinary. Men parked their cars, raked leaves off their lawns, shopped with their kids at the supermarket. I wondered if it really applied to all of them, even the ones who looked 100 percent nice. I stared as though staring would uncover it, this nameless sexual thing they all possessed. The feeling it gave me was disgusting but addictive, sort of like cracking your knuckles. I performed it like a duty, waited patiently for the thing to expose itself. Would it be just a glint in their eye? Would I catch them ogling pretty women and scratching the lumps in their crotches? I doubted that's what my mom meant. She was hinting at something tougher, darker, like meat you can never chew through.

The subway was a good opportunity for people-watching. There were so many men and they couldn't go anywhere. I tried to pick a different type with every journey. One day it was a big thug of a guy in a quilted ski jacket. He had a hard plastic case beside him that I assumed was a box of tools. I tried to see things in the harsh light of my mom's implications. I searched the train for the kind of woman he would have sex with. I found her; she was standing beneath a cell phone network ad, holding a vertical pole for balance. She had dark roots that gave way to brassy hair, skin that looked like it'd been through the washing machine and dryer. She was wearing a bulky winter coat but it stopped above her knee, revealing two legs in semi-transparent tights. The legs weren't thin by ballet standards, but they weren't fat either, and I imagined him wanting to touch them with his callused hands, rip off her tights.

Another day it was a tall man just a little bit older than Isabel; in fact, I figured he was the kind of guy Isabel would describe as hot. He sat across from me in a wool coat and a turtleneck, had a shadow of stubble around his mouth. There was something gentle about him—it may have been the feminine slope of his shoulders—but I wondered whether this gentleness was a facade. The right girl was sitting directly to my left; she looked sixteen, seventeen maybe, and was really no bigger than me. I stared at her nails, half moons of blue chewed to the nub, and imagined him on top of her, smothering her body with his weight.

The biggest challenges were the most normal ones. I studied the men who could've been my dad's friends. They had expensive coats and leather briefcases, that serious look of dignity in their eyes. I tried to get inside their heads, imagine dirty images on the screens of their brains. Did they just think about the female exterior, the plumpness of a bum, the perkiness of a boob? Or was this somehow the wrong track? I tried to think in anatomical detail, imagine a dark, territorial kind of lust that involved the female insides. I thought of pink, wet flesh and the need to split it open, to capture something even pinker, even wetter, up inside.

My imaginings grew more convincing with every effort—or at least I got better at concocting details that could keep me occupied for entire subway rides at a time. One evening, as I was heading home from a late rehearsal, my subject was sitting directly across from me, reading a *Metro* newspaper on his lap. He looked to be my mom's age and wore a tidy suit, although something about its shape and colour made me sure it wasn't as expensive as the suits in my dad's closet. He had pale skin for a man, and soft hair parted deeply to the side, so that it made a heavy slope across his forehead. The subway car wasn't crowded and I was the only girl in easy visibility. The reality was unavoidable: if this man was a man in the men-are-always-men way, and by deductive logic he would have to be, then I was the woman he was thinking about. The idea sent a wave of disgust to my chest, but there was another feeling too. A curiosity.

I couldn't see the man's eyes, so I focused on his brow and got to work. My brain stumbled over the first image, but I willed myself over it like a hurdle. I had to go on. He was pretending to read the headlines but he was really thinking about squeezing his thumb inside the waist of my jeans so that he could slide the button through its hole with his index finger. He'd pinch the zipper of my fly, then drag it downward tooth by tooth. With one hand on each hip, he'd yank my jeans down to my ankles. I hesitated over my underwear, but it would have to go too. I felt his hand, big, warm, strange, through the thin layer of cotton, then the shock of skin on skin as he dipped his fingers beneath the underwear, pulled it to the floor. He leaned me against the see-through subway divide, my bum white, my back arched, and pounded his body into me.

Just then he looked up. There was a millisecond where we stared at each other before I snapped my head down, focused on my hands. There was no way he could have read my thoughts. He probably figured it was a coincidence, that he'd simply got caught in the line of my absent-minded gaze. If this were true, he would be looking elsewhere now, probably back at the newspaper on his lap. Slowly I lifted my head, and our gazes collided again. I squirmed in my seat, fixed on the red upholstery beside me, felt like an idiot from head to toe.

He was suspicious now, I was sure of it; it was all beyond my control. But how suspicious was he? It was possible that I'd embarrassed him, that he was avidly avoiding me too. Maybe, if I lifted my head gradually, discreetly, made it seem like I was fixated on something to the right of his head, I could check one last time and get away with it. I lifted my head, found a suitable spot just over his shoulder on which to rest my attention. I hesitated for a second, then did it, moved my eyes sideways, where they instantly hit his. Again, we were staring at each other, but it was the expression on his face this time that made it unbearable. He was smiling at me slyly, telling me I'd been caught.

The subway pulled into the station, my heart thudding. The train stopped with a jolt and the man stood up, moved to the exit beside me. Thank god. He was leaving. As the doors opened, he dropped something, a wrapper, in my lap. I thought he muttered something as he dropped it, but it was so fleeting, the man pausing over me, the doors chiming, closing behind him. I stayed very still, worried other people might have witnessed this, feeling a morose responsibility for whatever it was in my lap. Still I burned with curiosity. I wouldn't touch it until the next stop. I bounced my foot, tried to keep myself occupied and instantly gave up. I looked down, grabbed the crumpled scrap of paper and unfolded it slowly. The name *David* was written in scratchy blue letters, and below it was a phone number.

I called Isabel on her cell that night. "What are you doing?" I asked.

"Just picked up some groceries. On my way home." There were sounds in the background, traffic. "What's up?"

"Do you want to come over?" I heard a car honk. "I haven't seen you forever."

"Oh, George. I would . . . I've had the craziest day and I have about a thousand pages to read tonight—"

"Dad's not home," I said. "And I need to talk about something."

"Oh." She paused. "Sure. Of course. Give me an hour."

Isabel showed up forty-five minutes later with a Spanish film and a bag of caramel popcorn. She wore a long, dark coat that tied at her waist, her wavy hair tumbling onto her shoulders. I wondered whether she ever tied it back when she wanted to look important. I worried she'd get mad at me if I asked.

"We don't have to watch it." She gestured at the DVD, placed it on the radiator.

We sat at either end of the sofa in the living room, our legs stretched in opposite directions, me on the inside, her on the out. She turned on the TV and pretended to watch it, but I could tell she was waiting for me to start talking, giving me time to prepare.

"Has Dad been away a lot?" she asked without looking at me.

"Same as usual."

I could feel the scrap of paper in my jean pocket. It seemed twenty times heavier than it actually was, like a piece of cardboard. I pulled it out and passed it to her without unfolding it.

"What's this?" She looked at me questioningly, reached forward to take it. I watched her open it, read it. "Who's David?"

I shrugged. I had wanted her to see it, but now the embarrassment was too much.

"Is he a boy at school?" Isabel smiled.

I shook my head, stared at the cushion beside me. I couldn't meet her eye.

"Well, who is he?"

"A man."

"A *man*?"

"On the subway."

"What?" She moved forward. "A man on the subway gave you his phone number?"

I nodded.

"What do you mean, a *man*? How old was he?"

"Old. Maybe forty."

"Why did he give you his phone number, Georgia?"

"I don't know," I whispered.

"Did he talk to you?"

I shook my head.

"Did he try to do anything?"

I wanted to tell her that I'd been staring at him, that it had been my fault for thinking like a perv.

"It was . . . I was kind of the one who started it."

"What?"

"I was looking at him. And then . . . he caught me."

"What do you mean you were *looking* at him?"

"Just looking." The sound of this was mortifying. I wasn't making sense. "I wanted to see what he was like."

"You were *looking* at him—okay." She lifted her hands to say so *what*. "I mean, were you *smiling* at him? Were you . . . making suggestive faces?"

"No." I shook my head with force. "We just . . . we kept making eye contact. It was only half on purpose. No. It wasn't on purpose, it just started to happen. And then I had to keep checking to see if he was looking at me. Do you know what I mean?"

She got up and paced around the living room. "Ugh!" She shook her head and stopped on a corner of carpet. "If a man ever bothers you on the subway, Georgia, you scream and press the emergency alarm."

"Isn't that only for fires?"

"No!" She came over to me, kneeled, took me by the shoulders. "Georgia, it's for your safety. Don't ever let a man make you feel uncomfortable. You get up and you switch seats. If he follows you, announce loudly that he's making you uncomfortable and threaten to pull the alarm."

"But isn't it a bit my fault for starting it?"

"Nah nah nah nah no!" She shook her head quickly. "You didn't *start* anything. Women are allowed to let their eyes rest on people without having to worry about their personal safety. What a creep! This stuff drives me crazy."

I stood on the subway platform the next morning and tried to name the feeling that drilled inward on both temples. There was something sour in my stomach; I was digesting the disorder in my head. Had I been responsible for provoking this forty-year-old David? The thought was largely ridiculous; I knew this in the rational part of my brain. I had done little more, in fact no more, than accidentally meet his eye three times. The guy was a perv. Still, there was something new inside me, a growth like an unsightly wart. Three measly glances and it had been unleashed, this thing my mom had hinted at. All it took to release it was my getting involved. The discovery gave me a terrible feeling. My mom had been a little right.

A subway pulled into the station. I stepped back from the strip of yellow safety bumps, let the tunnelled air storm my face. The train stopped and the doors opened. I moved forward in line, focusing on the clamour in front of me, trying not to step on heels. I crooked my head to the right to look into the car, see if there'd be anywhere to sit, and through the window I locked eyes with a new man. He was tall, grown up, ordinary. He looked away almost instantly, the way normal people do, but I froze. Why was my heart racing? People were moving around me, entering and exiting the train. Someone shoved into my shoulder and I stumbled to the side. The electronic chimes sounded, one, two, three, a flattened, downhill scale. The subway doors closed and the train left the station.

The platform cleared out quickly and the noise retreated too, but I had a hazy feeling of withdrawal, like half of me was somewhere else. I looked up at the time feed above the middle of the platform. I was an idiot. The next train might not be for another ten minutes and I was going to be late. I moved backward towards a bench, sat on its edge.

When I got to the Academy it was 8:57. I changed as quickly as I could, tried to ignore my unsteady stomach. I was halfway up the stairs when I stopped. Something was wrong. I looked down; I had forgotten my slippers. I ran back to the change room, cursing my stupidity with every step. I could see Roderick's face, the disappointment knitting his eyebrows. He wouldn't say anything, but one eye would squint a little more than usual. I would feel like an idiot for the entire class, maybe the entire day. I remembered my dad lecturing Isabel about being late once. She gave an excuse I believed, something about traffic or having to wait for a ride, but my dad shook his head and said there was no less considerate thing a person could do. His anger had been so profound that he hadn't raised his voice.

I took my ballet slippers from the pile of everything at the bottom of my locker and ran back up the stairs. I stopped outside the studio door and listened for piano music. I couldn't hear any, which probably meant the class was between exercises. If there was a good time to interrupt, this was it. I sucked back air to cool my nerves and pulled open the door.

Faces turned towards me from the floor. The girls were clumped together in the centre of the studio. They sat with their legs crossed or their knees hugged up to their chests. I turned in the direction they were facing and, instead of

Roderick, saw a man I didn't recognize. My relief was immediate, like a flicked switch inside my gut.

I found Sixty as soon as I sat down. She was a few bums away from me and she beckoned me with her head. I shifted around the group of bodies, hoisting my weight like a crab. I watched the man as I travelled. He was short, had shiny black hair and huge round glasses that reminded me of Petri dishes. He stood next to an easel that displayed a laminated poster of a floating triangle. Above the triangle was the title FOOD GROUPS and when I looked more carefully I saw it was divided into four sections.

"It looks like engine oil," Sixty whispered when I reached her. "Are they worried we're going to eat engine oil?"

Sixty must've been referring to the triangle's peak, where two canisters of indistinguishable liquids sat next to a candy that twisted into fish tails on both sides. FATS was the label beside it. Below that were the usual groups, PROTEIN, VEGETABLES, DAIRY and CARBOHYDRATES, with recommended daily servings beside each.

The man rubbed his hands together. He had dimples on his chin that caught the light.

"Are there questions?"

There was silence followed by giggling. I looked up. Molly poked Veronica in the ribs. Veronica lifted her hand. I could see three round moles on her arm, even as polka dots.

"Yes?" The man pointed at her.

"But it can't really matter if you're just gonna puke it all up afterward."

Everyone laughed except the short man. He shook his head to demonstrate his disapproval, waited for the giggling to subside. Molly lifted her hand. The man nodded in her direction.

She cleared her throat theatrically. "Do you know anything about the diet patch?"

"I saw that!" Anushka said. "It's supposed to speed up your metabolism."

"It doesn't work," Veronica said. "I have a friend who tried it and it just gave her a disgusting rash."

They looked up at the man. "What do you think, Mr. Cohen?" Veronica asked sweetly.

"I've never heard of this." He spoke slowly, deliberately, as though chewing up the letters of each word. "I don't know what it is."

"It's a *patch*," Molly repeated. "Like a big pink Band-Aid. You wear it here." She stood up and pointed to her midriff.

"I thought you were supposed to stick it to your butt," Veronica said.

"No." Molly made a face. "Well, maybe *your* butt."

"Hey." Veronica whacked her lightly on the leg.

"Hey, yourself." Molly whacked her back. "Butt Patch."

Veronica, smiling beneath her outrage, turned to the man for support. But he was nervously adjusting the arm of his glasses, eyes cast towards the floor.

The studio door clicked shut. We turned our heads. Roderick was standing in front of it and the laughter stopped immediately. He had a funny look on his face and I wondered how long he'd been standing there. He lifted his hands to shoulder level and leaned his body backward.

"Don't stop on my account," he said.

The man had straightened himself and moved to the easel. "I think we have just about come to the end, actually," the man said. He looked over the group as though asking a wordless question.

When no one said anything, he took the poster off the easel and began to roll it against his torso. The poster veered in an awkward diagonal, so that layers jutted out the side. Chantal got up and held the door for the man.

"Thanks for your presentation, Mr. Cohen," Roderick said.

"Oh." The man turned around, surprised. "You're welcome."

Roderick continued to stand there, looking at us distrustfully. He seemed to enjoy his suspicion, as if we had just denied something when he had the incriminating evidence hidden behind his back.

"I don't like to patronize," he began once Mr. Cohen was out of the room. "I really don't think that patronizing does justice to anything we're trying to accomplish here." He scanned our faces. "Did any of you find that lesson useful?"

I looked down at my stocking feet. My slippers were still bunched under my hand.

"Did anyone find that that was . . . how should I put this . . . ?" He sighed, looked up at the ceiling rafters. "A fair depiction of some of the food issues you've faced, or have maybe seen your peers face?"

Again there was an uncomfortable silence. I heard the dim purr of the studio lights.

"Come on." His voice was persuasive. "I mean, did you see that thing? That poster predates the car phone. The colour scheme alone is enough to kill your appetite."

There was a tentative laugh around the room and I felt it in my own throat too. Out of the corner of my eye I saw Sixty. She leaned back a little, loosened her grip on the knees she'd pulled to her chest.

"It's a Board of Education thing. The food talk. We have to arrange it every year." He started walking farther into the studio, using the barre like a banister. "And we have to hand it to them a little bit. Their hearts are in the right place. They see ballet students as being particularly vulnerable to issues about weight and body image, and they're just trying to protect you. Trying to do what's best."

He stopped. His back was to the barre and he lifted both hands onto it, so that his elbows made right angles behind him. It made me look at his chest. There was a button undone again, so I could see that same triangle of skin.

"But their efforts would be better directed elsewhere. Because, actually, you are among the most protected teenage girls on the planet. And do you know why?" He paused. "Because the ballet body isn't sexual."

There was giggling and shuffling around the room. I looked at my knees and felt my cheeks go warm.

"Go on, get the giggles out." Roderick smiled. "Let me know when we can go on."

We made a few more sounds.

"It's a cliché at this point, but it's one that bears repeating." He gripped the barre behind him. He had thick wrists and I watched the tendons tense. "Your body is your instrument; we've all heard this before. But unlike a violinist, with a single, cherished violin that can, worst-case scenario, be replaced, you get one body. That's it. So, if you'll pardon my French, don't fuck with it."

We giggled again. Sixty looked at me over her shoulder, her eyes bright.

"Dancers have to be thin. This isn't a newsflash to anyone. And if you're not comfortable with that, well . . ." He shrugged his shoulders, his eyes wide. "And it'll mean more work for some of you than others. That's just the luck of the genetic draw. There are dancers like Molly who'll never gain a pound their whole career, then there are others like"—his eyes skimmed our faces—"like Chantal, for example." He held his hand out in her direction.

She was sitting in front of me and I looked at her back. Other girls looked at her too.

"Chantal is an excellent dancer, isn't she? She has strength coming out of her ears. But . . ." He paused and tapped his finger on his mouth. "Chantal, could you come up here for a second?"

Chantal didn't move for a moment. Then, slowly, she placed a hand down on either side of her body and pushed herself off the floor. She took a few steps so that she was standing in front of Roderick.

"Face them," he told her.

Chantal turned around. She kept her chin level and her eyes focused somewhere indefinite above our heads.

"She's got long limbs and that's lovely. But her muscles are short and look what that does." He pointed at her legs from behind. "It adds a bulkiness to her thigh. How does that look, girls?"

Roderick pushed himself off the barre. He walked slowly along it, placing his feet pensively on the floor, as though each step was a new thought. I looked at Chantal. I couldn't see any emotion in her face. My eyes dipped down her neck to her body. The leotard she wore cut high up her leg and accentuated her small belly. It was more childlike than fat, a puddle of softness, not really extra flesh. Then there were her thighs, and I saw what Roderick was talking about, the bulkiness I didn't have, the meat that bowed outward above both knees.

"That was a question, ladies. Will someone grace it with an answer?" He considered our faces. "Georgia, tell me, how does that look?"

Roderick stared at me, waiting. I could feel the other girls looking at me too and my pulse quickened. I shrugged.

"No, no. You're not helping anyone by keeping quiet. Take a good look at Chantal's legs. Do they look like the legs of a dancer?"

I had no idea whether I was really supposed to answer him and all I could feel was my body getting hot. I looked at Chantal and saw that her lips were quivering.

"I'm not asking whether you like Chantal or whether you think she's a good person." Roderick laughed. "This is pretty objective stuff here and these are questions you girls will have to be comfortable with if you're going to succeed. So, Georgia"—he turned to me, dropped his arms to his side—"are Chantal's legs beautiful? Will they assist her in evoking weightlessness and grace?"

"No," I whispered.

"No." He nodded definitively. "They certainly won't."

He turned towards Chantal and, tentatively, I did too. Her lips quivered more now and she tucked them into her mouth. Then, in an instant, her eyes welled with tears and she ran out of the studio.

"Oh, Jesus," Roderick muttered. He turned away from us and walked towards the piano as we started whispering. "Okay, okay. That's enough. Will someone—" He pointed at Limor, who was sitting near the door. "Go make sure she's okay." He sighed deeply. "We better stop there. But that shouldn't happen." He pointed at the door, bounced his hand for emphasis. "She's only slowed things down for the rest of you. Really, ladies, this isn't personal. You'd better learn how to hear these things now, because trust me, I'm being gentle by the standards of the industry." He dismissed us and walked across the studio. He stopped. "Georgia?" His eyes jumped over the other girls to find me. "Thank you for your honesty."

We got up and made our way to the change room. Sixty put her arm around me and Veronica tapped me on the shoulder. "You did the right thing," she said softly.

Everyone whispered about Chantal as we moved through the lobby. Would Roderick get over it or had she lost his respect for good? When we got to the change room, we found her and Limor sitting on the padded bench. Veronica's box of Kleenex was between them and several sheets were balled up in Chantal's lap.

"What happened?" Limor asked.

We all looked at each other. Veronica stepped forward, moved through the group so that she was standing in front of Chantal.

"He was pissed," she said. "You really pissed him off."

Chantal lifted her head. Her face was tearstained but she shrugged to say she didn't care.

"Don't you remember what he told us?" Veronica continued. "About checking your emotions at the door?"

Chantal wiped her eyes. "I didn't mean to," she muttered.

Veronica rolled her eyes towards Sixty and me. "It doesn't matter whether you meant to or didn't. The point is that it's not fair to the rest of us."

Molly stepped forward. "It makes us all look immature."

I watched Chantal's face. A storm was brewing inside her and I thought she'd either dissolve into the vinyl cushion or start to scream. The other girls had moved to their lockers and I followed Sixty to mine. I hoped that Veronica would leave Chantal alone now, but she kept standing in front of her like she had a right to be there.

"Didn't you watch Molly and me last week?"

"You guys were so good," said Anushka.

"You're gonna have to learn how to do that," Veronica continued. "How to *take* it. Roderick should be able to say whatever he wants to you and you shouldn't even bat an eye."

"I can do that," Chantal mumbled.

Veronica and Molly looked at each other and started to laugh.

"I *can*," Chantal repeated.

"Yeah, right."

"I can! You'll see next time."

"What happens if you just fuck up again?" Veronica turned to address all of us, her eyes charged with distress. "We can't risk that."

"I promise," Chantal said under her breath.

Veronica shook her head. "We need, like, *confirmation*."

She moved to her locker and slipped her arms out of her leotard. Molly changed beside her and it felt like everyone was watching, waiting for Veronica to continue. Chantal just sat there looking helpless and angry. Her expression reminded me of a fever, a clammy whiteness of draining blood, like she was sweating and shivering all at once.

"You should come to Coffee Time with us after school and talk to the guys there," Veronica said.

Chantal shifted nervously on the cushion. Fear tightened her mouth and her voice sounded choked. "What do the guys at Coffee Time have to do with anything?"

Veronica glanced over at Molly like this was the stupidest question on earth. "You can practise on them."

"Practise what?"

"*Taking* it," said Veronica. Then she and Molly started to laugh again.

We met on the front steps at five o'clock. Sixty had brushed her hair a thousand times and parted it so deeply on the side that it swooped down to cover her left eye. Her lips were the colour of barbecue sauce.

"You look nice," she told me.

I had taken my hair out of my bun because I knew it would make Sixty happy, but I knew I didn't look nice. My hair was as limp as dental floss. We started to walk eastward as a group. Molly and Veronica were in front of us and they both had their hair loose too, Veronica's swinging halfway down her windbreaker and Molly's a heavy mass of curls around her head. Molly was wearing a leather biker jacket covered in zippers that Sixty had told me was really authentic. Anushka talked to someone on her cell phone behind us and Chantal dawdled beside her, her hands stuffed inside the sleeves of her raincoat. I tried to meet her eye to make her feel better, but she kept her focus on the sidewalk.

The Coffee Time was just around the corner on Jarvis Street. Yellow letters floated in a red bubble over a window that made up the whole wall. There was writing in the glass, frosty letters that said WE SERVE BREAKFAST FRESH. I expected it to smell like coffee inside, but instead it smelled more like sugar, as though the rings of doughnut icing made a vapour in the air. Veronica took stock of the situation. She glanced to the left, where a group of guys, maybe five or six of them, sat at two tables, then led us in the other direction. We sat down at a table against the window. Then she and Molly collected money to buy everyone coffees. I had tried coffee only once and its bitterness had pinched my jaw muscles and made it difficult to swallow. I wouldn't have minded a juice, but I worried that would look stupid, so I passed Veronica five bucks.

"Do you want a coffee?" Veronica asked Chantal.

"Yeah." Chantal dug into the pocket of her raincoat and dropped a bunch of coins into Veronica's hand.

I rested my elbow on the table and looked over at the guys. They were pretty much how Veronica had described them, had messy hair and dirty jeans, hooded sweatshirts that folded over their jacket collars. One guy got up and walked to the counter. He was wearing a giant pin-striped blazer over a T-shirt that said *Hello, I'm Lost*. His arms looked heavy as he walked and he moved his head rhythmically, like he could hear imaginary music. He got in line behind Veronica, and even though I couldn't see her face, I could tell that she was conscious of him behind her. She dropped all her weight onto her left hip and propped her fist there too, like she'd been waiting in line for a century. After a second, they started talking. Sixty nudged me and motioned towards them. "Look," she whispered.

Molly ordered the coffees while Veronica and the guy talked. She seemed to know just what to say to him, and even when she paused it looked intentional, like her silence was a graceful moment in a film. Finally Molly handed Veronica two coffees to carry and they came back to our table.

"They're in grade eleven. They want to get drunk at Allan Gardens tonight," said Veronica.

"Where's that?" asked Sixty.

"In Crack-Central. It's one of the most dangerous areas in Toronto," said Chantal.

"It's just around the corner," said Veronica.

Everyone laughed. Veronica sipped her coffee and pushed her hair over her shoulder. She sat back and looked at Chantal, who was fiddling with her sleeve.

"Maybe you should go talk to them."

Chantal lifted her head. I saw panic in her eyes. "Why?"

"Isn't that why you came? To show us that you can handle stuff?"

"Yeah."

"So?"

Chantal looked down at her coffee and pulled on her sleeves. "What do you want me to say to them?"

"God!" Molly exclaimed. "Just go over and make normal conversation."

"That's not good enough." Veronica flicked Molly's arm. "Chantal's here to show that she can control herself around Roderick."

"What do you mean?" asked Molly.

Veronica fiddled with the plastic tab of her lid, wiggled it up and down until it came off. "The whole point of this is for Chantal to practise being strong enough for ballet class.

So she needs to experience something even worse than Roderick's insults."

Her voice was quiet but full of purpose. Something about it frightened me.

"Like what?" Sixty asked.

Veronica moved in closer. "It should have something to do with sex."

The word stung me. We all sat motionless.

Veronica kept going. "She should go over to the guys and ask them if she can *do* anything for them."

"Oh, my god!" Molly covered her face with her hands. "That sounds so slutty."

Veronica slapped her hand against the table. "I'm being serious! Do you know how bad what Chantal did is? The grade eleven girls told me that when Roderick gets mad at a student, he can take it out on everyone."

We went quiet again. I wondered if this was true. Roderick had been annoyed in class today, but he hadn't gone totally crazy. Chantal was staring down at the table, so I couldn't see what she was thinking.

"But, like, what would she *do*?" asked Anushka.

"Whatever they tell her to."

Molly made a face. "What if they tell her to do something gross? Like . . . suck their dicks."

Anushka gagged on her laughter.

"This isn't funny," Veronica said. She turned to look at the boys' table. "She'll do exactly what they tell her to. That's the whole point."

I couldn't believe what she was saying. I was sure Sixty thought it was as horrible as I did, but her expression was blank. The other girls didn't say anything either.

"I won't do it." Chantal didn't raise her head and her speech was choppy, like every word hurt her throat.

"I thought you really wanted to be a dancer," Veronica said.

"Yeah. But this is stupid."

Veronica made a show of sitting back in her seat and flipping all her hair onto the other shoulder. "Do you know what Roderick said when you ran out of class?"

Chantal shrugged.

"He said that you have two big problems. Do you know what they are?"

Chantal shrugged again.

"Well, Georgia should probably remind you of the first one."

"What?" I sat up, startled. "What are you talking about?"

"Tell her what you told Roderick in class today. He was so pleased with you, remember?"

I looked away. I'd hated saying it the first time and it was too mean to repeat. I tried to laugh. "What's the point when we've already heard it?"

"The point is that Chantal doesn't get it. You were so honest in front of Roderick and you should be able to say it here."

"Come on, Veronica," I mumbled. "Can't we just hang out like normal people and finish our coffees?"

She looked at me meanly now, caught the smiles of Molly and Anushka, and they all started to laugh.

"Maybe you want to go talk to those guys instead," she said.

My heart beat harder. "What's the point of that?"

"I don't know. It sounds like maybe it'd be good for you."

"Yeah," said Anushka. "Georgia should go first and warm them up."

It was unthinkable. I wished Sixty would help me but she was focused on her coffee cup. Was it really a big deal to repeat something that'd already been said? It couldn't hurt Chantal any more the second time.

"Roderick said your legs were big," I said with my eyes on the table. "He basically said your legs were too big for classical ballet."

Veronica clapped her hands once, twice, with exaggerated slowness. I waited for Chantal to lift her head and face me, but she didn't move, just kept staring into her coffee.

"Your other problem is much easier to fix, Chantal," Veronica continued. "Just go over there and do what those guys tell you and you'll prove that you can take it at school." She looked around at all of us. "Who thinks she should?"

The others said they did. When I hesitated, Veronica glared at me.

"What do you think, Georgia?"

"Yeah," I mumbled. "She should."

Chantal slouched down in her seat and pulled her hands farther inside her sleeves. "Okay." Her voice was barely audible.

We decided she needed to be fixed up a bit so that the guys would take her seriously. Veronica and Molly grabbed their shoulder bags and pulled Chantal into the washroom at the back of the shop.

"Do you really think she should do it?" I whispered to Sixty.

Sixty looked worried. I thought she was going to say no, but then she nodded. "We can't run the risk of her crying again."

I sat back in my chair, watched the guys as they elbowed each other and talked. The thought of approaching them left a dead weight on my heart. When Chantal came back from the bathroom, she looked like a kid dressed up as a punk for Halloween. They'd put her hair in a side ponytail and tied the bottom of her shirt into a knot. Her lips had the same outer-space sparkle as Veronica's.

"All right," Veronica said. "Good luck."

Chantal stood there, not moving. Her gaze was more faraway than ever and all the blood had left her face. She glanced over at our table, as though searching for someone to intervene. I looked at the floor. When I lifted my head, she was already walking towards the guys' table. I couldn't believe she was doing it. When she was halfway across the room, the guy with the pin-striped blazer noticed her. He nudged his friend and they watched her approach. Chantal stopped a couple of feet in front of them. I became aware of the radio playing in the background, a woman's voice warning about a collision on the 401, and the clutter of other people talking.

I watched the boys' faces. They were vacant, angled up towards Chantal, and then in an instant they were laughing. Their mouths contorted in horrible shapes and they slapped one another's arms, laughed harder. Something in the sound was too nasty and I wanted to cover my ears. The next thing I knew, Chantal was running out the door.

NINE.

SIXTY WAS STANDING ON THE front steps of the Academy when I got to school on Monday morning. There were leaves on the ground now, clusters of them ringed around the sewers. She should've been wearing a jacket but had a big sweater thrown over her ballet clothes instead. I could even see the pinch of her blue leotard, the skin of her chest exposed above it. When she saw me, she flapped her hand in the air.

"It's starting," she whispered when I reached her.

"What?" I asked.

She took my hand, weaved her fingers between my fingers. I knew her skin was cold because it was the same temperature as mine. I wondered how long she'd been waiting outside. She led me through the side door and down the steps to the first-floor hallway. I inhaled a smell I was getting used to, something sweet to do with the heating system, like cafeteria cookies had been crumbled inside the vents. We got to the main lobby and she pulled me around to the bulletin board. There was a piece of paper thumbtacked to its centre. Sixty let go of my hand and wrapped her arm around my middle, her hand pressing into the zipper of my parka. She pulled me so that I was standing right beneath the sheet.

Four names were printed down the margin.

VERONICA ORR

ANUSHKA SAINI

MOLLY DAVIES

CHANTAL ARCHER

Beside each name was a time, and at the bottom of the page it said: PLEASE REPORT TO MR. ALLEN'S OFFICE AT THE INDICATED HOUR.

"This is it." Sixty had brought her lips close to my ear. "The Rodomization."

I turned around and met her eye. I nodded slowly.

The day passed strangely. I walked by faces in the hall and it seemed as if everyone knew about the list but was trying to look like they didn't. I felt like I had a headache without actually having one. I had already spent the whole weekend feeling bad about what had happened at Coffee Time. The rest of us had sat at our table for a while, expecting Chantal to come back to get her raincoat. When she didn't, I'd stuffed it in my knapsack and left it in my locker over the weekend.

My bad feeling got worse in math class. I looked at the parabolas Ms. McGuinness had drawn on the blackboard and felt my stomach loop up and down with their curves. Veronica sat two seats in front of me. Her posture was very straight and she kept tossing her head back in small waves, the way someone would in a shampoo commercial. Chantal sat down the row from me, three girls away. Everything about her body rolled inward, her shoulders tucked towards her chest. I brought my fingers to the bridge of my nose and pinched the tiny pads of cartilage on either side. Sixty was beside me and she gave me a strange look. I could see the opened page of her notebook on her desk, and instead of parabolas she'd drawn seven or eight palm trees.

Our afternoon timetables were adjusted to accommodate the appointments with Roderick. Repertoire class was cancelled and appointments were slated into the freed time, things like pointe-shoe fittings and physiotherapy. I hadn't been scheduled for anything, and at four o'clock I found myself with nothing to do. I walked along the winding corridor from the lobby to the change room, thinking about the list. The more I thought about it, the worse I felt. All the girls on it had been involved in what had happened at Coffee Time. I couldn't help but suspect that this was more than a coincidence. It was like Roderick knew what those girls were up to. They came into the studio, leotards snug on their bodies, and flaunted the sex that was taking over their insides.

They had boobs, and you could tell they were proud of them, didn't care who knew. Roderick hated it. It was an insult to ballet. It turned the line of an extended leg into something impure, made pervs out of everyone.

I peeled off my ballet clothes and put on my bra and underwear. I pulled on my baggy T-shirt, then my corduroys. I moved to the mirrors over the row of sinks, gave my reflection a cold reckoning. What if Roderick knew that I'd been involved at Coffee Time too? My stomach twisted with shame. I punched my fist into the ceramic edge of the sink and the pain burned up through my knuckles into my wrist. I needed to be so much more careful about my behaviour. I had to focus all my energies on being the kind of dancer Roderick respected. And I had to do more than that too. I had to make sure that he noticed.

I scrutinized my eyes and nose and mouth. The last thing I had to worry about was prettiness. I pulled sideways on my cheeks. My nose flattened and my nostrils stretched. Now my reflection was defensive, like a living, breathing hockey mask. I seized the bun at the back of my head with my whole hand, made sure it was firmly in position.

I took Chantal's raincoat from my locker, put it back in my knapsack and went to the lobby to check the schedule. Chantal's appointment with Roderick had started fifteen minutes ago. I climbed the stairs slowly to the third floor. I could catch Chantal as she left Roderick's office and maybe I'd run into him too. That way he would know that I wasn't running around with those other girls. I walked down the empty hallway towards the office. My running shoes made a squeaky sound on the floor that I didn't like. I passed the academic classrooms that hosted math, geography and French, before coming to the cluster of administrative rooms. Roderick's door was shut. I moved to the bulletin board beside it, pretending to be interested in whatever happened to be posted there.

Magazine clippings about the Academy were scattered across the cork. One full-page spread had a photo of Roderick correcting a dancer's position. She was standing sideways at the barre, a muscled leg stretched high in front of her. Roderick stood behind her, very close, as though his proximity was part of the correction. One of his hands was on her shoulder, pressing it down. His other hand wasn't visible but I knew exactly where it was. Dancers in that position will throw their hips off balance, trying to get a few extra inches of height out of the extended leg. Roderick's hand would be on her lower back, his fingers sinking into the muscles of her upper bum, trying to keep it level. I brought my fingers to my own lower back, pinched them into the same muscles. What would Roderick have felt touching this girl? I moved my hand around the way he would have moved his hand, putting pressure on the mound of round muscle curving under towards my thigh.

A door opened. I dropped my hand, pivoted towards the sound. Chantal stepped out of Roderick's office. She looked right at me.

"Hi." The word scraped up my throat, rough with embarrassment.

Chantal's mouth was straight as a ruler and she didn't say anything. Roderick stepped out into the hallway. "Hello," he said.

I took a shallow breath. "Hello."

He looked from me to his bulletin board and back to me again. I was supposed to explain myself.

"I was just—" I pointed at Chantal. "I was looking for Chantal."

"Oh." Roderick turned to Chantal now too, as though he had momentarily forgotten about her. He considered me again for a second and his focus dipped down my body. I hoped he noticed the looseness of my clothing, how it didn't cling to me anywhere at all. "Well, that's very thoughtful of you, Miss Slade." The corner of his mouth pulled up towards his cheek, a smile that crept backward. "Why don't you girls go have a little powwow? And have an easy night, okay? Give yourselves some time to rest." He stepped back into his office and shut the door.

Chantal and I walked up Church Street to the subway without saying much. I didn't ask her why she was walking to the subway instead of going up to the dorm room she shared with Sixty. I didn't ask her if she was okay because it seemed pretty clear she wasn't. Her breathing was heavy and disjointed, accumulating every ten seconds or so in that hiccup-sob medley that kids get in the wake of a temper tantrum.

She turned to me suddenly. "Why were you waiting for me?"

I pulled the raincoat out of my knapsack and handed it to her. She looked at me like she didn't understand. Then she accepted it slowly, as though worried I'd whip it away. When she mumbled *thank you*, I tried to smile. I desperately wanted to apologize for what had happened at Coffee Time, but I didn't know how. We walked into the station, went through the turnstiles and down the escalator without saying another word.

"I'm sorry," I said at last. "I thought what happened . . . what they made you do . . . I thought it was gross. I shouldn't have said that stuff."

Chantal didn't respond and I realized there was no way she'd forgive me. But as the subway pulled into the tunnel, she caught my hand between both of hers in a weird hand-sandwich. Her palms were soft and the clumsiness of the gesture made them pawlike. She was instantly embarrassed and let go.

"What's wrong?" I asked, once we were inside the subway car.

She glanced over her shoulder as though she was worried someone from school might be on the same car. "I'm on probation," she whispered. "I could get kicked out."

I couldn't believe it. "Is that what Roderick told you?"

She nodded, dipped her small white chin into her turtleneck. Her mouth started to do something complicated, as if invisible strings pulled it in different directions. She was fighting back tears. I took her hand and squeezed it.

"Is it because you cried in class?" I asked.

She shook her head and the tears started to flow. One sky-dived straight to the swell of her cheek. I fished into my ballet bag for Kleenex, even though I never carried Kleenex. It seemed like the appropriate gesture and it gave me something to do.

"Then why?"

"*Because*," she mumbled and grabbed her thigh to show me.

I shouldn't have asked the question. I could see the suffering on her face and it made me feel awful. Chantal loved ballet more than anyone. I suddenly didn't care what Veronica and Molly had said about her having no control over her emotions. Chantal had cried in class that time only because Roderick had basically called her fat. It would have made the steeliest dancer crumble. The only thing Chantal needed to learn how to control was her appetite.

"Don't worry." I tried to comfort her. "It's okay."

"It's not okay! You don't understand."

"I think I do." We locked eyes. I loved her sadness, the way it was so wrapped up in her devotion. "I think I can help you."

"What do you mean?"

"With your *problem*."

A dollop of hope rippled through her gloom. "How?"

"I can just—" I wasn't sure how to explain it. "I'll *help* you."

"Why would you want to do that?"

I didn't know how to answer her. All I knew was that we were a little bit alike, and that little bit of likeness set us apart from those other girls. We loved ballet in a way that cancelled out all the stupid things they worried about, especially sex.

"I think you're a really good dancer."

Her expression started to change. She looked surprised for a moment and then, slowly, ecstatic. "I think you're really good too," she said.

Isabel's conference was that Saturday. I sat on the landing of the stairwell, legs folded like a kid in kindergarten, and listened to my parents argue. My mom was in the kind of mood that my dad called operatic. It meant that she said the same thing over and over again and, as if this repetition wouldn't do the trick, made tormented gestures with her hands too.

"I wonder how you could think that's normal," my mom hissed. "Because it's *not*, Larry. It's not normal. It's not. It just isn't."

"Okay," my dad said. "Don't come."

"I won't. I wasn't planning on it. I will not be joining you. You and Georgia can go alone."

My dad and I drove downtown together. I couldn't remember the last time I'd been alone with him in his car and I wanted to make the most of the event. He was in a pissed-off mood, though, muttering little things to himself and then shaking his head as if the argument with my mom continued in his imagination. It was best that I didn't bug him. Outside the window, the street was lined with cars and skeletal trees clinging to sporadic yellow leaves. I didn't mind the silence. I was secretly in a good mood and I wanted to enjoy it. I was looking forward to hearing Isabel speak, and maybe even more than that, I couldn't wait to see Pilar. Isabel would introduce us and Pilar would shake my hand, say what a pleasure it was to see me again after so many years, and that I looked elegant and serene, the quintessence of a ballerina. I loved it when people told me that. If there was time, maybe the four of us would go out after the conference for a snack and I'd watch Isabel and her mom discuss how it had gone, hear all the things they said to each other.

The conference was taking place on the main campus of the university. My dad paid twelve dollars to park on university property and complained about it as soon as the money left his hands. It wasn't right that adjunct faculty were required to pour their earnings back into the administration's purse. I told him he was 100 percent right and he nodded appreciatively. We walked into a building where bald branches scaled the bricks, and then we went up a staircase that ascended so gradually it was awkward to climb, every step a little anti-climax. The conference room was full of people. We sat in the only available seats, near the entrance, and I scoured the backs of heads for a woman who might be Pilar.

Isabel spoke well and didn't seem nervous, except for one time when she stumbled over a word and lost her place, had to start back at the beginning of her sentence. I tried to listen carefully, to make sense of the long phrases and all the difficult terminology. She sounded wonderful in my opinion, but I tried to gauge her performance by the reactions of other audience members who might know more. When she finished, everyone clapped. I thought the applause was louder than it had been for the previous two speakers, but I wasn't sure. My dad turned to me and made a face I recognized, the whites of his eyes expanding in mockery, like clapping was a ritual he'd never understood. Still he clapped, and maybe more to make up for it, hands raised above everyone else's and muscled into clamshells to make extra noise.

Isabel met us in the foyer when the conference was over. I threw my arms around her and my dad patted her on the shoulder.

"Where's your mom?" I asked.

"Oh." Isabel frowned. "She couldn't make it at the last minute. She's interviewing a doctor, a psychiatrist, actually"—she looked at my dad—"at the University of Manitoba."

"Who's that?" he asked.

Isabel wrinkled her nose, thinking. "I can't remember the name. But they're starting a study together, something about genetic mapping in body-image disorders. It sounded pretty cool."

My dad nodded like he thought this was a little interesting, but not very interesting. Isabel told us that she had to go out with her colleagues but that she'd make it up to me another time. My dad and I walked out to the parking lot together. I felt extremely disappointed by the whole afternoon. It was only four o'clock but the dark sky was already dropping towards us. The dreariness of the coming evening made me lonely. I didn't want to deal with my mom, so I decided I would go to the public library. I could browse through coffee table books on ballet and look for information on nutrition and dieting to help Chantal. When my dad and I got home, I grabbed my knapsack and went right back out the front door.

I hadn't been outside for more than a minute when my mom came running after me. Her hair was piled on top of her head and she'd stuffed her pyjama pants into a pair of Eskimo boots. She asked me where I was going.

"Out," I said.

"How was the conference?"

I kept walking. If she cared about the conference, she should have come herself.

"Did you meet Pilar?"

"Of course," I lied.

She grabbed my hand and forced me to turn around and face her. "What was she like?"

I yanked my hand away. Why in the world was she asking me this? My mom had met Pilar a bunch of times and it was stupid that she cared about her anyway.

"She was so nice," I said. "She sounded really smart and I thought she was as beautiful as Isabel."

My mom looked stung. Good, I thought, maybe she'd learn how to mind her own business. But then she went on. "Did she and Dad talk?"

I was so sick of all her questions, her excuses, her suggestive tone of voice. "What is your problem, Mom? Why can't you just be normal about things!"

She blinked hard and her eyes froze into two black jewels. She said nothing. Then she turned around and walked back into the house.

The following Monday, Molly wasn't there at the start of our technique class. My eyes kept going from the clock above the doorway to the empty metre of barre between Sixty and Sonya Grenwaldt. It was possible that she was only late. Molly lived in Mississauga and she took the GO train in to school each day. But I had a strange feeling, a numbing draught between my bones. I told myself that it was reasonable to consider her late, until it was forty-five minutes past the start of class. When forty-five minutes had gone by, I told myself it was reasonable to imagine other possibilities. Any number were conceivable. There could have been an accident on the tracks and all the trains could have been cancelled. She could've caught some kind of virus over the weekend and be lying on her couch in front of the TV. There may have been a family emergency, which probably meant one of her grandparents had died. I pictured Molly in a long black dress, standing beside her very tall father and her mother, who wasn't really that tall at all.

People whispered about Molly after class, but I stayed on the periphery of the commotion, head down as I zipped up my jeans and wormed my feet into my sneakers. Sixty was beside me, getting dressed too, and was similarly quiet. When I was ready to go for lunch, we locked eyes.

"Come," she said.

I followed her up the back staircase to the residence hallways. We moved solemnly, as though our muscles dragged from exertion, didn't speak; in fact we barely met each other's eyes.

"There are a thousand possible explanations," she said. "Kids miss normal high school all the time."

We huddled on her top bunk and called Molly on her family's land line. It was a 905 area code, so I pictured a wide street without a sidewalk, a basketball hoop with a beard of snow. We pressed our heads together, divided the receiver between our ears. There was the dull purr of the ring tone.

"Yeah?" The voice was male and sounded teenage.

I nudged Sixty to get her to talk.

"Is Molly there?"

"Uh." There was something like a grunt on the other end. "No."

"Is she . . . do you know if she's coming to school today?"

"Uh, no."

Sixty shrugged helplessly. I tried to think tactically, find the best question to exact clues.

"Is she okay?" I asked.

Sixty and I hovered over the silence, my temple pressed against her forehead. I felt the clammy adhesion of skin. We heard the voice breathe.

"I guess. Yeah."

We thanked him, hung up the phone. I leaned back on Sixty's pillow. My silence felt superstitious, as though saying the wrong thing would make the wrong thing a possibility. But I had a strange feeling. Molly was a sex girl and I knew this had something to do with it.

Metal scrapped in the keyhole. The door opened and Chantal stepped into the room. She saw Sixty first, then me, and her expression changed between the two moments. I remembered I had three books in my knapsack on weight-loss methods that I'd found at the library, but I couldn't give them to her in front of Sixty. Chantal moved farther into the room and opened the mini-fridge. She took out a snack-pack of chocolate pudding and then reached into the mug on top of the fridge for a spoon.

"*Chantal*," I said.

Sixty looked at me strangely and Chantal froze. I was as surprised by my outburst as anyone. Chantal hesitated for a moment, an embarrassed muddle in her eyes, but then she dropped the spoon back into the mug and looked down awkwardly at the pudding. She made a crude show of noticing something she hadn't before, something that displeased her. I could tell that Sixty was about to ask me what was going on, but Chantal interjected.

"There's something on the bulletin board for you, Georgia. Some kind of note."

On the bulletin board in the main lobby was an envelope with my name on it. Veronica and Anushka were sitting on the bench, and they watched me as I took it down, untucked the flap. Sixty stood closer to me than necessary.

"It might be nothing," she whispered.

"I know."

I read it to myself first. *Dear Georgia, I'd like to meet for a consultation. Studio A at 1 pm. Ballet attire.* The writer had signed off with a dash at the bottom of the page followed by two lazy initials, R.A.

I looked up at Sixty, who was reading over my shoulder. Her eyes stayed on the page for longer than they needed to. Was it pity or envy? Veronica and Anushka had come towards us, and Veronica pushed in next to Sixty.

"I have no idea what it's about," I said.

Sixty nodded slowly, thoughtfully. I worried that she didn't believe me, but then I wondered whether I believed myself. Technically I didn't know what this consultation was about; I certainly couldn't articulate it in a sentence or break it into points. But I did have some idea, a notion slippery and unsure. My strategy was working. Roderick saw that I was different from the sex girls and he had singled me out for more attention.

Veronica lifted her head. It was lunchtime, so she'd taken her hair down and she made a big show of it now, pulling all of it over her shoulder so that the ends dipped into the neck of her shirt.

"Maybe he has the hots for you."

Anushka looked me up and down and laughed. Sixty squeezed my arm and shook her head.

"Don't worry," she whispered.

I walked to the change room. Staring at myself in the mirror over the sink, I faced a new challenge. How should I try to look? Roderick respected me, on this point I was certain. But I was struck by a conflicting image: the beautiful ballerina in the photo I'd found online. Roderick had held her tightly, clasping her around the waist. Was her beauty something he forgave her for, or was it one of the reasons he liked her?

I pulled a clean pair of tights up my legs, straightened the seams on both sides of my bum. I tried to move quickly but I couldn't. All I could hear was Veronica, the way she'd said *hots*. She'd only been trying to be funny, but still. Was there the slightest possibility that Roderick could have the hots for a student? It seemed like one of those crazy legends that kids loved to believe, like crocodiles in the sewers or gangs that steal your kidneys. What did it mean to have the *hots* anyway? I repeated the word aloud. It sounded like a pant. Dogs panted because they couldn't sweat and maybe men had the hots when they couldn't sweat enough, looked for cool things to cure their bodies. Girls. The idea gave me the creeps.

When I got up to Studio A the door was open and the room empty. The top of the grand piano was open and it made a slope beneath the window, smooth like black ice.

I called out softly, "Hello?" Nothing. "Hello?" I walked in. I placed my pointe shoes on the floor against the mirror. What was I supposed to do now? I could just sit in the corner, stretch my legs as I waited. But that didn't seem good enough. Roderick had to see me working, sweating, training my muscles whenever I could. A real dancer would never entirely stop practising. She'd roam the world with her chest lifted and her stomach sucked into nothing. Her inner thighs would burn with every step, sending the tips of her toes out on permanent diagonals.

I moved to the centre of the studio. In the mirror I saw a tiny navy leotard, and because my tights were a creamy pink, as washed out as the sunlight in the window, I looked a bit like a floating body. The room expanded around me. When Roderick came in, we'd be so alone, just the two of us with all this unused space. I hated myself for feeling funny. Cooler girls handled this kind of situation like it was absolutely ordinary, shrugged off the men who leered at them the way you'd shrug off a bug on your shoulder. I forced myself into a first *arabesque*, my favourite static pose. I looked at it in the mirror. The line of my leg was long and slender and my foot flicked up from my ankle like an inverted comma. I looked perfect.

"Bigger."

Roderick leaned against the frame of the doorway. His arms were folded across his chest and he held one leather shoe crossed over the other.

I looked back at my own reflection, let the effort sprout up my calf so my supporting leg was fully rotated. I straightened my hips so that they rested evenly above my foot. I pulled up from my stomach, made myself taller. I felt the new space inside my elbows, between every rib.

"See, right now—" Roderick was walking into the studio, moving downstage towards the mirror. The soles of his shoes made light clacks against the wood. "Right now you're doing a *first arabesque*. And that's fine. Your body's aligned, the shape is nice, there's great extension behind." He had reached the mirror and now changed directions with a military sharpness. "But the difference between the kind of *arabesque* that gets you a position in a *corps de ballet* and leaves you floundering there for the rest of your career, and the kind of *arabesque* that casts you as Giselle or Juliet on the finest stages of Europe—London, Paris, St. Petersburg—well, that difference isn't something you'll attain by admiring yourself in the mirror."

The heat across my cheeks was immediate. Roderick had stopped now, was standing in front of the mirror just at the spot that blocked my reflection. Moisture gathered in the nook of my lower back and I wondered how long I had before it would show through my leotard.

He raised the toe of his shoe and lowered it with a clap. "I'll be the first to harp on the importance of strong technique. It's our craft. It's what sets the standard for what we do, what makes this a skilled and complex art form and not, say, modern dance." He chuckled. "Of course there are still some ballet schools in the world that graduate students with flapping wrists and overextended *à la secondes*. But if you ever want to be promoted past the *corps* in a good company, your technique needs to be so basic, so second nature, that it's there to be taken for granted. Dancing is not *doing* an *arabesque*." I could see him shift his weight. "You have to let the *arabesque* do *you*."

This sounded funny. It sounded like sex. He had a look on his face like he knew all the secrets of the world. It made me feel transparent. If I danced perfectly, the sex part would evaporate. I pictured an *arabesque* in its most real terms, no longer a position that could be assumed by human limbs but an entity in and of itself, a thing, a creature.

"You're thinking too hard," Roderick said. "And god only knows what about." He began to walk towards me. He moved behind me and tapped the curving end of my foot. "From here. Extend from here."

I kept my face fixed determinedly forward and tried to stretch from my toe. I heard him shuffle in a little closer. Then I felt the warmth of his hand underneath my calf.

"From here."

He was touching me. His hand was in one place, stationary, but I could feel it everywhere, the way sunlight hits you all at once. I tried to extend from my calf as he had instructed, and the muscular effort made me push into his hand even more.

He chuckled. "There you are."

He let go of my calf. I felt a shiver of relief as I strained to maintain the height of my leg. But then his fingers were back. They moved in single, spidery steps along the underside of my leg.

"Now continue to extend all along here. That's right."

His fingers reached my knee, paused and then stepped onto my inner thigh. The feeling was magnified now, the intensity of his touch on this sensitive part of my leg. It became more acute with every finger-step, until he was halfway up my thigh. Was I supposed to tell him to stop? The sensation throbbed in both directions, upward from the point of contact and downward from my groin. Still his fingers climbed, approached the junction with my body. I held my breath. Then, in an instant, his hand was gone.

"See. You just can't think about these things. It makes them sound ridiculous." He walked away from me and leaned against the mirror again. "You have to actually *do* them."

"Yeah." My leg dropped to the floor.

"You think it sounds ridiculous?"

"What?"

He gave me a strange look. It was sly, almost accusatory. He turned away from me and walked towards the corner of the room. I pretended to practise the new *arabesque* positioning but my body was numb. When Roderick got to the corner, he whipped abruptly back around.

"I know these last few weeks haven't been fun for you girls—trust me, it's been no picnic for the faculty either."

I didn't understand for a minute, and then my brain sort of woke up again. He was referring to the other girls, the ones who were in trouble.

"There's nothing really more depressing than having to dash young people's dreams." He shook his head as though disapproving of himself. "But it'll be a miserable awakening for them otherwise. A harsh blow now has that much longer to heal. Of course, that doesn't make any of it any easier to do. But I just keep telling myself that if I can't, hand on heart, see the student getting into a company upon graduation . . . well, it isn't in anyone's best interest, and least of all hers, to let her stay on at the Academy." He paused, rubbed the back of his neck. "Right?"

"Yeah," I said.

"So then it really just becomes a question of trusting what you believe in."

He started to walk towards me. My nipples hardened against my bodysuit. Something in his manner scared me. I imagined him reaching out and grabbing me from the front.

"What do you believe in, Georgia?"

"What do I . . ."

"Tell me what you believe."

"Um, lots of things. I guess."

"Really?" He was about a metre from me now and he stopped. "Just a moment ago, when I told you that you had to *be* the *arabesque*, what did you think about that?"

"Uh, I—"

"Did you think it was a useful image? A useful way of thinking your way through the movement? Or did you think—if you'll pardon my French for a second—did you think it was bullshit?"

"Um . . ."

"Go on. Be honest. Tell me what you thought."

"I thought it was a useful image."

He gave this a firm nod, looked me straight in the eye. "Okay. Now tell me the truth."

"What?"

"Tell me what you really thought."

My spit felt gluey in my mouth. I waited for his expression to change again, for him to guide me towards what he wanted me to say. But a grin was carved deep into his face. If anything it was broadening.

"I . . . um, I don't know."

"You don't know?"

I shook my head. I had an idiot face just then, twitchy and self-hating.

"You're worried, aren't you? Hey, it's understandable. It's a nervous place to be. What with lists going up and our having to let a student go." He paused. "You have nothing to worry about." The words arrived slowly, significantly, his eyes fixed on mine.

I must have moved my head in a way that betrayed my confusion, or at least the need for clarification, because he lifted a hand to silence me.

"You're not going anywhere. So let's not worry about that. What you need to focus on is your application. You need to start approaching your work with a fullness, an openness, that I haven't seen yet. It'll take an incredible amount of courage." He stepped towards the studio door. "You know we decide casting for Junior Showcase at the end of this term. Somehow I imagine you as a particularly beautiful Manon in Kenneth MacMillan's ballet." He glanced at me over his shoulder and walked out of the room.

When I saw Sixty that afternoon, she pulled me into the girls' second-floor bathroom.

"What happened?"

I looked into her penny-coloured eyes. I wanted to tell

her everything. She'd remind me how ballet teachers were supposed to touch us, how it didn't mean anything at all. But I backed away from her, bumped into the lip of the sink.

"He just wanted to check in."

"What do you mean?"

"Nothing, basically. I don't know—it's hard to explain."

"I'm really good at understanding things."

Her eyes were big with worry and again a part of me wanted to throw my arms around her neck. What was stopping me? Something about what had happened felt too private, a weird mix of bad and good.

"We talked about technique class. He gave me some corrections for my turns."

It sounded like a lie. I could hear the weakness in my own voice, a decibel away from cracking.

"Oh." She held the door open for me. "That's good, I guess."

On the subway ride home I thought about Roderick and it made a strange buzz through my body that I didn't like. I wanted to cross my legs, knot my intestines, force the irritation out of me. The warmth of his fingers was just a frequency away; I had only to fine-tune the dial, and my memory came through sharply. I imagined it over and over, reprocessing the sensation even when I wanted it to stop. It felt awful, but something satisfied in the awfulness, like pulling hairs from your leg one by one. Mostly I remembered the pressure, the push of his skin through my tights. His fingers had come so close. I couldn't decide whether that was okay, and this is what made me furious, my inability to make sense of it all.

My dad wasn't home, so my mom and I had to have dinner alone. We sat across from each other on stools at the kitchen island and ate the packaged lamb curry she'd bought at the organic shop around the block. She stared at her plate and bounced her leg under the table. She wouldn't meet my eye.

"I'm sorry I was rude," I said.

She nodded slowly. We were quiet for a while. Then she said, "I've only met her a handful of times, you know."

"Met who?"

She rolled her eyes as though her meaning was obvious. When I didn't respond she said, "You know who. It's only human that I'm curious. Did she . . ." She paused, one eye narrowed in deliberation. "Can you tell me what they're like together?"

"What are you talking about, Mom?"

"Your dad and"—she dabbed her mouth with her napkin, then let her hand drop to the counter with a thud—"Pilar. How did they greet each other? Did they hug?"

"I . . . I don't remember."

"Did she ask after me?"

"Why do you care?" I whined.

She held my eye sharply. "You could be a little understanding, Georgia. That's all. It's complicated when marriages end . . . abruptly."

"Nothing ended abruptly!"

"If you say so."

This was the most infuriating response imaginable. "Of course I *say* so! It's the truth! It's what you've told me a thousand times!"

I stormed out of the kitchen and ran up to my room. Why had I apologized at all? Any effort with my mom was useless because she was determined to see things the way she wanted to, let herself stay miserable forever. I turned on my computer and stared at the screen. My thoughts swam in the neon light. I couldn't let my mom bug me now. If I wanted to figure out anything about Roderick I needed to get hold of myself. I clicked on the Academy's website and went straight to Roderick's headshot. What was it that I was afraid of? I traced the pad of my finger over my lips, leaned in towards the keyboard. I typed DO OLDER MEN LIKE TEENAGE GIRLS into the search bubble in the corner of the screen, pressed Enter and sat back.

The screen loaded 1,340,000 hits. I read the first page. WikiAnswer informed me that such men were "immature predators," and that a preference for young women was indicative of "low self-esteem, lack of ambition, emotional confusion and creepiness." Another site explained that it was a natural biological phenomenon, that men were programmed to be attracted to girls at their most fertile, which occurred somewhere between the ages of fifteen and twenty-two. On the second page was an advice forum for teenage girls where a sixteen-year-old who signed off as *Lovelorn*

Lolita asked how to break the news of her thirty-five-year-old boyfriend to her parents. A Dr. Marcus Sternberger, child and adolescent psychologist, informed her that she was the victim of a statutory rape, and that she should seek help immediately. On the third page, I found a study conducted by a group of professors at Duke University in North Carolina. The study surveyed 650 high school teachers across twenty-five states and concluded that "being surrounded by beautiful young women put male teachers at risk of growing dissatisfied with their wives, which often resulted in marriage breakdown." And on the sixth page I found an article called "Doing the Prof" written by a former English lecturer at an unsaid university. He relayed stories of dodging the advances of various wide-eyed undergrads who stalked him during office hours, until he finally succumbed to the efforts of one particular raven-haired beauty, a twenty-year-old philosophy major who would become his future wife.

I pictured this dark-haired girl visiting her male teacher, his designs growing in barely perceptible increments, one day enjoying a shared smile, the next day imagining a kiss. These things didn't happen in big bangs. They didn't inflict upon reality like a horrible accident or an unforeseeable flash flood. They progressed directly out of the ordinary. There was little chance of a surprise attack; the consequences were too big. Roderick would never grab my boob or ask me to have sex with him; it was just too risky. If he actually did have the hots for me, he would try things so slowly that I almost wouldn't notice at all. It would start just the way it had started, Roderick's fingers moving in a perfectly appropriate way, leaving just enough space for him to bail at any moment, for both of us to pretend that nothing weird was going on.

I sucked air deep into my lungs. All I had to do to protect myself was watch Roderick closely. If I was always a step ahead of his designs, nothing could happen to me. I rubbed my hands up and down my thighs, felt strength in my palms again. The more that I knew, the better. It reminded me of something I'd heard about Napoleon, that military genius lies in knowing your enemy's next move. I needed to know as much as possible. I changed into my pyjamas and came back to my computer. I reopened the Google window and typed TEEN SEX OLDER MAN into the search bubble.

The hits loaded. The first was titled *Fuck Her Good*. I looked over my shoulder to double-check that my door was shut tight. I moved in closer to the screen and double-clicked on the first site. Hot pink saturated the screen. Then *Welcome to Fuck Her Good* loaded in across the top of the new page, with *Watch Them Get Fucked Good!* written in a puffier font on the left. Spanning below it was a girl, a girl who looked Isabel's age, with stringy brown hair that hung in her face, although her face was not the first place my eye went. The girl was glisteningly naked and her body stretched all the way across the frame. She was lying on her stomach but pressing her bum high up towards the camera. Her bum was amazing, two smooth cushions taut over the bulge of rounded bone. Then, between them, a tiny orb of darkened skin was thrust into the spotlight. I stared at it, amazed that she was letting me stare at it. I moved in closer to the screen, tried to see more of it, tried to make out the tiny folds of skin around it. But the image was dizzying up close. I looked at her back. It swooped into a catlike arch, a delicate ridge of vertebrae just barely visible down its centre. Her skin had a twinkle to it, like she was covered in a very fine layer of craft sparkles. By her arm was the shadow of breast, dipping in a pointy globe towards the floor. She looked backward into the camera with a sleepy look in her eye, as though she wasn't quite sure whether she was meant to be awake. Her lips loosened like a kid who can't breathe properly through her nose. *Mandi* was written in an elaborate red cursive underneath her, then: *A young slut named Mandi teaches you to get an older man's attention. Download video here.*

I moved my cursor to the download and double-clicked. My heart beat faster in my chest. The blank screen of the QuickTime Player popped up into the centre of the page. It framed a small circle with a rotating bullet lodged inside its border, like a skater lapping a rink. Then my computer was making noises, man and woman noises, loud grunting moans. I fumbled for the volume dial, but my thumb slid over the serrated edge and the grunts were instantly louder. I slammed down on the screen and jumped into my bed. I waited to hear shuffling in the hallway, felt a certain terror that those sounds would have been audible from the bathroom, possibly from my parents' bedroom.

When I didn't hear anything, I loosened my grip on the fistfuls of comforter I'd grabbed in my hands and tried to fall asleep. I couldn't. I saw interwoven limbs. There'd been two bodies rocking across the screen and so much skin it'd been impossible to tell what belonged to whom. What kind of men looked at stuff like that? I brought my hands to my sides and felt my body through my pyjamas. I rubbed my legs against each other under the blanket to see how soft they felt. It was like sex was in everything, lodged in men's heads and drowning in women's bodies. I curled into my extra pillow and wondered whether sex was in ballet too. It was the most horrible idea imaginable, but it didn't gross me out as much as it should have.

TEN.

THERE WERE TWO WEEKS OF school left before the Christmas holiday and I had my work cut out for me. I needed to find the perfect balance of focus, a way of working effectively on my dancing while all the time charting Roderick's moves. The two were not unrelated; improvements in my dancing would only make him like me more. This made my job easier. I worked as hard as I could in ballet class, holding my legs in the air until the muscles trembled like moth wings, letting sweat rain down the gully of my spine. I would show him that I had all the strength to master the MacMillan choreography, that I possessed the stamina for the demanding partner work, the presence to carry the role. At the same time, I watched for any changes in his behaviour. On the surface there appeared to be few. He directed class with the same casual scorn, stopping to pick on unassuming victims before retreating to his corner of the room. Occasionally our eyes would meet and he'd acknowledge me in the ritualistic way we'd established, a shared look like a silent alliance, pitting him and me against the rest of the class. When I turned to face away from him, the pleasure would linger, sticking to my face the way gum does if you blow a stupidly big bubble.

Once Sixty caught me midway through one of these expressions and gave me a weird look.

"What's so funny?" she asked after class.

"Oh, nothing."

"But you were laughing about something in the middle of *adage*."

"Was I?"

She bugged her eyes. "*Yeah*."

I took a step away from her, longed to tell her the truth. But this was impossible. How could I explain my special situation with Roderick? I could barely make sense of it myself.

I followed Sixty to the change room. Everything was quieter since Molly had left school. The entire subject felt bandaged in something gauzy and thick, like a mess of blood would leak everywhere if we unwrapped it. People checked the bulletin board regularly, worried about themselves. We laughed less in the change room, and Veronica generally left Chantal alone. Today was different, though. Veronica whined about how bored she was and fell back on the cushioned bench like a heroine in a play.

"Boredom striketh!"

Anushka climbed on top of her so that her legs straddled Veronica's waist and the two of them pretended to have sex. Everyone howled with laughter.

"Let's see what the Coffee Time guys are doing after school," Veronica said. "I would kill for a beer."

"Hell yes," said Anushka.

Veronica sat up and looked over at Sixty and me. Sixty nodded enthusiastically.

"Should we say hi to your boyfriend?" Veronica called out in Chantal's direction.

Chantal didn't look at her, didn't say anything at all.

I turned back to my locker. I had to get out of this Coffee Time trip. I'd planned on going to the Academy's library after repertoire class to borrow the DVD of Kenneth MacMillan's *Manon* and to print out the food schedule that I'd made up for Chantal. I dawdled with my jeans and sweater so that I was the last dressed and Sixty had to wait for me.

"I can't go after school," I told her when we were alone.

"Why not?" she asked.

"I just . . . My legs are kind of sore. I think it might be shin splints."

"Oh no!"

Her sympathy stung me. I wasn't being a good friend. I should tell her everything I was discovering about Roderick and warn her that aligning herself with the sex girls could jeopardize her position at the Academy. But instead I just told her not to worry about me.

I went straight to the school library after class. I didn't want to see everyone and have to explain why I wasn't going along. The librarian helped me find the DVD, a recording of *Manon* done by the Royal Ballet in 1982, and then I printed out the schedule that I'd designed at home.

Chantal was waiting for me, as we'd arranged, in her dorm room. I changed out of my ballet clothes in her room and talked her through the schedule. She needed to lose weight quickly but she needed her energy too, so I had her eating mainly fruits and vegetables.

"You can't pig out at dinner," I said. "No matter how hungry you are."

Chantal nodded solemnly. She folded the schedule in half and put it inside the bottom desk drawer, the one that was hers. I remembered something else I had in my knapsack for her. I pulled out my copy of *Dancing on My Grave*. Normally, I would never have considered lending it to anyone, but it felt right helping Chantal, wonderful even, as though a secret about my own dancing could be wrapped up and cherished in her success.

"I've marked the parts where she stops eating. Read them whenever you have a craving."

Chantal took the book from my hand. She handled it with extreme care, as though I'd passed her a valuable heirloom. She pointed at the black-and-white dancer's feet on her corkboard, the ones I'd noticed on the first day of school.

"Those are Gelsey's." Her eyes were bright.

Somehow I felt like I had always known this. "If the book doesn't do it, you have to promise to call me before you put *anything* in your mouth."

"I promise," she whispered.

That night, I took the DVD of *Manon* down to the basement, where my mom wouldn't bother me. I watched it over and over again. The story was so tragic; a young French girl accidentally destroys her only meaningful relationship and dies as a hooker in the swamps of Louisiana. The music sounded like beauty on the edge of disaster. I stayed up until midnight and tried to work my way through the famous first act *pas de deux*. Manon is in love for the first time. She awakens in her Paris boudoir and is overcome with the happiness of existence. I found a broom in the laundry room and used it as my supporting man.

Sixty was waiting for me in the lobby when I got to school the next day.

"I think I got drunk last night." Her face glowed with pride.

"How do you know?"

"You *know*. You start to feel really wobbly and amazing."

I tried to look as pleased about this as she was, but the truth was that I didn't understand. It was the worst possible time to be messing around. Roderick was in the process of casting Junior Showcase and a bad move now could affect the size of the part you got. Sixty kept talking. She told me how the Coffee Time guys had bought a two-four of Molson with fake ID, and how they'd all huddled outside the Palm House at Allan Gardens and sucked them back as fast as they could.

"When it got too cold out, we poured all the beer into our water bottles and walked up to Bloor Station and hid in the bathroom and drank the rest. Veronica and a guy called Steve went into a stall alone and stayed there for fifteen minutes." She beamed. "I didn't think we'd make last call for dinner, but we did somehow. Eight o'clock. We thought people could tell we were drunk, so we told the residence mom that we'd gotten flu shots that afternoon and that they made us feel weird."

"And she believed you?"

Sixty shrugged. "I guess."

Roderick announced in technique class that the casting for Junior Showcase would be posted before the Christmas break. He said that while a small role wasn't a death sentence, we should nonetheless consider it a marker of our progress.

"Casting is something of a barometer. A low reading means I see trouble ahead."

Everyone talked about this in the change room. We'd heard rumours about girls in higher grades. Ana Hernandez had graduated the year before and was already a first soloist with the Frankfurt Ballet. She'd danced a solo from *Paquita* in her Junior Showcase. Linda McAdams had been scooped up by the San Francisco Ballet before she had even finished grade twelve. She'd been cast as *Don Quixote*'s Kitri in her Junior Showcase.

"I heard that sometimes he just doesn't cast you," Veronica said. "That's how you know."

"Know what?" Sixty asked.

"That you're kicked out."

It was a horrible thing to consider. Anushka fixed her bun beside me and I breathed in her hairspray, a cloud of damaged fruit and rubbing alcohol.

"You must be worried." Veronica tapped Chantal's shoulder as she made her way to the sinks.

Even though the contact lasted less than a second, Chantal flinched like she'd been attacked by a bug. Veronica's words really pissed me off. Chantal had been working so hard on so few calories, and the truth was that Veronica wasn't half as good a dancer. She just had a better body.

"Leave her alone," I said.

Veronica stopped in her tracks. She turned around to confront me, and everyone else in the change room stared at me too.

"I mean, I don't really think she has much to worry about," I muttered.

I had never noticed how icy Veronica's eyes were. They were the chemical blue of antifreeze.

"How are your shin splints?" She smirked at me, didn't wait for an answer.

I established a routine from there on in. I came home every night and had dinner as quickly as possible. It was usually just my mom and me, and sometimes we barely exchanged so much as a word. When I finished eating, I went down to the basement and rehearsed *Manon*. I made my way through the first and second act choreography, learning the partnering with the broom and faking all the elaborate lifts. By the second week of December, I had started Act III, the most tragic part. Sometimes at the height of a sustained balance, I'd close my eyes and feel the heart of the ballet emanate from inside me. I was Manon. I was French but exiled far from home in the wilds of newly colonized Louisiana. My arms were feeble and intentionally shaky. Soon I would die on stage, damaged, deserted and disgraced.

Chantal often called me while I was rehearsing and I'd pause the DVD to talk to her. She'd lost almost six pounds since I'd given her the schedule and it was crucial that she avoid the rebound effect. All the books I'd found on nutrition warned about it.

"I'm really hungry, Georgia."

"You're not," I assured her. "Your body's sending you mixed messages."

"Are you sure?"

"Did you read the parts in Gelsey's book?"

"Yeah."

"Didn't they inspire you?"

"I guess."

"Just concentrate on the role you want the most in Junior Showcase. Don't let yourself think about anything else."

When I finished rehearsing, I went up to my room and sat at my computer. Roderick's face saturated the screen and I gave myself a moment to really observe it. I could see it clearly now, the place where he was handsome. I imagined our first rehearsal for *Manon*. He would walk into the studio with the same crumpled look on his forehead and watch me dance from the corner of the room. I'd be suspended over a *développé devant* when he'd stop the music, move towards me. *You're doing it all wrong*, he'd say. My arms would be arced over my head in fifth position and he'd take hold of one bicep, wrench it backward about an inch. His hands would drop to my rib cage, seizing it on either side so that I could feel his fingers between the bones. *You're leaning back*, he'd say. He'd push into the hollow slats of my torso, force my weight forward. The trick would be to show zero resistance. Otherwise I might piss him off and this could bring a spiral of bad things. So I would need to seem compliant, even encouraging. He'd move his hands up farther, so that an index finger grazed the underside of my boob. Would it be intentional or accidental? Our eyes would meet. I'd give him a couple of moments to move his hand of his own accord. If he didn't, I would have to subtly take control, lifting from my stomach so that his hand slipped to somewhere more acceptable. Then our rehearsal could resume.

The casting for Junior Showcase wasn't posted until the last day before the holidays. I was at school earlier than usual and I walked into the lobby, a whack of cold pressure in my chest. I saw the notice on the bulletin board immediately. *Manon* was the first ballet listed and next to it was my name. I had been cast in the famous Act One *pas de deux* with Nathaniel.

I looked at the ceiling and breathed in the enormity of the news. My lips inched upward, a childish smile that felt bigger than my face. I scrutinized the list some more. Chantal had been given a beautiful solo to learn from *Coppélia*. Sixty and Anushka had been cast in a pretty duet from *La Bayadère*, and Veronica was one of many cast in a *corps de ballet* segment from Balanchine's *Serenade*. I went to the change room and put on my ballet clothes at the slowest possible speed. The happiness flowed through me, making my limbs heavy and my head light. Maybe this is what it felt like to be drunk. I heard the door of the change room open. I was a little annoyed to have my private celebration interrupted, but when the intruder turned the corner, I saw that it was Chantal. We threw our arms around each other and said congratulations so many times that it was hard to tell whose voice was whose.

ELEVEN.

ON THE FIRST DAY OF Christmas holidays, the sky turned as white as the ground, so that the whole world looked anemic. My mom set the furnace too high and a film of static electricity lifted the hairs on my arms. Sixty was leaving for Argentina to meet her dad that afternoon and I felt a dull softness on both my temples, the throb of encroaching boredom. I slid around the house in my socks, trying to see how long I could go without lifting my feet off the floor. I ended up in the kitchen, where the linoleum made this easier. My mom had made a list of possible activities for me and posted it on the fridge with a magnet from our dentist.

It was my least favourite magnet, shaped like a giant incisor tooth, with a dented top and big, leg-like roots. It gave me the creeps. I pushed the magnet aside and looked at the list. I hated it already, hated it from a tightening knot in my stomach. When I saw that the first idea was to pick up my mom's dry cleaning, I crumpled the sheet into a ball and tossed it into the recycling bin.

For the first few days of the break my mom was attending a seminar at the university, so I had the house to myself until she came home in the late afternoon. I took scalding showers in the morning and sat in my towel in front of my computer, leaving beads of water dotted on my shoulders, my wet hair heavy like an animal on my back. I checked my e-mail first. Chantal had gone home to Saskatchewan for the holidays, so she e-mailed me now instead of calling. She was becoming increasingly disciplined and made only small mistakes, like having one too many bites at dinner or accidentally drinking a regular pop. I wrote back one-liners that I knew would encourage her, things like *You're almost there!* and *You'll do better tomorrow!* and *I actually prefer Diet Coke!*

I Googled Roderick over and over again. I found pictures of him with different haircuts, longer layers that grazed the back of his neck, messy bits that hung in his eyes. He was much younger in some and his face had a clumsiness to it, a goofy smile that favoured one side, like his features hadn't quite figured out the best place to settle. I wrote GIRLFRIEND beside his name in the Google bubble and searched for more pictures of him next to women. I wanted to see what they looked like, the women he had loved, see if they were tall and beautiful, if they had wide shoulders and prominent wrist bones, wore silky things that gaped off their backs. Or would they have frizzy hair and Japanese running shoes; would they be looking sideways, beyond the camera, impatient to get back to their intellectual lives? Would any of them be teenage girls?

At some point amidst all this wondering, I'd scroll down my website history and, turning away for a second as though I wasn't completely aware of what I was doing, let the cursor hook on www.fuckhergood.com. The screen was like paper towel laid over pink Kool-Aid, instantly absorbing a spill. Then came Mandi. She materialized in two round phenomena, bum and head, a crescent of tanned back in between. My eyes dipped from one end to the other, trying to take her all in at once. I had discovered that if you clicked on the Free Tour button on the top right corner of the webpage, you could meet Mandi's friends too. There was Jordan, who sat with her legs akimbo, rubbing a Popsicle between her boobs. She was smiling, sticking out her purple tongue as if to prove that the Popsicle wasn't just for her chest, that it had been in her mouth too. There was Puma, with white blonde hair and complicated underwear that didn't cover anything that underwear was supposed to cover. And there was Valeria, who was hard and oily, a rhinestone floating over her belly button like a shimmering star. She lay on her side, her knees folding open with the looseness of a baby's while she pressed a long, white-tipped fingernail between her legs. But Mandi was my favourite. I loved her face, the sleepy weight of her eyelids, the soft indifference around her mouth. It hung open just the right amount, looked wet without being slobbery, as if her saliva were made of something thinner than usual. The bones of her bum amazed me. They were so visible, flexing up into the camera, tightening her flesh into two perfect humps. Then, between these humps, that mysterious circle, dark and colourless at the same time, impossible to really see and yet still the focus of the picture.

I took off my towel and went to the full-length mirror on the back of the closet door. I got down on my hands and knees and faced away from my reflection. Arching my back, I brought my chest lower to the floor, trying to bring my bum up higher. It wasn't a difficult pose for a dancer. I turned around. The position was just about right, my body cat-like and defenceless. But my expression was important too. I tried to remember what was so alluring about Mandi's face, the way she looked quiet and available and completely ready for sex.

Later in the week, when my mom was done her seminar, I came down to the kitchen in my pyjamas and she made us pancakes for breakfast.

"These are gooey." She looked down at the fried dough she'd piled on my plate. She took my fork from my hand, pressed the tines into the surface of the top one. It made a squishy sound and she laughed. "How did I manage to make them so gooey?"

"They're fine, Mom." I took the maple syrup from the fridge door and handed it to her. Then I sat down at the kitchen island, watched her lay the frying pan in the sink.

"Are you still mad at me?" she asked with her back turned. Then she sat across from me and drizzled maple syrup onto her pancakes. "Are you going to let me get you something for Christmas?"

"I don't really need anything."

"No?" Her voice lilted musically. "You don't want some new ballet clothes or some books or . . . some jewellery?"

"Not really."

"*Georgia*. Since when don't you like presents?"

I shrugged.

"I could get you some nice pyjamas or, I don't know, a housecoat or . . . do you need new underwear?"

I looked up from my plate. My fork clanked on its surface.

"What?" she asked hopefully.

All I could picture were the bright strips of fabric that stretched over unexpected parts of Mandi and Puma. I couldn't imagine what it would be like to own clothing like that.

"Underwear?" she asked.

It didn't seem right to let her buy me things when I was so angry with her, but the idea of sexy underwear made my palms itch. "If you *really* want to get me something."

She started to smile. "Of course . . ." She pressed her lips together. "That seems like a pretty nice idea. Some new underwear. A camisole or something. Some simple lingerie."

"Yeah. Lingerie."

"We could go out one afternoon this week. Get you properly fitted." She was bouncing her legs under the island and she tapped me with her big toe. "Is there . . . is there any particular reason you want underwear, sweetie?"

"No."

"There isn't . . . oh, I don't know, there isn't someone special in the picture? Someone you care about? A new boy?"

I looked out at the backyard, felt my cheeks burn.

"Oh." Her voice slid melodically through the syllable. "So I'm right." She paused. "Do you want to tell me about him?"

I shook my head. There was a lump in my throat.

"You can talk to me about these things, you know. Anything."

I nodded hard. I could feel the serrated ridge of my top teeth as I bit into my lip.

"What's the problem, sweetie? Does he . . . Is it . . . ? Does he know how you feel? Does he not like you back?"

I shook my head.

"Okay." She popped off her stool, took her *Number One Mom* mug over to the coffee machine. I heard the quiet glug of the pour, the simmer of the burner as it yearned for the pot's replacement. "So there's a different problem. Does he have a girlfriend?"

My attention was still outside, caught on the orange seat of my old swing, the patch of silver ice beneath it. I didn't shake my head this time.

“Oh.” There was a glint of satisfaction in her tone. She moved around behind me, placed her mug down in front of me, hugged me from behind. “He already has a girlfriend.”

I considered correcting her, but the words didn’t come.

“Well.” She swung a little sideways, so that our hug dipped to the left. Then she released my shoulders and kissed me lightly on the crown of my head. She reached for her coffee and walked to the sliding door. She gazed out at the snow. “You’re very young. Girlfriends are usually pretty temporary.” She stayed still for a few moments, like she’d reminded herself of something that pushed her thoughts far away. Then she turned around and faced me. “We’ll go underwear shopping tomorrow, okay? I actually need a bunch of new things too.”

She took me to a department store at Yonge and Bloor. She said that they’d have all the quality labels there, and that if I didn’t find anything we could walk to the boutiques on Bloor Street. We took the escalator up to the third floor, the lingerie department, and she led me along an aisle, the floor milky and impenetrable, smooth enough to skate on. We passed display after display of hanging silky things, transparent panties that dangled from plastic hangers, bras trimmed with forests of lace. The light made jewels in their creases. The air smelled like cellophane, cardboard and Christmas trees.

At the desk a girl with peroxide hair and long nails was talking on the phone. She reminded me of Puma, and as she raised a finger to indicate she'd be a minute, I let my eyes dip down to where her tank top met her breasts. The skin on her chest had a painted quality, tanned and tinged with orange. I could just see the top of her black bra, crunchy, reinforced lace peeking over the seam of her shirt.

She took me to a fitting room. I took off my shirt and she wrapped a tape measure over my bra. She smelled like sweet artificial strawberries, and as she leaned over me I saw half moons of white under her arms, small clumps of congealed goo. Her breasts swung right beneath my face as she measured me and for a second they grazed my collarbones. I didn't move.

"You're tiny." She looked at the coordinates on the tape, then up at me. "In a good way." I smelled nicotine on her breath. "Do you have a boyfriend?"

"Yeah." I flicked my hair over my shoulder. "But he's a lot older than me."

"Oh." She leaned away from me, surprised. "That's cool. My boyfriend's a lot older than me too."

My mom had assembled two piles, black satiny stuff for herself and things she thought I'd like. I thumbed through them. They were mostly cotton and lightweight, panties with full bums and pretty eyelets, soft-cup bras you could fold delicately away. They were all wrong, and the wrongness of them, their inadequacy, throbbed from a spot just below my navel.

"What?" My mom picked up a particularly pretty pink camisole, ran it between her fingers. "You don't like these?"

I didn't answer. The sales girl took a step forward. She was frowning in my mom's direction. She turned to me.

"Give me a sec."

She came back a few minutes later with a handful of underwear, laid them out on the fitting-room table. They were thongs and G-strings in slippery nylons. Some had trinkets fastened to their sides, others had sequins sewn into different shapes on their fronts—hearts, diamonds and hot lips. I pulled out a pair with a zebra pattern and white fur trim along the top.

"It's what they're all wearing," the girl told my mom, taking a silver one from the pile and handing it to me. It felt like a bathing suit. I looked at the crotch; it was a long, narrow triangle, like a skinny bandage. "That stuff"—she pointed at what my mom had selected—"it's really more early twenties."

"Oh," my mom said. She dipped her hand into the pile and pulled out a satiny red thong. She draped it on the back of her hand like it was worth a lot of money, considered it for a moment with a curious affection.

"I know." The girl reached out and snatched it from her. "It's so not your thing."

My mom opened her mouth as though she were going to contradict this, but she stopped herself mid-thought. Her hand fluttered to her neck, fiddled with her pearl.

"Here." The girl handed me something else, a bra on a hanger. It was black and made of rough, substantial lace with a plastic finish. Even empty, the cups retained the shape of small breasts. "This'll give anyone cleavage."

I chose four thongs and three bras. That night, I laid them all out on my bed and tried to figure out which combination Roderick would like best. I'd done more Internet research and knew that part of the appeal of younger women, aside from their hard bodies and prettier faces, was that they'd wear skanky clothing that men pretended was beneath them but secretly yearned for. If Roderick had a girlfriend his age, she'd wear the kinds of underwear my mom had chosen—silky, discreet things that needed to be washed by hand. I took off all my clothes and slipped on the shiny silver thong and the hard, moulded bra. I opened my closet door and examined my reflection in the full-length mirror. The nylon string disappeared inside my bum cheeks and then reappeared to make a T along my lower back. I pulled at it, let it snap my skin.

I opened my bedroom door and listened. I could hear the murmur of my mom talking in the kitchen. My dad was at a hospital fundraising dinner, so she must have been on the phone. I walked down the hallway. The lights were off, but I could make out the bright skin of the naked Goya on the wall. I went down the stairs, planting a foot meticulously on each step, letting the sprigs of carpet absorb my soles. Behind me, I could feel the glowing half moons of my bum, tingling with nakedness. I tiptoed across the main-floor hall towards the basement stairs. I couldn't see my mom but I could hear her. She was saying *I know* over and over again into the receiver. *I'm going to. I can't take it. I know. I will.* I shut the basement door behind me.

I took the *Manon* disc out of its laminate envelope and slipped it inside the DVD player. I selected my *pas de deux*. Manon lifts herself from bed and steps slowly across the stage. The first strains of violin warm bit by bit until they swell into overlapping outbursts. I pushed my arms away from me, my fingers sifting through the air in a sinewy slow-mo. I stepped into the first *attitude* position. I looked at the TV, where the ballerina held the same pose, her slip floating around her legs. The basement's dim overhead light blurred the screen right below her and I could just make out my reflection in the TV, the parallel line of my leg and then, instead of a costume, the gleam of my white bum.

TWELVE.

I LEANED AGAINST THE RADIATOR in the Academy's lobby and waited for Sixty. She had called me the night before, spoken in a voice of dreamy exhaustion—jet lag she'd said—and asked me to meet her before our first ballet class that morning. She said she had something to tell me. I pressed my legs into the radiator so that I could feel the columns of heat through my jeans. In my new thong, I pictured it burning long red stripes from my knees all the way up to my hips.

"Hi." Sixty stepped into the lobby from the residence stairwell. We hugged. Her cheeks were darker and I thought

I could smell coconut sunscreen through her shirt. "You look good," she said. "Older."

I clenched the muscles of my bum so that I could feel the string of material between my bum cheeks. I felt like I looked good. I felt older too. We walked down the main hallway of the Academy, hand in hand. She told me about her dad's new house in a city called Mar del Plata, about a terrace framed with jacaranda trees that had creepy purple petals. There was a steep, rocky path to the beach down which she'd tumbled twice.

"I really had one of those moments where I was like, *okay, that's it, my leg is broken, my career is over.*"

"Is that what you had to tell me?"

Sixty stopped. "No."

We were standing in a quiet nook between the main lobby and the stairwell, and no one was around. She pulled me in close to her so that I was looking up into her face.

"I almost did it," she said.

"What?"

"It."

"Oh."

"On the beach."

She waited for me to say something. I didn't know what to say. I was so close to her face but I couldn't understand her expression, the funny knot of her mouth.

"He was a lot older than me."

"How much older?" I asked.

"Eighteen."

"Oh."

She told me the story. He was the son of her parents' friends. There'd been a dinner party on a boat.

"He came up behind me. He put his hand right there." She reached around to the back of my neck and traced a finger along its invisible hairs. I shivered. "He said he'd been watching me all night. He said he thought I was a model."

We started moving down the hallway. I listened and looked for Roderick. It made a liquid feeling inside my chest, the constant tipping of anticipation. Sixty was still talking. The boy had taken her to the beach the next night. They'd drunk sweet vermouth from the bottle. He'd rolled on top of her out of nowhere and started to unbutton her jeans.

"It was weird."

"Good weird?"

"Yeah." I heard a tremble in her voice. "I guess."

"What do you mean?"

"Nothing." She shook her head. "It was good."

"How far did you go?"

She looked down at her shoes and shrugged.

"What?" I asked.

She stayed quiet. When she lifted her head, she looked as though something made her nervous, frightened her even. "His eyes went funny."

"Like funny how?"

"Like brain-dead funny."

We stood there looking at each other. I saw diamonds in her irises. For a second I thought she might cry. But instead she moved her eyeballs upward and rounded her mouth in a small O.

"Like that?" I asked.

She kept going, bringing her eyebrows together while she moved her head back and forth like a dunking bird. It made a violent picture, one body beating into another body, but then, out of nowhere, she started to laugh. So I laughed too, even harder than she did.

"Like he could only think with his dick!" she said.

"Oh my god!" I laughed so hard my stomach burned. "Gross!"

We turned the corner into the main lobby and I thought about Roderick. I imagined him rolling his body on top of mine, the feel of his fingers as they reached down and fiddled with my fly.

Sixty squeezed my hand. "Look," she whispered.

I followed the tilt of her chin towards a girl in the middle of the lobby, sitting on the covered bench. The girl looked down at her lap, so that I couldn't see her face, only the silhouette of her mousy bun. It was Chantal. She turned her head abruptly, not towards us but in the other direction, as though she'd heard a sound coming down the opposite hall. A man and a woman approached her. Sixty pulled me back into the hallway so that we were more or less hidden behind the dividing wall. Chantal was getting up to greet the couple, but she moved with a troubled slowness, shifting her weight onto her arm and using it to help her up. When she was finally on her feet I saw what was wrong.

"Oh my god," Sixty whispered. She pressed her fingers into the soft part of my arm.

Chantal's body had deflated. Two sticks jutted from her jean skirt, thighs barely wider than calves. It gave a sense of backwardness, her legs getting thinner where they should have swelled. Her knees exploded in the middle of it all, two doorknobs of bone. What had she done? Chantal took a step towards the couple and the man put his arm around her, squeezed her from the opposite shoulder like he was helping her to walk. The woman moved behind them, her skirt a frenzy of floral drapes, keeping a pace away. She was about the same height as Chantal, although the wideness of her hips in comparison made her look like a different species. These must be Chantal's parents. Sixty and I watched silently as they moved in a sluggish threesome down the hall towards the stairway that led to the faculty offices.

I didn't see Roderick until ballet class. When he walked into the studio, my heart pumped furiously. His collared shirt was rolled up at the arms and his hair looked a little unruly, like he'd been rubbing it with his hands. He greeted us with a clipped hello and proceeded almost immediately into the first exercise. It wasn't what I'd been expecting. Where was the welcome-back speech full of insidious smirks and warnings for the new year? I did my *pliés* and *tendus* and waited for him to look at me with sex in his eyes. But his expression had a blankness I'd never seen before. He wasn't even sneering. I scanned the barre for explanation and noticed that Chantal wasn't in class.

All the dancers cast in solos and duets were supposed to have a preliminary meeting with Roderick after class, but when we'd finished our *révérence*, sinking to the ground in voluptuous curtsies, he announced that he'd have to reschedule.

"I'll post something on the board tomorrow." He was already halfway out of the studio.

I'd been looking forward to this extra time with him in a smaller group and felt another pang of disappointment. It would have been an opportunity to observe his behaviour. How else was I going to prepare myself for the advances he might make when we were alone? I rolled off my leotard and tights in the change room, pulled on my zebra thong. I took out my bun and brushed my hair in many hard strokes. I borrowed Sixty's new Argentinean lip balm, Rosa Mosqueta, made from wild roses in the Patagonian mountains. On the top of the tin was a flower the colour of dried blood, its printed petals unfurled beyond the rim to drape over the side. I unscrewed it and spread my finger along the surface of pale moth-coloured wax, rubbed it into my mouth. I looked at my reflection and pictured Mandi. I allowed my lips to part in two lazy pillows. I licked them so that saliva would congeal over the gloss, make shiny beads of wet. Rosa Mosqueta tasted like soapy Plasticine.

I walked back through the lobby and up the stairs that led to the faculty offices. I tried to focus on thoughts of Roderick, but I couldn't stop worrying about Chantal. I pictured her legs again, the tiny wobbliness of them. It gave me a horrible feeling. I looked down at my own legs. Hers had been just a little bigger than mine before the break. She was supposed to diet until she reached my size; that's what my schedule had planned for. What had gone wrong? A dim worry started to clamber up my middle, made a nasty kind of ring in my ears. Had Chantal told people about the schedule? What if she made it seem as if she was doing as I had instructed? There was no one in the hallway. I walked down it, squeezing my bum muscles together so that I could feel the black string between them. Roderick's office door was closed. I went closer to it and something moved behind me. I turned around. Chantal was standing by the doors to the stairwell. I hadn't seen her from the front yet. Her cheeks were depressed, making concave saucers on both sides of her face. She took another step towards me, moved her lips like she was rolling something around in her mouth, maybe trying to moisten it.

"Hi." She looked at me expectantly. When I didn't respond, she gestured down at her body like it was a prize on a game show. "Look."

"What?"

She stared at me like I was crazy, smiling all the while. The smile pulled on her skin, stretched it like chewing gum. "What do you think?" she asked.

I shrugged.

"I owe you the biggest thank-you," she said.

"For what?"

"For everything! For helping me."

I felt like I couldn't move. She didn't look real to me, more like a stick-figure come to life with the face of an old lady. "I didn't really help you," I muttered.

"Georgia!" She took another step towards me and tripped a little. If she fell, she'd break every bone. I could imagine the sound it would make, a hundred eggs cracking on the marble. "You did!"

I heard something from Roderick's office, shuffling on the inside, a conversation nearing the door. I bolted for the stairwell, pressed my body against the perpendicular wall so that I wasn't visible. The door opened and voices stormed into the hall.

"You'll hear from us soon," a woman said.

"Let's just go," a man said.

"Fine." It was Roderick, exasperated. "If you really think that will help your daughter."

Footsteps travelled towards me. I pushed my body off the wall and ran down the stairs.

THIRTEEN.

Chantal wasn't at school the next day, and Roderick was strange in technique class again. I tried to use my eyes as an invisible leash, pull his focus onto my body. But everything about his behaviour had a vagueness to it. He talked us through the exercises, moved his hand as though to demonstrate, but it swung with all the enthusiasm of a dead fish. I thought about what I'd overheard outside his office, the meeting with Chantal's parents, and worried again that my name had come up. Maybe Roderick was ignoring me intentionally. I pushed my lips together hard, tried to smother my frustration. It wasn't fair. Chantal had practically lost her mind, and there was no way I could have prepared for that. I'd thought I was helping someone normal and it made me furious that she had gone so far.

On Wednesday, I was crossing the main hallway on my way up to the residences to meet Sixty. Roderick was crossing from Studio A towards the stairwell that led to the faculty offices when he saw me and stopped.

"Georgia." I'd caught him off guard and he seemed surprised, almost embarrassed. "How are you?"

"Good." I was instantly hot and I stammered. But his expression appeared to be warming, and this gave me confidence. "I'm good. How are you?"

He breathed in so that his torso lifted, his crisp dress shirt filling with more chest. Then he exhaled audibly and shook his head. "I'm okay. I'm okay. Thank you."

I realized, in that instant, that he wasn't okay. He was distracted, upset. It was an opportunity to mention Chantal, make it seem like I was as shocked by her condition as he was.

"I saw Chantal," I blurted.

"Oh?"

I kept going. I'd happened upon her in the lobby. She'd been with her parents, and I didn't know what to think. He considered all this without reacting, his face a deadpan moon. When I ran out of things to say, I could feel my nerves catch up with me. Roderick looked pissed. Had I said the wrong thing?

"Don't worry about Chantal. She's going to be fine." His tone was firm. "This happens more frequently than anyone is willing to admit, and invariably things are fine."

"Oh. Good."

"She'll be back in class within a month." His voice softened. "So don't worry, okay?"

"Okay."

"Are the other girls—they aren't worried, are they?"

"I don't think so."

"Good. That's good." He took a step away from me, stopped. "Because there's really nothing to be anxious about. I see this happen virtually every year and it always resolves itself quickly. Why not tell the other girls—" He cut himself off and shook his head.

"What?" I asked.

"Nothing." He was still shaking his head. "Nothing, Georgia."

"Did you want me to say something?"

"It's a shame, that's all." His jaw was tight. "Another talented young woman getting herself in a mess when this whole thing was completely avoidable."

"Is that what you want me to tell the other girls?"

"No." He laughed once, falsely. "God forbid we should actually talk about these things."

"About what?" I asked gently.

He gazed up dramatically, as though the topic was too big to broach. I thought he was about to walk away again, but just thinking about it seemed to trigger his anger and he took a step towards me, lowered his voice. "You remember that presentation you watched? The one with the food groups?"

I nodded.

"Well, that's where this kind of nonsense starts." He punctured the thought with his finger in the air. "All Chantal needed was a little *real* guidance. But instead, we send thousands of mixed messages and wait for things to get really bad. What it is, is unbearably childish!"

I looked deep into his eyes. It felt like he had taken my own thoughts and transformed them into words. This is exactly what I had tried to do, help Chantal in a reasonable way.

"You know," Roderick continued, practically muttering to himself, "anorexia hardly existed when I was at ballet school. Do you know why?"

I thought hard. The right answer would impress him. "Was it because the idea of a perfect dancer's body was different then?"

"No." He shook his head. "No, the standards were identical. It's because the girls had daily weigh-ins. Because they were told to keep thin. Because it was something that was talked about openly. There was no shame in it." He looked back at the ceiling, as though remembering a better time. Then his chin dropped like a drawbridge and he fixed me with a hard stare. "Ballet is about beauty. Is there something wrong with that? Is there something demeaning about that?"

"No," I said. "No."

"Because people seem to like it, ballet. Women seem to like it. The company has giant gross profits every year and 70 percent of its patrons are female. It's not like we're talking about titillating lonely men at gas stations. And it's not like you girls have been kidnapped and coerced into this.

Is there anyone pressuring you to be here? Are your parents forcing you?"

"No."

"Not at all?"

"No." I spoke firmly. "Not at all."

"No one's bribing you with a bigger allowance or the promise of—what are you kids driving these days—a Mini Cooper when you turn sixteen?"

I laughed.

"Is there something you'd rather be doing than ballet?"

"No."

"Anything you want more in the world than to become a ballerina?"

"Of course not," I said, grinning. "Nothing."

"So who are we to tell you that you don't know what you're talking about? That you've been manipulated, like children, against your will?"

He was very close to my face now. I stayed absolutely still.

"Sorry, Georgia." He backed away and ran a hand through his hair. "Sorry to get carried away with all that, but this stuff just"—he tightened his hand into a fist and bounced it in the air—"it just really ticks me off, you know?"

"It's fine." My hair was down and I moved my hand through it softly, let it rest on my shoulder. What was he seeing in me just then? How much did he like it? "People don't realize how complicated everything is."

"You're absolutely right. The process of training dancers is incredibly complicated." He paused, considered me more carefully. "You've grown up a little over the break. There's a new maturity about you."

"Oh." This was it, the kind of comment I'd been waiting for. The thrill of it tickled.

"We'll start *Manon* next week. Maybe Monday afternoon. I'm really looking forward to it."

"Me too."

"Good."

He walked towards the hall. I turned and watched his back. My eyes dipped below his belt.

When we walked into Studio A for ballet class on Monday morning, there was a woman sitting in a chair against the mirror. Roderick was standing over her, gesturing. Sixty's fingers found my arm and squeezed and we exchanged a look. Roderick had a no-visitor policy in class. He didn't mind an audience in rehearsals but maintained that class was sacred, that it needed to be a kind of sanctuary where we could push ourselves and make mistakes without fear of being judged.

I sat on the floor beneath the barre and pressed my legs into a diamond so I could get a good look at the woman, figure out why Roderick had made an exception. I had a weird feeling about her right away. Maybe it was her size. She wasn't big in a fat way. Her dimensions seemed perfectly proportioned but slightly exaggerated, so that she left the impression of a statue, everywhere larger than life. She looked professional. Her hair was dark and framed her face in manicured layers. She wore a tidy grey suit that tapered at the waist and had flat, oversized buttons on the jacket. An open leather folder rested in her lap, and her large hand was cupped over the paper holding a silver pen.

Roderick had finished speaking to her. He stood at her side and watched us set up along the barres. For a moment, I wondered whether she could be his girlfriend. But this seemed impossible. There was a formality between them. Roderick almost looked uncomfortable. His hands rested on the sides of his thighs with an unnatural heaviness, as if he had placed them there deliberately and was willing them to stay. And the woman was about his age, possibly older. If Roderick had a girlfriend she'd be as young and beautiful as Gelsey Kirkland.

I pulled myself into middle splits but twisted my body sideways enough to keep looking at her. There was something comfortable about her face, something verging on the familiar. Her nose had a funny thinness to it, the bone visible from bridge to tip like the piping of a tent. She tapped her pen against the notepad in a way I liked. There was a composure in the gesture, a natural authority. I looked down at her calves, planted on the floor. She had short muscles that bulged like pears. She didn't look like a dancer.

Finally Roderick cleared his throat. "Good morning, Year Nines. We have a visitor in class today." His tone sounded apologetic. "Dr. Navarro is a professor at the University of Toronto. She studies—sorry," he said, turning towards the woman, "I hope I've got this right—the genetic etiology of food-related—"

"Oh, no." The woman laughed and colour rose on her cheeks. "That was just a title," she said to Roderick, "the title of a study I've been . . ." She faced us. "I study cultural theory, which is . . . the media and society and ideas about that." She brushed a hand in the air in front of her as though she thought this was the most worthless thing a person could study. "Please don't mind me. I'm just here to watch quietly." She squeezed her shoulders inward, made her body smaller. "Very happy to be here," she added with a sheepish shrug.

Navarro. My heart raced as I repeated the name in my head. The coincidence caught in my throat like a large pill you can't quite swallow. Could it be? I looked at Roderick for more information, but he had walked to the piano and was now demonstrating the first exercise.

This woman was Pilar. The coincidence felt like the luckiest fluke imaginable and my heart pounded with delight. But was she here because of me? I knew Isabel talked about me sometimes. Maybe she had mentioned something about ballet that triggered Pilar's interest, seemed related to all the feminist stuff she wrote about in books. I did my *pliés* and watched her. She seemed only half real, like if I blinked for long enough her features might change and she would become someone else. She was different than I'd imagined, not the idea of her but the particulars, as though an infinitesimal difference in every feature culminated to change the result.

I bent forward from my hips in a deep *port de bras devant*.

When I came up, she was smiling in an absent-minded way, as though her smile were a light she'd left on in an upstairs bathroom. I wanted her to look at me. But did she know who I was? Had she seen a recent photograph? Suddenly, I felt a desperate desire for her to have seen a picture of me, for photographs of my face to have popped up at various moments in her life.

Roderick was distant throughout class. He kept his voice low and gave us few corrections. When we finished the last exercise he thanked us for our hard work, something he never usually did, and walked over to Pilar. They exchanged a few words. Pilar stood up and looked around the studio. I tried to do the things I was supposed to, stretch out my calves and hamstrings, go over the steps that I'd screwed up, but I only wanted to watch her. I saw wonder in her eyes, as though we were a flock of strange birds she'd never encountered before. Roderick gestured towards the door. She hesitated but allowed herself to be ushered out.

I had to talk to her. I picked up my water bottle and started to walk out of the studio. Sixty clambered after me.

"Where are you going?"

I shook my head. There was no time to explain. Pilar was standing right there in the lobby. She leaned against the metal rail above the covered benches. Roderick appeared to have just said goodbye, was walking away from her as she fiddled with her notes. I mustered all the courage I had and moved towards her. There was a funny imbalance in the moment, like I was approaching a celebrity who had lived on a poster on my wall.

"Hi," I said.

Pilar looked up from her notes and right away I could see my sister. There was Isabel in the feline distance between her mother's eyes. Pilar seemed embarrassed for a moment and then, with some difficulty, she found a smile. "You must be Georgia. I thought I recognized you in there."

Her voice was full and throaty. I thought I remembered it. We shook hands like two strangers until she pulled hers away. She glanced down at her notes as though they might prompt her, then back up at me.

"It's nice to see you again. Last time I saw you, you were—" She levelled a flat hand at hip level.

"Oh, yeah," I said. "I grew."

Pilar nodded as if to say *that's that*. "Your dancing was nice," she added after a moment, her eyes shifting over my head. "You girls are so talented."

"Thanks." It was Sixty. I realized she was standing behind me.

"You're very musical," Pilar said to me. "It's lovely to see."

"Oh." I beamed. "I come from a family of musicians. On my mom's side, I mean."

"Is that right?"

I noticed a stiffness in her voice. We fell silent again. Why did this feel so weird? I wanted Pilar to like me right away. I wanted to remind her of a smaller version of Isabel. I couldn't think of anything more to say, and after another awkward moment there was nothing else to do but turn around and leave. But then Pilar asked if we had a few minutes to spare and could answer some questions for her research.

Sixty and I followed her to the covered benches and sat down. She opened her leather folder and uncapped the silver pen.

"Right. So"—she looked down at her lap—"don't mean to seem formal with the notepad or anything, I just might want to scribble a few things down. For my own reference. Is that okay?"

We nodded.

Pilar asked us whether we remembered the first time we'd seen ballet. I told her about the beautiful Sugar Plum Fairy in *The Nutcracker* and Sixty relayed a similar story about seeing *The Sleeping Beauty* with her mom in Rome. Pilar asked how long after that we started dancing ourselves and whether we could remember why. We both responded that it was pretty much right after but stumbled over the reason.

"It just . . . I don't know," Sixty said. "You did things when you were little."

Pilar wrote something on her notepad. I wondered what she was writing. She proceeded to ask us about a typical week of school. My voice sounded strange as I answered. I was conscious of it as I spoke and then I lost my way in my own words. Sixty interrupted me to disagree over the order of certain classes and how much time we spent sewing pointe shoe ribbons in the evenings. Pilar listened carefully, her chin cocked slightly to the side.

"And food," she said, as if this followed naturally. "Tell me about what you eat. Do you watch your weight at all?"

It was a weird question and it made me feel uncomfortable right away. More than uncomfortable. Suspicious.

I wondered if this was exactly why she was here. Had word of Chantal leaked out already?

Pilar rolled her hand forward, encouraged us to speak. "I mean, do you girls discuss dieting with one another?"

"No." Sixty answered for both of us. "We're like this naturally. We don't think about it at all."

Pilar asked us a few more things, like whether our families were supportive and whether we had any time for extracurricular activities. Finally she closed her folder and thanked us for our help.

"I'll be around on and off this week, so hopefully we'll chat again." She stood up as though to go, but then she hesitated. "I hope this isn't awkward, Georgia. I guess it's . . . it's an unusual situation. But I want you to know that I don't hold anything—" She rubbed her forehead. "What am I trying to say?" She looked straight into my eyes. "Just that . . . it's nice to meet you again after so long."

I watched her walk away. Sixty came up close to me.

"Your stepmom?" Her voice was a whisper but full of excitement.

"She's not my stepmom."

"That was strange. What she just said." She linked her arm through mine. "What do you think she meant?"

I shrugged. We started to walk across the lobby.

"It sounds like she really doesn't like you."

I let her arm drop. "Why would you say that?"

"I don't mean it's your fault. I mean—"

"What?"

"It just sounds like something bad happened, that's all."

"No." I frowned. "I don't think so."

But Sixty just looked at me and said nothing.

That afternoon, Nathaniel and I waited in Studio C for Roderick. We were supposed to have our first rehearsal for *Manon*. I lay on my stomach with my legs in a froglike shape behind me. Boys never stretched as much as girls did, and Nathaniel just paced, digging his feet into the floor like he thought he could move the wood veins. He looked down at me a couple of times like he wanted to talk and slippery wedges of untrimmed hair fell into his eyes. I looked away. I needed to prepare myself for what was ahead and couldn't be distracted by an immature conversation. Roderick would walk in at any second and I would pay attention to all the details, the things he would say, the way he'd say them. If he was going to try to touch me again, it was unlikely to happen now, with Nathaniel in the room. And it was too soon in the rehearsal process for Roderick to risk too much anyway.

After twenty-five minutes, his head finally appeared around the door.

"Georgia, Nathaniel. Sorry."

I flipped over and sat up. Roderick stepped into the studio, and my heart, as though pressed by a button, started to beat faster.

"But I'm going to have to postpone again. I've just . . . I've got to run."

"Oh." The disappointment weighed on my chest. "Okay."

"Really sorry. Something popped up."

"It's okay."

"Yeah," agreed Nathaniel.

"Good. You guys are great." He placed a hand on the edge of the doorway, swung his body around. He looked back over his shoulder. "I'll find you two tomorrow to reschedule." He winked at me and left.

I felt miserable as I pulled off my leotard and tights in the change room. I tried to console myself by rationalizing the situation. Roderick was under a new kind of stress. Chantal might be a legal problem and it sounded like her parents blamed him. Who knew what they might do? Roderick had a lot on his mind right now and it had absolutely nothing to do with his feelings for me. But the sad ache in my stomach surged despite this. Roderick's behaviour felt different. I was supposed to be carefully charting his advances and now they had all but disappeared. He had been very honest with me in the lobby the other day, but it wasn't the same. He hadn't tried to touch me. He hadn't even looked at me in that hungry way that I'd finally got used to. How could someone's behaviour change so quickly? I dragged my feet as I left the change room. It was more than disappointment; I felt like I'd been tricked.

My mom and I ordered pizza that night. She opened a bottle of wine she admitted was much too nice for a weeknight and told me not to tell my dad. I drank a little to make her happy even though the wine didn't taste like much more than apple juice that had been sitting in the fridge too long. She went out into the backyard without her jacket. I watched her light a cigarette but my mind wasn't really on her. I thought of what Sixty had said, that something bad had happened. What kind of bad had she meant? The sky was a sheet of grey, pinned without a seam, and the smoke from my mom's cigarette drifted in white ribbons underneath it. Pilar hadn't been how I'd imagined her, not half as noble or nice, and what she'd said at the end unnerved me. Was it really so unusual to meet your dad's first wife, the mother of your sister? I knew of families that were ten times as complicated, with strings of wives and stepmoms younger than the kids. But Pilar's voice had quavered as though it perched over something terrible. I watched my mom, the smoke, and wondered.

"How's that boy you like?" my mom asked once she'd stepped back inside.

"Okay."

"Have you had a chance to get to know him a bit better?"

"Not really."

"No?"

"He's really busy."

She tapped me under the kitchen island with a flexed toe. "Busier than you?"

"He's kinda had some problems lately." I wondered where Roderick was right now, whether he was eating dinner too. "He's going through a rough time."

"Oh." My mom bit into her pizza. "Have you thought of doing something nice for him?"

"Like what?"

"Ooh. I don't know." She rubbed her chin. "What nice things can you do for a boy . . . ? Does he live in residence?"

"No."

"He's from Toronto?"

"No."

She laughed a single laugh. "So where does he live?"

"Um." I looked down at my socks. "In a residence. It's just a different residence. It's not a part of the Academy."

I thought I saw a look of doubt on her face, but in a second it was gone.

"Well, hmm. He's probably a little homesick. Probably misses some of the comforts of home. Why don't we bake him something?" She stood up, smoothed a hand down the front of her skirt. "Cupcakes."

"Cupcakes?"

"Sure."

"Aren't cupcakes kinda babyish, Mom?"

"Oh no no no. Cupcakes are girlie definitely. But that's not babyish, no. It's very sexy."

"Oh."

"And we'll do them just the right way, make them extra feminine. A vanilla base with a thin layer of pink icing. Edible reminders of your sweet little self." She smiled.

We ended up only having chocolate cake mix and no red food colouring to turn the icing pink. My mom poured the sack of flour too quickly, so that it overflowed the measuring cup and ended up all over the floor. Then, after waiting twenty minutes for the smell of baking chocolate, I realized the oven had been preheated to only fifty degrees. My mom leaned against the counter, propped a powdery hand on her hip, laughed.

"You know in theory I would say yes, I absolutely made cupcakes before, made them dozens of times when you were a kid. But when I actually think about it . . . I can't remember a single time." She blew a strand of hair out of her face. "Now when you give them to him, hold the plate out like this." She widened her eyes and held out an invisible plate at an exaggerated height. She had a peaceful expression, as if the cupcakes were an offering of tranquillity. "And say: 'Would you like a cupcake?'"

"Mom?"

"Yeah?"

"Does Pilar hate you?"

I could tell she was surprised. She let the imaginary plate drop, rubbed her hands together like they were cold.

"You can imagine how complicated it was when your dad's marriage ended. That was very difficult for Pilar, and I . . . well, I can understand that she might blame me a little."

"You were *there* when their marriage ended?"

She turned her chin an inch, eyes fixed on me. "Yes, Georgia. You knew that."

Her tone was flat, bare. I didn't know what she was talking about.

"It's not something I'm particularly proud of," she continued. "But it happened."

I stared at her dark eyes, tried to make sense of what she was saying. "But I thought you didn't meet Dad until after his divorce?"

"No, Georgia." She looked like she was about to say more, but after a second she seemed to change her mind and just shook her head instead.

"How did you know him?" I asked.

"I audited a seminar of his at the university."

"You mean he was your teacher?"

"Well—" She hesitated and I thought I saw new colour in her cheeks. "In a way."

We left the cupcakes out to cool on a plate my mom had gotten as a wedding gift. It had a fat border of gold grapes, the vines crossing like train tracks. I worried it'd be too nice to take to school with me, but my mom assured me it was hideous junk. I sat on the floor of my room and made shapes with my fingertips in the carpet fibres. I imagined a classroom, my dad standing in front of a blackboard. He was younger, thinner and his hair had pigment I had only seen in pictures. His students were talking, girl students, raising their hands and asking questions. One of them was my mom. I reached for a pillow and squeezed it between my legs. Something *bad* had happened. Did this have something to do with it? The idea made me feel gross and it didn't make any sense because my dad wasn't like that. He wasn't the kind of man who thought about girls that way.

I got into pyjamas and wondered if I should call Chantal. I wanted to make sure she was okay, but the thought of actually talking to her, her breathy desperation on the other end of the line, freaked me out. She'd been so weird that day in the hall. I turned on my computer and sent her a quick e-mail instead. *How are you feeling? Hope you're okay.* Then I crawled into bed and thought about Roderick. He'd be touched by the cupcakes and I'd be back at the forefront of his mind, his favourite student in the whole grade nine class. And, I whispered to the ceiling, *the one he wants to put his hands all over and have sex with.* I stuffed my face into my pillow to muffle my laughter.

FOURTEEN.

I WALKED DOWN THE HALL towards Roderick's office, the plate of cupcakes between two clammy hands. It was 8:45 in the morning and I'd already drunk a Diet Coke. I could hear my heartbeat, light and irregular, like the pitter-patter of mice inside a wall. I knocked on his door. There was a pause. Then the doorknob turned and he was standing in front of me. He didn't look good. His face was pale and there were slug-like shadows under his eyes.

I held the plate up a little higher. "Would you like a cupcake?"

"Oh. Wow." He looked down at the mounds of stiff white icing.

"Vanilla on chocolate. They should be good," I added.

He smiled with some difficulty. "Thank you. A little early for so much sugar but—" He took one from the top. "I'll save it for my lunch."

I lifted the plate some more. "I made them for you. They're all for you."

"Oh?"

"To cheer you up. I know you're under pressure."

I passed him the plate. For a second I thought he might not accept it. But he did, with two uncertain hands, supporting the ceramic as though he didn't quite trust it.

"Sorry, Georgia. This is . . . it's really nice."

"I thought something sweet to, you know, sweeten—"

"Yes, this is really . . . really thoughtful of you. I'm not quite thinking straight this morning, I'm afraid. I just have a million things—"

"Oh, I understand. Totally. Can I do anything to help you?"

"No, that's—" He closed his eyes for a second. "It's nice of you to offer." He looked down at the cupcakes. "These are very sweet. And I've really appreciated your patience with *Manon*."

"That's nothing," I said. "No problem."

"Listen, I have another meeting about all this business at five this afternoon, lawyers and the whole circus. But with any luck I should be through by six. Let's plan on mapping through the first half."

"Okay. Sure."

"I'll tell Nathaniel and we'll meet in Studio C at, say, six-thirty?"

"Great."

I looked at his wide hands holding the plate. I reached up and touched one. I couldn't believe I'd done it, but there was my hand on top of his. I let it sit there for a second. It was just long enough to feel his skin, process the reality of it. Then I pulled my hand away. I looked up at his face and saw the vastness of what had happened. Was there embarrassment in his eyes?

"Feel better." I spoke shyly, turned away.

The rush of it hit me as I walked down the hallway. I had touched him! I had touched him without provocation, reached out and done it on my own. The feeling blasted through my body.

Pilar was sitting in Studio A again when we came in for our ballet class, but this time there was another woman sitting in a chair beside her. This woman looked younger than Pilar yet older than my mom. She had frizzy hair that'd been smoothed into a ponytail. She held a ringed notebook in the crook of her elbow and pressed the end of her pen into her cheek.

Roderick introduced this new woman as a professor from Manitoba and said her name so quickly that I didn't catch it. He seemed quietly enraged as he talked us through the exercises. I tried to dance with an extra serenity, hoping my calm mood might improve his. I was careful to avoid his eye. Acknowledging what had transpired between us would be a mistake just yet; it was better to let it alone. Pilar and the other woman whispered to each other and wrote things down. I saw them point at Veronica and Sonya. When their whispering got particularly loud, Roderick stopped his demonstration and turned to them.

"Oh, sorry." Pilar covered her mouth with the tips of her fingers.

I was meticulous getting ready for our rehearsal that evening. The pressure was physical, like a weight strapped to my back. I had given Roderick a gigantic green light, done something that could seriously alter our relationship. His behaviour would change accordingly and I had to be prepared for it. Who knows what he might do? He would be making all kinds of assumptions, thinking he could touch me just as I had touched him, out of nowhere and for no reason. I pulled open my locker door and quivered at the possibilities. Maybe he was in his office now, plotting the things he might do to me. I would have to act like I wanted it. It was crucial that I show no resistance until the second before it went too far.

I looked through my locker for the right leotard. There was no fooling around now. If I wore a normal one, it would look suspicious, clashing with what I had done. I took out the sexiest one, a shiny Lycra high-cut on the thigh. I pulled it up over my body and went to the mirrors. I looked at myself from behind, at my bum, and thought of Mandi. I arched my back and tried to recreate those two enticing curves. I made my eyes Roderick's eyes and felt a tremor of excitement. This was how he would feel when he looked at me.

In Studio C, I tied my pointe shoes on carefully, taking time to wrap the ribbons at identical levels on both ankles. I stood at the barre in fifth position. Nathaniel wasn't there yet. Maybe Roderick would get there before him and the two of us would be alone. What would Roderick do? The *pas de deux* involved a deep back bend onto a *tendu à l'arrière*. It was a beautiful piece of choreography, buttery, loose, capturing Manon's unquenchable thirst for experience. But the thing about back bends was they made it difficult to breathe. If Roderick wanted zero chance of resistance, it would be just the position to wait for. He would come very close to me, place a hand on my chest. At first this would be under the pretense of getting me to release tension in my upper rib cage, but then he'd get braver. He'd inch his fingers down the front of my bodysuit, maybe even slip the straps off my shoulders. I would be paralyzed, gasping for air. If the studio door was closed, he'd pull down the top of my bodysuit, bring his lips to my chest. There'd be no way of resisting him.

I worked on my back bend over and over again, tried to pinpoint the exact spot of helplessness. It was tough on my stomach muscles, but my stomach muscles were strong. After doing this at least fifteen times, I caught a glimpse of the clock above the doorway. Roderick was thirty minutes late and Nathaniel was nowhere to be seen. I sat on the floor. I decided to watch the clock for five minutes straight, hoping I could exhaust myself of stares the way a baby might exhaust itself of tears. When five minutes had gone by, I looked away. The motion reminded me of something—a solar eclipse when I was a kid, my mom drawing all the curtains in the living room, walking me to school in the early morning with our heads down. It had been torture then, every second a test of self-control. But now I had real discipline, and when I finally looked back up at the clock, it was a half hour later.

I dragged my body off the floor. It had become dark outside, was getting dark inside too, the light in the studio straining against the blackness of the universe. The windows were dank, oily, the room a fluorescent bubble. I went to the change room, threw on my clothes and left. I walked up Church Street to the subway, a clear feeling inside me, one I didn't have to struggle to name. Anger. It was indisputable now: something had changed between Roderick and me. It wasn't right or fair. How could he have failed to show up for our rehearsal? How could he stop all his perviness after pursuing me for so long?

I heard my mom humming when I got home, a nearby hum like she was right in the hallway. She wasn't in the hallway, though, or even up the staircase. I dropped my stuff on the landing and turned around. She lay on the floor in the living room, her body bent like a broken hanger, an unlit cigarette in her hand. Her hair was spread over the carpet like the tassels on a jester's hat.

"What's wrong?" I moaned.

Her body stiffened. I had startled her. She sat up slowly and I was relieved when she shook her head and rolled her eyes at herself, like she was perfectly aware of how strange she looked. I stepped through the alcove, pointed at the cigarette.

"What if Dad sees?"

Her eyes followed my finger as if she had forgotten what she was holding.

"Oh." She pushed herself off the floor. "Don't worry about that, sweetie. He won't be home till late." She walked past me and took her coat from where she'd left it on the banister.

"You're going to get caught," I said. "Dad's going to catch you eventually, you know."

She stared at me as she fitted her arms into her coat sleeves. I expected her to be pissed off, but she wasn't. Instead, compassion warmed her eyes and she sighed very slowly, like I was the one who had done something wrong. "Fine, Georgia. Let me get caught."

Her tone could have driven me crazy. When she'd gone out to smoke, I noticed a cardboard box by the bookshelf. I walked over to it and saw that it was half full of books. Her books. I waited until she came back inside and listened to her plod up the staircase, the sound of her closing her bedroom door. I lifted out the first book, a collection of modern poetry in a dust jacket that was turning yellow. Beneath it was a travel book on the forests of Germany and beneath that a novel with the image of a cloudy bottle on the front, a turned-over glass beside it. She'd written her name on the first page of each. I packed them back exactly as I'd found them and sat down beside the box, let my head rest on a flap of cardboard.

Where was she taking her books? The spines in front of me, the ones left on the bottom shelf, were her old textbooks, *Cognitive Psychology*, *Abnormal Psychology*, *The Principles of Developmental Psychology*. Beside that was a leather-bound book with embossed writing down the side. Her PhD thesis. I pulled it off the shelf. I hadn't looked at it in ages, but when I was a kid, probably before I could even read, I used to sit with it on my lap for hours and pretend that I understood everything and could expand upon her theories. My mom would laugh miserably and tell me I could explain the whole damn thing to her. I ran my thumb over the gold text, let it tickle the grooves of my fingertip, and stopped at the date: 1996. I would have been five years old then. I swung my head sideways, caught the mock-Tudor ceiling beams in a dizzy line of sight. Why didn't that sound right? I was sure my parents hadn't married until my mom was finished her PhD and then I was born after that. Could they have made a mistake at the printer? I rubbed my finger into the 6 as though it might change.

I tried to think clearly, dig up a memory of my mom as a student. She had been around a lot when I was small; I could see us in the kitchen together, me colouring on a scrap of newsprint and her perched on a stool by the phone, one foot up on the wall so that its hind legs rocked back precariously. I could hear her more than see her in this scene, her voice the same except for its volume, which was exuberant then, seemed to fill up the whole room. If the date was right, if my mom had finished her PhD in 1996, and PhDs took, say, five years to finish, then she would have started it in 1991, the year I was born. Maybe that was the weirdest part of anything. Who would start a PhD the same year they were having a baby? I counted out the months backward on my fingers. I was born in July of 1991, which meant my mom had gotten pregnant in November of 1990. If she'd started her PhD that September, then she would have been at the university for only two months when she'd become pregnant. Two months wasn't a very long time. If she'd met my dad because he was her teacher, then he would still have been her teacher, her *married* teacher, when they made me.

I fell back onto the carpet. My head felt light. Was this a possibility? The thought was too awful for words. I didn't know where to start. It couldn't be as creepy as it sounded. It couldn't be like that pervy story in *Doing the Prof*. It was different when you did a PhD. You were an adult and school was like a job. I tried to figure out how old my mom would have been to prove that, at very least, she'd been properly grown up. I went into the kitchen and did the math on the erasable message board. She was thirty-eight now, so fourteen years ago, when I was born, she would have been twenty-four. That meant she'd have been twenty-three when she got pregnant. Oh god! Isabel would be twenty-three this year.

My heart beat harder. How could it have happened? I imagined my mom as I'd seen her in pictures, with black hair and gold-hooped earrings, but I dressed her in Isabel's clothes now, pencil skirts that went up to her rib cage. She smiled at my dad because he was an important professor. She smiled because she wanted him to like her and she wanted to do well in his course. What had my dad thought? He wasn't like those men who leered at girls on the subway. He didn't think about girls that way at all! Maybe my mom had instigated everything. Maybe she'd been just like Veronica, the kind of girl who walked around with loops in her hips and her long hair everywhere, forcing people to do what she wanted them to.

I went up to my room and dialled Isabel's number. Luckily, she answered the phone herself.

"I have some important questions to ask you," I said.

"Okay, boss."

"Don't laugh. This is serious."

"I'm not laughing."

"And it's going to sound weird."

"Consider me warned."

I took a deep breath. "If you were to have sex with one of your professors, would that be illegal?"

"Jesus, Georgia!" She laughed. "Where did that come from?"

"Please, just answer the question."

"I guess, no, it wouldn't be *illegal*." She laughed again and paused. "But it would definitely be against the university statute."

"What does that mean?"

"It means that if anyone found out, the professor would lose his job."

"And you'd get kicked out of school?"

"Uh, no." She paused. "No, I don't think the student would be held accountable."

"But what if you were just as responsible. What if it was the girl who seduced the professor?"

"Even so," she said. "Things are complicated when a figure of authority's involved. A relationship like that, one that's so . . . fraught with status, well, it can be traumatizing for the weaker party. The rules are there to protect the student, so it falls upon the professor, the one with power, the one *employed* by the university, to do the right thing." She paused. "What's all this about, G? Where did it come from?"

"Nowhere," I said. "Just curious."

"Come on, Georgia. Let's hear it."

"It's nothing. I just . . . I saw something on TV."

We said goodbye and I curled onto my side and stared at the wall opposite. I heard Sixty's voice again. Had something *bad happened*? I said the word aloud—*teacher*—and it sent a shiver down my back. My dad had been my mom's teacher and they had had sex. I imagined a teacher trying to have sex with Isabel and it made me so mad that I punched the mattress. I got under the covers, squeezed my knees to my chest. I wanted to fall asleep immediately, just like that, in my jeans and sweater. But the image of my mom dressed in Isabel's clothes was like a headlight shining on my eyelids.

I saw an adult hand, a male hand, wide knuckles over squiggles of hair, approaching her. What had she done? Her black eyes were paralyzed and the bigness of them, deadened by fear, kept me awake for ages.

Roderick was standing in front of the bulletin board, head thrown back, when I stepped into the lobby the next morning. I stopped on the spot and watched him. I felt different than I ever had. My anger made me solid because that's exactly what it was, something clear, hard, factual. Roderick was in the wrong. He had told me he'd be somewhere and then he just hadn't shown up. The clarity of this gave me confidence as I stepped towards him.

"Georgia." He glanced over his shoulder when I got to the bulletin board. "Good morning."

I shot him a look and half-shrugged, waited for him to apologize. But he turned back to what he was reading. It made my blood hot. He untacked a schedule from the board and nodded a wordless goodbye. I couldn't believe he was just leaving. "Where were you yesterday?" My voice was quiet but all rage, a scream with the volume low.

Roderick paused. The skin between his eyebrows made a W. Then it came, the light on his face, like his memory had been plugged back in.

"Oh, jeez. Our rehearsal." He shook his head at himself. "Did you wait long?"

"Yeah." I looked at the floor. I suddenly felt overwhelmingly sorry for myself and the pity clogged my throat.

"Oh, dear. I had a meeting and then—" He brought two fingers up to his temple, moved them away from his head in one piece. "It just must have slipped my mind. I am really sorry about that, Georgia."

I pressed my lips into my mouth, tried to push my feelings down. It was good that he felt bad.

"Really I . . . There's no excuse for that kind of forgetfulness. I'd want to kick the shit out of any teacher who did that to me." A smile crept into his voice. "Do you want to kick the shit out of me?"

"No," I mumbled.

"Are you sure? Here"—he stuck his face out on an angle—"one blow across the nose and we'll call it even."

"It's okay."

He smiled at me for another moment. "Well, I'll be on my guard. You might change your mind. Listen"—he looked at his wristwatch—"six o'clock, Studio C. You have my word."

"Do you want me to tell Nathaniel?" I asked.

"No," he answered slowly, like he was making up his mind as he spoke. "No. Let's make it just the two of us. There are some tricky technical things I'd like to nip in the bud."

At ten to six, I was at the barre in Studio C with my pointe shoes on. I was excited beyond words, but I wouldn't let the feeling take control of me. I wasn't going to be disappointed this time. Roderick's intentions were what counted. He wanted to rehearse with me alone; this is what he had told me. If something got in his way again, if he was distracted by the Chantal fiasco or had to meet with one of his lawyers, I wouldn't take it personally. I would shrug it off and do my best to get him back on track the next time I saw him, remind him of everything he wanted from me.

But five minutes later he stepped into the studio. I was practising a balance in *retiré*, and he waved a hand at me, telling me to continue. I focused on my placement and wondered whether his eyes were climbing up and down my body. I was certain they were.

"You don't have a . . ." He motioned towards his thighs while he stared at mine. "A practice slip?"

"No." I looked down at my uncovered legs, embarrassed. "I didn't know I was supposed to."

He walked across the room to the TV and CD player, where he fiddled with the pile of CDs. I hoped he wasn't annoyed.

"Let's start at the top. Have you had a chance to watch it?"

"Yeah."

"Do you need a refresher?" He pointed at the TV.

"No." I shook my head. "I know it."

He looked somewhere between skeptical and impressed, took his hands off the DVD player and backed away from it. He came towards me with a chair, set it down in front of the mirror.

"The bed," he said. He cued the CD with the remote.

"Can I . . . can I have a minute?"

"Of course." He smiled. "Take all the time you need."

I sat on the chair, facing away from him. I needed to focus because so much hinged on this rehearsal. I imagined the intensity of Manon's happiness, let the feeling course through my body to put me in the right mood. I signalled to Roderick to start the music.

Something about the first strains of the *pas de deux* reminded me of crystal chandeliers clinking in the wind. Manon's joy was so powerful it could smash into itself and shatter on the floor. I pushed myself off the chair and stepped into the first position. This was the key to her movement, the doom that floated behind her like a scarf she'd tied around her neck. I moved across the room. My feet were doing what they were supposed to do and I imagined that my arms had been injected with helium. When I got to the spot where Nathaniel should have been, I mimed our interaction as well as I could. In a phrase of music the actual *pas de deux* would start and I wouldn't be able to continue without a partner.

"Good, Georgia." Roderick pointed the remote at the CD player and paused the music. He turned to face me. "That was good." He looked me straight in the eye. "Now I want you to try it again and see if you can find a little more space in here." He brought his hand to his sternum and spread his fingers over the top of his rib cage.

I danced the segment again, careful not to collapse in my chest. It felt different this time. I was twice as conscious of him watching me. You would think that would make me less focused but it did the opposite. I took the feel of his eyes on me and let it put fire into every step. I understood something new now, that he could see me as Mandi and Manon at the same time. His eyes could rove up and down me in two ways, admiring my dancing while still wanting something else. The discovery did something wonderful to me, like I was finally free of an embarrassment that had weighed down my whole personality.

When I got close to the *pas de deux* part, I assumed that Roderick would just stop the music again, but instead he stood up and positioned himself where Nathaniel would be. He held out his hand. I took it and lifted my leg in the first partnered *arabesque*. I kept going even though I couldn't believe what was happening. Roderick was dancing with me. I stepped in towards him. The next bit of choreography was a supported sequence of turns. Would he put his hands on my waist like my partner was supposed to? I waited for the impact. He seemed to hesitate and I wondered whether he was going to stop. Maybe the situation had suddenly struck him as inappropriate. But then, in an instant, his hands were on my waist. The feeling reverberated through my entire body. I *plié*d in fifth position. His hands took control of me as I turned and turned and turned.

"Ignore the music," he said. "You're helping me too much and the extra effort is sending you off balance. Try it again and trust me."

He squeezed my waist. He was so much bigger than me and his hands could feel so much, everything from my hips to my rib cage and most of my stomach too. If he moved his hand up just a few inches, he'd land on my boob. I could feel sweat trickle down my lower back. I *plié*d and turned again.

"Better. That was better." He walked back to where he'd left the remote and stopped the music. "You know what's great about you, Georgia? You know how to take direction."

"Thanks," I said.

"Are you tired? You look a little tired."

I tried to tell him that I wasn't but he kept talking.

"Why don't we call it quits for the night? I'll draw up a rehearsal schedule tomorrow so that we don't lose momentum with this. It's looking good," he added as he made his way towards the door. "And again, really sorry about the other night. And the night before that too." He held my gaze significantly for an extra second, then looked at his watch. "You know what?" He squinted a little, poked the air with his index finger. "Let me drive you home."

"Oh." My stomach buoyed. "Why?"

"Well, if you don't want a ride—"

"No, it's just . . . Are you sure it's not too out of your way?"

He chuckled, shook his head. "I think I owe you a detour to Montreal at this point, young lady."

We walked down the front steps of the Academy together. The night felt hushed yet untamed, the sky static but powerful as a magnet. It was too much to think about, the enormity of this happening, so I just sucked back the air's sweetness, let it shatter in my lungs. A memory knocked—me, the night before, drowning in the sadness of waiting. It seemed like a distant dream.

"I'm parked down here."

We walked down the sidewalk. We were alone, the echo of Yonge Street, car engines and dinner crowds behind us. I was conscious of each step, of my shoulder in line with his upper arm. He carried a briefcase in the hand closest to me and I could smell the leather in the thawing air. The handle squeaked every third step or so and I thought of this as one and the same, smell and sound, the meaty odour and the yelp of metal.

"This is me." He stopped in front of a red car.

I wasn't sure why, but it wasn't what I had expected. There was a prominent dent along the side, vaguely the shape of a fish, and the car seemed smaller and rounder than the kind I imagined he'd own. He took keys out of the front pocket of his briefcase and unlocked the passenger door. I slipped inside. When he shut the door, I took advantage of the private moment to look around. The interior was tidy. I was particularly impressed with the cleanness of the carpet, a thin fur of synthetic grey, as though people wiped their feet before they got inside, with none of the wrappers, papers and parking stubs that were all over the floor of my mom's car. On the back seat was a neatly folded newspaper.

Roderick ducked into the driver's side.

"So what distant suburb of the Greater Toronto Area will I have the pleasure of visiting tonight?" He turned to me and grinned. "Ajax? Oakville?"

I laughed and told him the address.

"Well, I'll hardly atone for anything then." He fit the keys into the ignition. "I just might have to drive you home a second time."

He turned the ignition and brassy classical music came storming from the car speakers. His fingers slipped over the volume dial, turned it to the left.

"Do you like Mahler?"

I fiddled with my seat belt so that it sat right between my breasts. "Yeah."

He pulled out of the parking spot, tackling the steering wheel with a flat hand, making two smooth circles. I sat up straighter in my seat. If something was going to happen, it would happen here, in this car. Again it was too much to think about. I needed to talk.

"Where do you live?" I asked.

"Me?" We pulled out onto the street. "Not too far from school. Close enough to walk, really, but—"

"Yeah." I nodded as though walking was somehow ridiculous. "On what street?"

"Just on Richmond. A building past Spadina."

"Oh." I looked out the window, tried to make it seem like I was casually interested. "What number?"

He paused and I felt his eyes on me. I was asking the stupidest questions. I should make up some kind of excuse, pretend that I had a friend who lived on the street and that I wondered whether he knew her, but then he started to smile.

"Eighty-three. Why? Do you know the area?"

"Yeah. Well, a bit."

He looked at me and smiled more. "I'm lucky I have one friend at the Academy, Georgia."

I hummed as if this were only of minor interest.

"Yes," he sighed theatrically, "I'm lucky I have you. Things are . . . well, they aren't going so well for me these days."

"I know." I looked down at my lap. "I'm sorry."

He made a clicking sound with his mouth. "Yeah, well, so it goes, I suppose. What can we do?"

I tried to smile reassuringly, but his eyes were focused on the road again. He was confiding in me. Would this lead to something else?

"It seems that I'm a bully," he said finally. "A bully." He shook his head. "Did you know that, Georgia? That I bully young women?"

"I don't think you do that." There had been a meanness in the question, but I knew it wasn't directed at me.

"No? Well, I wasn't aware of it either. I thought we were in the business of graduating more professional dancers than any other school across the country. But no, news brief, that's actually immaterial." Roderick whacked the steering wheel with the back of his hand. "What matters is that sometimes, occasionally, I forget to mince my words. That instead of censoring my thoughts and undermining you girls as artists, I actually treat you with respect. Apparently, the Board of Education doesn't like that too much, me treating you with respect."

I nodded solemnly.

"Do you like it?"

"What?"

"My treating you with respect. Like an artist. Like an intelligent human being?"

"Of course." I looked at him so that he'd feel the weight of my sincerity. "Of course I do."

I could see the ligaments in his neck tighten. Sometimes in ballet class, if he felt a student was dancing with extraneous tension, he would flutter his fingers gently from her shoulders to the nape of her neck, encourage her to let go. I wanted to do that to him, to reach out and dip my fingers under the collar of his shirt.

"And that's the worst part, the most ironic part. I'm accused of bullying while they . . . they put words in your mouths!" He knocked the steering wheel again. "You girls feel manipulated. You have no self-esteem. You're suffering psychologically—I'm not kidding you. The Board of Ed claims to know it all." We stopped at a red light. "I can't imagine what that feels like. To be a trumpet for someone else's cause." His voice was quieter now, troubled but curious. "Tell me what it feels like."

"I . . . uh, I don't know exactly."

"It must—I mean, it must just infuriate you."

"Yes. It does."

He seemed to like this answer. "You know, some people would even see this as inappropriate. Me driving you home like this."

"Oh. Really?"

"Amazing, isn't it? That someone could distort something so innocent?"

"Yeah," I said quietly. "Amazing."

We pulled up in front of my house and I thanked him for the ride.

"We'll start regular rehearsals next week." He rubbed the back of his neck, his fingers inside his collar at exactly the spot I'd been yearning to touch. "Providing I don't get sued in the meantime for . . . god, who knows, inciting starvation."

"Can they do that?"

"They can try to do anything. But they have no case. Don't worry. Beatrice—I mean, Mrs. Turnbull—is rallied behind me and we're getting very good advice."

"Oh, good. That's essential."

"Yes. It's essential." He looked at me, his face unreadable. "And you will be beautiful as Manon. I'll invite all the right people."

I lifted my knapsack off my feet. It was coming, something was coming now.

"There are some exquisite extensions in that *pas de deux*. We'll showcase those gorgeous legs of yours."

My cheeks burned. I couldn't stop them.

"You're blushing."

"I'm sorry."

"You don't have to blush."

"I—I know that," I stammered.

"Ballet isn't about that."

"Okay." I nodded hard.

"Don't ever be embarrassed about your physical beauty. It will ruin your presence on stage."

I focused on the folded cuff of my jeans.

"Tell me you won't be embarrassed."

"I won't be," I said quietly.

He laughed. "Look me in the eye and say it properly."

I raised my head. His eyes were dark. "I won't be embarrassed."

"Good." He wore a private smile now, as though I'd done him a favour. "I care about your career. I really do. I don't want you to fall victim to these idiots who try to regulate everything and make ballet as banal as their own lives."

"Oh." What else should I say? "Thank you," I added.

"Good night, Georgia."

I thanked him once more and said goodbye. If he was going to put the moves on me, this was his last chance. I walked up the path to my front door, moving slowly. He could get out of the car and come up behind me, grab me by the waist. I took another step and imagined him ogling me from the driver's seat, staring at my bum through my jeans, his fingers tapping the steering wheel in indecision. Should he come after me or should he resist? I moved as slowly as possible to give him time. He was probably kicking himself for not trying something earlier. It would be trickier now, the logistics of it. My parents could be in the living room and if he startled me I might scream. He'd have to tiptoe up behind me, maybe cover my mouth with his hand. I'd struggle silently, flail my arms as much as I could, but he was so much bigger. He'd pin my arms to my sides, drag me backward. Before I'd know it, we'd be back in the car.

I took my house key out of the front pocket of my knapsack, brought it up to the keyhole. I turned around to see what he was doing. But he was pulling into the opposite driveway to turn the car around.

There was a note on the fridge from my mom. *Headache–bed–pad thai.* I opened the fridge and took out the brown paper delivery bag, still stapled closed, a bill splotched with see-through grease on its front. I heated the pad thai in the microwave and tried to eat. But my stomach felt lined with raw nerves. I put my plate in the fridge and went upstairs. My mom's bedroom door floated over a sliver of light. I hesitated for a second and then knocked.

"Yeah?" she said.

I opened the door. She was sitting up in bed, reading. Only the lamp on her bedside table was on and it cast a long shadow across her face and neck, so that she looked like a gloomy photograph. Her expression enhanced the effect, eyes sinking under two apples of darkness. I realized it was the expression she usually had these days, as though something inside her had shrivelled up.

"How are you feeling?" I asked.

She managed a nod. "Okay."

"Do you want me to get you an aspirin?"

"I took some already."

I leaned into the doorway. She was wearing a tank top with silky straps and I saw her again in Isabel's clothing. I needed to know what had happened, the truth of what my dad had done. But how could I ask? She rested her book on her lap and adjusted the pillow behind her shoulders. Her sadness looked different tonight. It worried me now and I could feel it more clearly, like a pebble pressing into my toe.

"Mom?"

"Yeah?"

I ground the ball of my foot into the carpet. I was afraid of my own questions. I knew what men were capable of now, the way their lust set the rules for everything. Girls could feel it even when nothing was said. I had accepted this. I had seen it in Roderick and accepted it, and maybe this was something my mom had never done. And then she let the unfairness make her miserable.

"Is something up?" she asked.

"No," I whispered. "Good night, Mom."

"Good night," she said, and looked back down at her book.

A few hours later, I was trying to sleep and not succeeding. I closed my eyes and looked for a cool, quiet place inside my head to curl up, but my mind felt humid and overcrowded. The word *gorgeous* made an amorphous cloud of sound, everywhere and nowhere, whining like mosquitoes by my ears. *Gorgeous* was not a ballet word. Roderick had chosen it deliberately.

I tried to picture Roderick's naked body. I focused on one part at a time. I made out two wide shoulders and the undulation of chest beneath, pectorals like flattened mounds of dough, chocolate chips of nipple. There would be hair somewhere but here the image got confusing. Would it be curly or straight and how much would it cover? Colour compounded the problem, not so much of the hair, which I imagined must vaguely match that on his head, but of his skin. What was the colour of male skin? It couldn't have any of the pinkness of mine, none of the pale softness of girl flesh that snuggled beneath T-shirts. I aged him across his ribs, painted crystalline formations of sun damage, bluish shadows of veins. But when I spliced his head on top, the picture wouldn't stick together. Head and neck didn't match, like one of those kids' games where everyone draws a different body part.

Why had Roderick driven me home? I flipped onto my back violently, let the mattress suck me in. The ceiling was truth and I stared at it. He had pretended the ride was a spur-of-the-moment apology, but we both knew this wasn't true. The act was big, too big, outweighed the size of the offence. Roderick had wanted me in his car. He had wanted to do *something*. Normal teachers didn't drive students home anymore; there were probably even statutes against it. I flashed back to the feel of sitting there, the worn upholstery under my legs. There'd been a smell, wires and car dust—I could almost get it back. *Some people would even see this as inappropriate.* What had he been trying to say?

I was back on my side, curling into the memory. At the time I'd seen it as a statement, but now, replaying it, it didn't sound like a statement at all. *Some people would even see this as inappropriate.* Roderick had been asking me a question. Possibly several questions at the same time. Did I see it as inappropriate, and was inappropriate okay? The statement had been a test, a test any child could identify, but one that had stupidly, unforgivably, eluded me.

My thoughts moved slowly, carefully, letting the clues fall into place. Roderick knew it was dangerous to put the moves on me. He wasn't inside my head like I was, had no proof of how I might react. In his mind I might be a cluster of girl nerves, innocent and wired tight, frightened of the world. I might wind down the window and scream my tonsils red, open the car door and hurl myself into traffic, tell my parents and destroy his career. He was a smart man, a rational man, and hare-brained risks were unthinkable. He needed to ensure that I'd be compliant, that I was up for his moves.

It was up to me to fix this, to give him what he was too scared to take. Roderick had probably driven home in a huff of disappointment. He was sitting in his condo now, drinking whatever he drank normally, perplexed by the inconsistencies in my behaviour. I had caressed his hand in the hallway and now I was acting like a prude. His guard would be up and I'd have to proceed carefully. What I'd have to do is find that narrow space between his new doubts and his real desires and slip inside it. I'd have to pinpoint the very second I became irresistible to him, the second his eyes went funny and he started thinking with his dick.

I went downstairs to the drawer in the telephone nook. It was a mess of papers, receipts and elastic bands, but I found the leather case of my mom's digital camera. It'd been a gift for her last birthday and I'd seen her use it only once. I took it back to my room. I placed the camera on my desk, on an angle so that it faced my bed, and examined the view on the back screen. It captured the top of my pillows, two rectangles of ivory cotton like giant tablets of chewing gum, and the white headboard against the pale pink wall. The desk was too high. I scanned my room for something better. My bookshelf. I took four large books off the bottom shelf: *An Encyclopaedia of Technology*, *The Pop-up Book of the Human Body*, *Balanchine's Stories from the Ballet* and a French–English dictionary. I made a tower of them in front of my bed, placed the camera on top of it and inspected the viewfinder. The image sat perfectly, capturing the lilac comforter and the space just immediately above the mattress.

I turned off the overhead light in my room and replaced it with my desk lamp and the lamp on my bedside table. I selected the timer setting on the camera and the automatic flash. I took off all my clothes and started taking pictures. I had no problem recreating Mandi's position, sticking my bum up at just the right angle so that it was curved and taut and exposing the skin in between.

The printer and camera software were on the computer in the basement, so I waited for my parents to go to bed before I tiptoed down. I uploaded the photos and chose four. I printed them and made sure I'd deleted everything before I went back to my room. At my desk, I picked my favourite, one where my eyes had the sleepy look of Mandi's eyes and where my bum looked bright from the flash. I placed it on top and slipped all four photographs into the front pocket of my knapsack.

I waited until the end of the day to minimize the risk of distractions. It was Friday, so by four o'clock traffic had thinned in the stairwells and most of the staff had pattered off to their cars. I walked down the faculty hallway and knocked on Roderick's door. When I heard his voice, I stepped inside.

"Oh." He looked up at me. His eyes were soft and inky. He was sitting at his desk. The window was open a crack and his hair had a rumpled look. "Hi, Georgia."

I pulled on the edge of my jean skirt, forced the waist onto my hip. I told myself to speak. "Can we talk?"

He looked perplexed. "Of course." He put his pen down and straightened a couple of papers. "Now isn't actually the best time, though. Is it something that can wait?"

"Well." I looked down at my feet. I'd painted my toenails that morning with a polish that Isabel had left in the bathroom and I imagined the muggy purple beneath my sneakers, like a row of squarish bruises. "No, I don't think it can."

He turned towards me now, more curious than annoyed. He crossed his hands in his lap and gestured in the direction of the extra chair. "You don't want to sit down?"

I shook my head.

"Okay. Do you want to shut the door?"

I'd forgotten about the door. I turned around and shut it promptly.

"So?" He opened his hands and left them that way for a second. "What's going on?"

I took a deep breath and lifted my chin. I would start the way I'd planned, with a smooth, clear statement. But his eyes made this difficult. They were right there, dark and liquid, and my heart pumped. My mind whispered, *this is real, those are his eyes*. The air knotted in my throat. I cleared it with a thin fake cough.

"I'm all ears," Roderick said.

Now I was self-conscious. The feeling was lawless, spreading everywhere at once. I looked back at my sneakers. I wished I could enter again, exterminate my stupidity.

"Georgia?"

I looked up. Roderick's forehead crinkled with a teasing sympathy and he leaned his face into his hand. "Take your time. It's okay."

"Thanks." I nodded once. "Okay."

I gazed past his head and out the window. His office looked out onto another building and I could just make out the silhouette of a computer and a desk. It occurred to me that I had never thought about this building before, never questioned what kind of offices it housed. I held my chin up and felt my earlier resolve blow in like a weather front, irrepressible and smooth. I closed my eyes for an invisible second so that I could have a moment alone. There was a coolness in my head, sharp as a newly sucked mint, and I revelled in the clarity.

"So." He lifted the hand from his face. "Tell me."

I took a step towards him, then another. I reached out and lifted his hand from where it rested on his knee. It was heavier than I'd expected and the logistics of lifting a hand that didn't know where it was going were a little weird. I had to take another step towards him. When his arm was roughly at a forty-five-degree angle, I forced myself to meet his eye again. He looked surprised, maybe a little tense; the side of his face turned to me in a question. I paused. Then I felt it, the resistance in his hand. He sat up straighter, pulled it away.

"What did you want to talk about?" he said firmly.

I looked down at my blouse. It was going wrong already.

"Georgia, maybe we should talk another time."

"Us," I said quietly.

"I'm sorry?"

"I want to talk about us." I couldn't meet his eye.

"I'm not sure I understand what you mean."

He *did* know what I meant. I felt a charge of confidence, looked up and met his eye. His expression wasn't what I'd been expecting. It was jumpy, alarmed. He scratched the top of his head.

"Do you want to chat tomorrow?"

I looked at him, kept my eyes level. "I know what's been going on," I said.

"Regarding . . . ?"

"Regarding me." I willed myself to continue. "Liking me," I whispered. My eyes dropped to my sneakers.

"Liking you?"

I kept my head down. I'd said it. He knew what I meant and I had only to bide my time for a second, wait for him to absorb it and take action. After a moment I looked up.

"I know how you've been . . ." The dryness in my mouth stung. My voice had cracked into breath. "Interested."

Roderick's mouth opened just a little. His eyes were on me and a familiar expression flashed across his face. It was his sneer, subtler than normal, but recognizable all the same. "Georgia, I don't know what you're talking about."

Horror came over me. I didn't know what to think. He looked me in the eye. I struggled to keep speaking.

"Just . . . I mean about the attention." I had to say more. "There's been a lot of attention."

"Oh." The sneer was instantly gone. "You feel I've been . . ." He paused. "You're saying there's been pressure. Too much pressure."

My stomach was contracting, caving in towards my spine. My stupidity banged like a second pulse. I had done everything wrong. He hadn't understood. I looked down and made the sickening realization that I wanted to cry, that I was going to cry.

"Hey," Roderick said. "Hey." His voice was gentle.

He got up and pulled over the chair I had refused earlier. I took a step backward without looking up, let my body sink into it. The embarrassment was unbearable. I rubbed my hands over my cheeks, pushed my fingers into the recesses beneath my eyes as though pressure could stop the tears.

"Hey," he said again. He leaned down a little, put his hand on my shoulder. "This can happen. The program is so intensive. Really. This is . . . I see this all the time."

I swallowed a sob. His hand was all I could think about. He slid it down so that his fingers were on my upper arm and he squeezed through my blouse. Every increment of the squeeze brought him closer to me. He shifted his weight and the cuff of his shirt grazed my shoulder as he moved away. He went back to his chair, wheeled it towards me. We were almost knee to knee. I could feel his pant leg on my calf.

"Hey." He ducked his head down, tried to get a glimpse of my face. "Everything all right in there?"

I sniffled, nodded.

"Good."

He put his hand on my knee, patted it. Air snagged in my throat. He was touching me. What did that mean? Maybe I hadn't screwed up. This time I wasn't going to chicken out like a freak. I moved to the very edge of my chair. Just a foot separated our heads and I searched his expression for signs of alarm, but he seemed pleased that I was relaxing. So I moved in more, put my hand on top of his as my face lifted towards him. In a single motion, I placed my lips on his lips. It was the strangest second, blind mouths pushing against each other. I could feel resistance in his muscles, so I lifted his hand and put it on my boob. I held it there for a moment, training it to stay. I moved my lips and things got softer. We were kissing. The realization hit me like a slap and then I was falling backward. I felt the seat of my chair as it rolled away from me, and my spine pounded as I hit the floor. The pain was the deep ache of bone. He stood over me, staring.

"Christ." He ran his hand through his hair and his face shook. The anger in his eyes was terrifying. For a second I thought he might hit me, but he rolled his shoulders back, as though keeping the impulse lodged in his arm. Then he walked out of the room.

I didn't move. Everything had been so fast. Had he pushed me away? It was impossible. I wasn't thinking straight. He would come back and apologize.

My lower back hurt and I felt dizzy. Had my head hit the floor too? I picked myself up and tried to remember my plan. I took the photos from my back pocket, realized I'd forgotten a paper clip. It was important they didn't get separated. Through my jean skirt, I pulled off my underwear and tights. I wrapped my underwear around the photos. The zebra pattern made a beautiful ring that held the paper in a coil, made it look like an ancient scroll. I opened the top drawer of his desk and placed it inside.

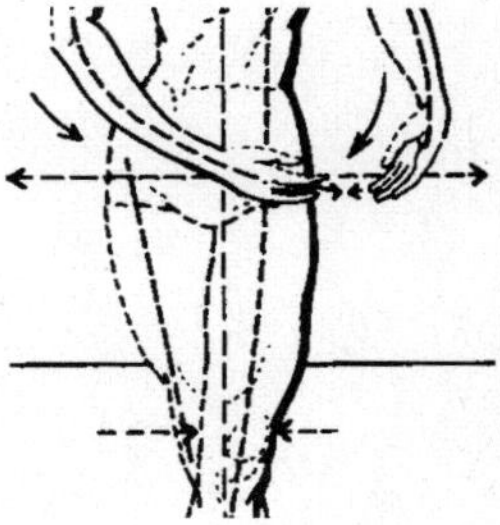

PART 2

FIFTEEN.

I AM STANDING ALONE ON the sidewalk. I have read the sign a thousand times now but the fact of it is still abstract to me. SCHOOL CLOSED. It's an idea that's not quite convincing, like a smudge in the sky someone says is a galaxy. I look up and there's an appropriately puffy cloud, white and organized, with storybook contours that don't bleed into the blue. Sixty has joined a group of grade nines in front of the portico. Their conversation is a hum to me, a shapeless drone without words. I listen to this as something both dim and sharp pulls on the muscles in my chest. I force the feeling down, knowing how easily it could well up and find my eyes, spill out as tears.

Sixty looks over her shoulder and beckons me with her hand. I shake my head. I see the others behind her, Veronica and Anushka. They move their hands as they speak, their expressions earnest. Veronica crosses her arms over her parka and shakes her head with grown-up disapproval. Anushka bites her lip and nods. Do they suspect that I have something to do with it? The feeling in my chest is rising. It's hot and spiteful but not something I can name. I shake away images, snapshots fragmented like jigsaw-puzzle pieces. My hand on Roderick's thigh. The skin of his face up close. The back of his shirt as he left the room.

I feel warmth in my hand, a tug, and realize Sixty is standing beside me. Her shoulder rubs against mine and the closeness is saddening. I am still a million miles away.

"Chantal," she whispers.

"What?"

"We have to find her. This is probably all her fault."

She tells me the group of them have discussed it. Chantal is the root of this mess. Her parents must have sued the Academy, and school would need to be cancelled throughout the trial.

"It's probably a regulation," she says. "So that more girls don't stop eating. Like, while the case is on." Sixty nods. It's a private nod, as though she's considering her own assessment. "We need to find out." She pauses for a moment, taps her foot on the concrete as she thinks. Then her face flushes with an idea. She reaches into her shoulder bag and pulls out her phone. "Call her."

I hesitate. My stomach knots and I avoid her eye. I fight off another memory, the strangeness of Roderick's lips on mine.

"It's important," Sixty adds. "She's ruining things for everyone all over again."

I take the phone and punch in the numbers quickly, as though the whole thing will be easier if I get it over with fast. It rings once, twice, and there's a voice I don't recognize. I tell her who I am.

"Georgia?" the voice repeats as a question. "This is Chantal's mom."

I don't like the way she says it and I worry instantly that she knows my name, has heard all about the eating schedule.

"Thanks for calling, Georgia. Chantal will appreciate it so much."

"Oh." I look at Sixty. "Great."

"Will you be able to visit? I'm sure Chantal would love that."

"Um . . . visit where?"

"Oh, I thought the school would have told you. We're at the Hospital for Sick Kids."

The knot of worry yanks hard enough to snap. "Why?"

"Chantal's been admitted into the eating-disorder clinic here. She's quite sick, I'm afraid."

I don't know what to say. I fumble with the zipper of my ballet bag, but my fingers have gone clumsy. I mime a pen at Sixty and she pulls one out of the front pocket of her knapsack. She takes off her glove and offers me her palm. I bring the nib to the fleshiest part so that I don't hurt her and take down the room number. I thank Chantal's mother and hang up.

Sixty looks at her hand. "What's that?"

"She's in the hospital."

Sixty's eyes widen. "Let's go." She hooks her arm through mine and pulls me in the direction of Church Street.

We walk up Church, retracing the steps I'd taken only half an hour earlier on my way to school. I remember the feeling I'd had then, cold head and empty stomach, like the blood wouldn't flow. I hadn't eaten dinner or breakfast, and my sleep had been a membrane of worry. I could think only of Roderick, of what I was going to do.

Now, if it's possible, I feel worse. The squares of sidewalk are sinister. I see splotches of ancient gum like malignant moles, and the background greyness is flat and mean. Sixty is speaking to me but my stomach twists. How sick could Chantal be? How angry is Roderick? I imagine the phone ringing in my kitchen. My mom is at the table, elbows planted on either side of the newspaper, but she gets up, drifts sleepily to the telephone nook. Roderick introduces himself and tells her I've done something horrible. She must come down to the Academy at once. I see a pale fear wash over her expression, the baby quiver of her bottom lip. I scan the traffic for my mom's white Toyota. It's not in front of us, so I stop dead in my tracks and turn around. It's only a little after nine and the cars are bumper to bumper. Then I see it, the back of it, hugging the curb to turn right onto Alexander Street.

"What are you doing?" Sixty asks.

I drop my ballet bag and run towards the car. I'll stop my mom before she gets to the Academy. I catch a clear glimpse of the car's rear just as it completes the turn and read the licence plate. It's all wrong. I stop, breathless. My pulse unwinds a notch. My eyes are hot and damp.

"Hey." Sixty has picked up my ballet bag and met up with me. She clocks my tears but doesn't question them, helps hoist the knapsack onto my back. She squeezes my hand. We resume our walk up Church Street.

We take the subway all the way to the hospital district at Queen's Park. Sixty talks and I drift in and out of listening, like she's a movie I'm not enjoying. My head feels heavy on the inside, a shimmering thickness I can't clear. I look at the faces in front of me, and only after several minutes do I realize that I'm looking without seeing, that one is a woman with heavy eyeliner, one an old man with a cane. I try to compensate by focusing intently on the man's features, noticing the fleshiness of his nose, the way his glasses magnify his eyes. But my brain swims elsewhere. Roderick's eyes. I had waited in his office for an hour, thinking, or just hoping, he might return. I'd picked up his pen and poked it against his desk, rotated it from top to bottom, poked it against the desk again. I had opened his desk drawer and checked on my underwear. I had stared at the doorway till my heart felt like it was falling and my eyelids felt coated in lead.

Sixty pulls me up an escalator and onto the street. She tolerates my silence, probably thinks she understands it. We walk into the lobby of the hospital. Everything has the industrial sheen of the newly renovated, sharp edges and uncluttered spaces, pearly floors illuminated by skylights. We find the elevators and go up to the eighth floor. The nursing station is empty. We walk past it and turn down the first hallway, following the numbers to Chantal's room. Sixty knocks on Chantal's door and a voice tells us to come in.

We step into pale green curtains, turn right to avoid them. A woman is sitting at the far end of the room and she motions us towards her. I catch a glimpse of a sleeping girl as we pass between the wall and the drapes. She is so small. The lump of her body ends only a metre from her head, and in the crook of her arm lies a doll with yellow hair and retractable eyelids. The girl's head lolls sideways onto the pillow and I see the tube branching up into her nostrils, a moustache of glass. It scares me. What if Chantal has tubes too?

But Chantal is sitting upright. She greets Sixty and me with something close to a smile and her face has the look it normally does, like she's hiding a rare secret. She doesn't have much in the way of cheeks left; they sink into the cavities of her skull and her eyes glide above the way ice cream floats in soft drinks. Her arms are even stranger, tiny cylinders that look painted with blue threads. Sixty shoves into me intentionally, waits to meet my gaze. She's trying to tell me she's grossed out. I turn back to Chantal and wait to be appalled by the look of her. I scan her up and down and try to muster some disgust but instead have a thought that surprises me: Chantal doesn't look that terrible. She's underweight, sure, but when I picture her before, the bulge of tummy in her bodysuit, I realize something I can never tell anyone. She looks more like a ballerina now.

There's an open book in her lap that she lifts from the spine to show me. It's a collection of photos from the New York City Ballet.

"I rented movies, bought a convenience store out of magazines." Her mom gestures to a pile of them on the windowsill. "But it's got to be ballet."

I pretend to find this amusing and move to the top of the bed, sit down beside Chantal. I look over at the DVDs. They're all blockbuster stuff and the magazines are what I expected, *Seventeen*, *Cosmo Girl* and *Teen Vogue*. I look down at the black-and-white image of a dancer in a *penchée*, her legs splitting into a perfect vertical line, and want to laugh at how clueless her mom is. Sixty stands beside the bed, fiddles with the movable table.

"Why don't you tell your friends about how well your treatment's going?"

"It's going well," Chantal says.

"The doctors think she'll be better soon," her mom adds.

Chantal catches my eye like she's trying to tell me something. "*Mostly* better," she corrects.

I look over at her mom, worried that she's seen this. But her mom is straightening a vase of flowers under the TV.

"I'm going to pop downstairs for a moment. Do you girls want anything from the cafeteria?"

We say no thanks and Chantal's mom grabs a tan-coloured purse from the armchair beside her. I feel very awkward as soon as she's left the room. Chantal keeps shooting looks at me and it feels like I'm dodging bullets. But Sixty isn't paying attention. Her eyes move over Chantal's body like she can't make sense of it, doesn't want to believe it's real—the way a kid looks at a dead cat by the side of the road. Finally she takes a step towards Chantal's bed.

"Why did you do this to yourself?" Her voice is strange to me, whispery.

"Do what?" Chantal says.

"This." Sixty gestures to Chantal's body and her face gets choked with feeling.

"I didn't do anything."

"You *did*." Sixty shakes her head and there's so much swirling in her eyes that I wonder if she'll cry. "It's not right. It's terrible."

"It's no big deal," Chantal says. "Right, Georgia?"

They both look at me now. I've never seen Sixty like this before, the panicked muddle of her face. I warn Chantal with my eyes, hope to god she'll keep her mouth shut.

"She'll get better," I tell Sixty. "That's why she's here."

Chantal blinks, then gives me that look again, like we share a thousand terrible truths. I'm so relieved when her mom comes back into the room. She thanks us for coming and I hug Chantal to say goodbye. Her arms stay clasped around me longer than I want them to and I even jostle my shoulders a bit, try to shrug off her bones. I check to make sure Sixty hasn't noticed, but her eyes are glued to the twig-like shapes under the blanket, what's left of Chantal's legs.

Outside the hospital on University Avenue, the sun makes gleaming marble of the statue in the middle of the road while cars curve around either side of it like they're magnetically repelled. I stare at it, breathe in heaps of cool air. I want to find the exact spot where light waves start distorting the statue's appearance, infecting the matte stone with particles that twinkle. Sixty is saying a lot of stuff about Chantal that I don't want to hear.

"Are you okay?" she asks.

"I don't feel well."

The instant I say this, I feel worse. The gleaming particles fill my vision and I feel the blood leave my head. I hunch over football-style, hands on my thighs.

"Georgia?" Sixty's hand is on my back, her voice distressed. "What's wrong?"

For a second, I can't answer. The particles swirl in mangled figure-eights. I feel doomed to watch them or pass out. I close my eyes. Slowly, I straighten myself up, take a minute to let the air settle in my lungs. I tell Sixty that I feel well enough to walk but that I want to go home. She takes my arm on our way back to the subway, probably thinks I'm just upset about Chantal too.

When I get home, my mom is sitting at the kitchen table. There's an open book in front of her but she seems to be reading the silt in her coffee mug instead, staring into it as if it might tell the future. She looks up at me without surprise.

"Your school just called me."

Blood saps from my face. "Who?"

"One of the secretaries. Didn't catch her name." She takes a sip of coffee and then looks back into the mug as though the image might have changed.

I move to the door that leads to the backyard, face the glass and wait. If it's coming, it's coming now. I'm anticipating the awkward way she'll bang her mug on the table, tell me we need to talk. What word will define what I've done?

"Are you friends with her?"

"Who?"

"This poor girl in your class."

I've been holding my breath. I realize this as the air leaves me in a warm pant. I turn around. My mom's eyes shine with worry.

"It sounds like your teacher was involved in it." She shakes her head. "Terrible."

I mutter a sound of agreement.

"You don't worry about your weight, do you?"

The concern on her face is touching and ridiculous simultaneously. If only my weight were my problem. I shake my head.

"The secretary said your academics resume tomorrow," she adds. "But ballet is cancelled all week."

I go up to my room and sit on my bed. I focus on the actual sitting, my folded legs in front of me, because that's all I can do. When I stop concentrating on my body I see Roderick. It's Friday night and he's driving home in a panic. What is he thinking? I try to read his feelings on the image of his face. Is he mad or sorry or disgusted or upset? Each possibility scares me more than the one before and then they're multiplying out of control. I flip onto my stomach and try to make it stop. I push my fist into the tender spot between my ribs. Something is wrong with me. I sit up again and think of my spine, my legs, but the nausea is back. I grab for the wastepaper basket and open my mouth to vomit. But the feeling has moved to my heart. It's racing so fast it hurts. If it gets any worse, my body won't handle it, can't handle it. *Stop*, I whisper, *stop*, *stop*, *stop*, *stop*, *stop*. I want to cry but my eyes feel hard as golf balls. I put my head on the pillow and watch the ceiling. I try to breathe and breathe and breathe.

I open my eyes to sunlight. For a moment I think it's morning, but I turn on my side and see the steely pallor of late afternoon. I look down at my clock radio; it's just after five. Above the radio sits a glass of water, and I have a dim memory of my mom's hand on my forehead, her slipping in to check on me. I lift the phone off my bedside table and dial.

"Hello?"

"Isabel?"

"Hi, George. What's up?"

The sweetness of Isabel's voice, the familiarity, is too nice. I start to cry.

"George? What's wrong?"

I don't say anything. I can't.

"Georgia?"

"Something's wrong," I manage.

"I can hear that," she chuckles. "Tell me."

"I can't tell you."

"Oh?"

"I think something's really wrong with me right now."

"What? What's wrong with you?"

"I can't tell you."

"Well, I think you can. I think that's why you called."

"I . . . uh . . . I did something . . . I did something really bad."

"Okay. That's okay. You can tell me."

"Ballet's cancelled all week."

"What happened?"

I try to control my sobs. "I . . . I did it."

"Did what?"

"Cancelled it."

There's a single, sharp laugh. "You cancelled your ballet classes, George?"

"No." I say it slowly. "I made them . . . I *caused* them to be cancelled."

Isabel pauses. "How did you do that?"

"I . . . I went to his office."

"Whose office?'

My molars are grinding into each other. I swallow hard. "Roderick's."

"Okay. Your teacher." She pauses. "Yeah?"

"You don't understand. We . . . there's something with us. Something between us."

"I don't understand." Her tone is still gentle, but I hear a difference this time, a twinge of concern.

"We . . . I mean . . . it's been building up forever."

"What has?"

"Something happened with us. In his office."

"What happened in his office, Georgia?"

"Something. I did something."

"Georgia, I think you better tell me what's going on."

"I can't."

"Yes, you can. Right now."

I'm crying again. "You can't tell Dad. Or anyone."

"Okay."

"Promise?"

"Yes, I promise."

"Like, really promise for sure?"

"Georgia. This is serious. Take a deep breath and tell me exactly what happened."

"I . . . I kissed him."

"*What?*"

"But it didn't go right."

"What do you mean you *kissed* him? Like, on the mouth?"

I sniff hard. "Yeah. I thought he wanted to."

"Oh my god," she mutters. "Why did you think that?"

"Because . . . it's hard to explain. I thought he'd done things before."

"What things?"

"Before that."

"Georgia, did he *touch* you?"

"Yes . . . well, no. No."

"Yes or no?"

I wipe my nose with my fingers. "Not for very long."

"What!?"

"But not . . . *you know*."

"No, no, I *don't* know." She sounds frantic. "You need to tell me. Now."

"I made him do it."

"You made him touch you?"

"I . . . I don't know."

"Did he . . . god . . . did he . . . ? He didn't force himself on you?"

"You're not listening!" The tears pour out with my anger. "I . . . I might be in a lot of trouble."

"For what?"

I am crying and gagging at the same time, and it's making horrible noises.

"Okay, sweetie, okay. You haven't done anything wrong. It's going to be okay." She pauses and I keep crying. "I'm going to call you back in ten minutes, okay? Don't worry and don't go anywhere. I'm going to call you right back in ten minutes."

I hang up the phone and stare at my clock radio. In eight minutes the phone rings.

"Hi," I say.

"I'm coming right over. I should be twenty minutes." Her voice is different now, organized. "I'll sleep over at Dad's tonight and then we'll take care of things tomorrow morning."

"Oh." I like this, the efficiency of her manner. "But don't tell Dad. Or my mom."

"I won't. I'll just tell them you're feeling down and want my company."

"And you'll help me tomorrow? We'll make sure Roderick's okay?"

"I'll take care of you. We'll take care of everything."

"Okay," I say. "Thanks."

That night, Isabel sleeps on an inflatable mattress on my floor. I can't sleep, so I watch her in the darkness. Her hair fans over the pillow in shadowy undulations and the light from the street pulls two stripes along her cheekbones. If she kissed one of her professors he would not leave the room. He would take her in his arms and stay with her forever. But Isabel is not a ballerina, and this changes everything. I listen to her breathing and feel calmed by the consistency of it, the touch of my sister's voice in every odd inhale.

SIXTEEN.

In the morning, Isabel borrows my mom's car and we drive south and west. I ask her where we're going and she tells me not to worry, that I'll find out soon enough. She eyes me skeptically after saying this, as if expecting me to object, and though I hadn't been intending to, her expectation is unnerving. I look out the window and wonder if I should complain.

We turn down a residential street and then another. Salt rubs the city white, clings to the bottoms of everything. It's an older neighbourhood; the houses are tall here, and often semi-detached, and most haven't been completely restored, so vines overgrow and paint peels elegantly from front steps. There are virtually no driveways, and instead of lawns, slender pathways lead immediately to front doors. Isabel slows down and scans the curb for a parking spot. I watch her hand on the gearshift, the long taper of each finger. She manipulates the knob, up, across and down, making half the letter H, and we reverse smoothly between two cars. She undoes her seat belt and looks at me. Her expression is full of different things. I see a guilt that's trying to redeem itself, trying very hard to be stern.

We walk along the sidewalk, retracing the direction in which we drove. I could ask her where we are, whose house we're going to, but I let her lead me without speaking. And just as I think this, she stops in front of a house. It's a pretty house, narrow like the others and maybe not as tall, with a hemplike rug over the front steps. The small porch is painted green, the rich green of pine trees, and a metal shovel leans against a corner by the door. I follow Isabel up the path towards it. Again she wears that look, half apology, half attack, as if she's grappling with a duty she dislikes. I expect her to reach up and press the doorbell, but instead she holds up her ring of keys and selects one with a yellow band around its head for identification. She fits it in the lock and I follow her inside.

"Mom?" she calls out gently towards the staircase.

Pilar appears on the landing. Her hair is damp and she's wearing wide-legged pants that sit high on her waist in the latest style. She pads down the stairs, and the wood creaks beneath her stocking feet. She puts her hand on my shoulder and the look she gives me has a doubleness in it too, as tender as it is firm.

"Let's go sit down." Pilar gestures along the hallway.

I turn to Isabel. My face demands to know what's going on.

"Just come," she says, and then she and Pilar are moving down the hallway as if it's assumed that I will follow them, as if there's zero possibility I will do anything else. I should stand still and insist that Isabel tell me what we're doing here, but my feet are too muddled to decide anything. They are propelled through a white corridor, walls high as cliffs. Pilar's house. I've imagined it so many times, but I can't feel any satisfaction at being here. The circumstances make everything too strange, and the strangeness fills me with worry. What has Isabel told her mom? I follow them into a living room. The floors are a hardwood that's almost black and worn to reveal the odd nail, but this is contrasted with modern furniture, a chair the colour of a tomato, a low couch in a metal frame. There are books everywhere, lining two of the three walls, and their spines make a kind of mosaic, mismatched colours like shards of broken art.

Isabel and I sit down on the couch, Pilar on the tomato chair. She leans forward so that her wrists cross over her knees and folds her fingers together between her legs. She looks extra big in this position, like a football coach hunkering down to talk to the team.

"Don't be mad at Isabel," she starts slowly. "Her decision to tell me wasn't a personal one. It's a legal one, because you're under sixteen."

Isabel is looking at me from across the couch. I can see her in my peripheral vision. But the realization weighing down on me is like sinking. I sink through the cushion and its frame. I sink through the floorboards and the basement.

"I know how difficult this may be for you to talk about. But it's really, really important that you do." Pilar pauses, unmoving. "If you want Isabel to leave the room, that's fine."

Isabel reaches out to touch my hand. I flinch. My heart is racing, trying to catch up with my brain. Maybe my heart is the last part to believe what Isabel's done to me, the scope of her betrayal.

"I'll go, George," she says quietly. "Do you want me to go?"

I can't look at her, can't talk to her. The rage thumps through my body. If I say anything, I'll scream.

"Georgia," Pilar says, "can you tell me what happened between Roderick and you?"

I hate the sound of his name on her lips. I stare at her wide mouth and imagine stitching it up the middle, sewing it shut with thick black cord.

"You don't have to start with what happened in his office. You can start with something that's easier to talk about. Maybe the first time he did something that upset you. It must have been confusing." She raises an eyebrow, tilts her head to the left. "Do you want to talk about that? How it felt to be confused?"

I look down at the seam of my jeans. I wonder what would happen if I stood up and walked out the front door. Would Pilar run after me? Would she bar the way? I picture her muscled arm across the doorway. I could lift my leg high enough to kick it, but her strength is different. It's the brutish strength of size.

"Do you want to talk about that, Georgia?"

I look up at her and shake my head.

"Okay." She unfolds her hands and props her body back on the seat. She looks over at Isabel for a second and then places a hand on each thigh. "Is there a reason you're afraid to tell me? Did Roderick give you a reason to be afraid? Did he tell you not to tell anyone?" She pauses again, her eyes on me steadily. "Did he threaten you with . . . with something to do with ballet? Did he say something like, oh, 'If you tell anyone, I won't give you any good parts in the next recital'? Or, 'I'll make sure you don't get into a good company'? Or 'I'll ruin your career'?"

I'm looking at the floorboards now. In each dark strip are veins as fine as hair strands. Even wood looks fragile in this room full of lies.

"No?" Pilar crosses one leg over the other. "Or maybe, maybe it happened the other way. Maybe he said that if you do something for him, if you do what he asks without telling anyone, he'll make sure you get into a good company? That he'll"—she pauses and illustrates her thought with a rolling gesture—"make you a star? Because that's very typical. That's part of what these predators do. They manipulate. They threaten. But you have nothing to worry about. Roderick won't be able to hurt you. I promise." She pauses, hoping I might speak. Finally she shifts her position, leans forward on her knees again so that she's lower, closer. "We've had a lot of problems with Roderick already. I'm sure all you girls at the Academy know that. He's threatened other students this year. Not in quite the same way—" She stops for a second, catching herself from going on. "Everyone will believe you. No one will think you've done anything wrong." Her lips pull inward, an expression that's as much a frown as a smile, and her forehead is heavy with empathy. "So please, Georgia, take a deep breath and talk to me. You'll feel so much better."

I do take a deep breath. I look straight at her, though in my head I'm pointing daggers at Isabel. "Nothing happened."

Pilar takes a second to absorb this, an empty look in her eyes. Then she nods once, twice. "Nothing happened?"

I shake my head.

Pilar's eyes dart to Isabel. "Then what did you tell Isabel yesterday?"

I feel a pang between my ribs. I finally turn and look at my sister. "I made it up."

"You made it up?"

"Yeah."

"What did you make up?"

"Everything."

Pilar stares at me. "Why would you do that? Why would you make something like that up?"

I've moved out of the corner of the couch a bit and I lean back on the cushion, let myself take up even more space. Why would I make something like that up?

"For attention," I say.

"You made it up for attention?"

"Yes."

Pilar looks at Isabel again, and while I can't see my sister's expression, I know the two of them are working against me with their eyes.

"You're confused," Pilar starts again. "Roderick has done something very wrong, and right now, it's very normal that you're confused about it. But we're going to need your help, Georgia. I need you to think about that, okay?"

I shrug.

Pilar looks at her watch. "Okay." She presses her hands into her thighs and stands. "Now I have to get to the university."

I stand up and walk to the doorway. Pilar and Isabel stay in the living room and I listen to the inflections of their whispers. What will Pilar do with what I've told her? Something tiny in me is burning. I should demand to know what she's thinking but I don't know how. I picture the mechanics of it, stomping one foot on the floor and then the other, pushing fists into my hip bones.

"Do you want a ride to school, George?" Isabel leans in from the hallway. Meekness lightens her tone. "Your academics start back this afternoon, right?"

Her face looks the same to me. I know it's as beautiful as it's always been, that nothing physical has changed. But the girl I'm looking at isn't Isabel. Isabel had all my trust. And this girl in front of me, a beautiful girl with a dark honey braid on her shoulder and grey eyes like saltwater pebbles, has trampled on me. I let the door slam in her face.

It takes me over half an hour to walk to the Academy. Sixty is waiting for me on the front steps. As soon as she sees me she stands up and waves and a gust of wind carries her hair into her face. Blind fingers scurry over her cheeks. I am so happy to see her, even though there's guilt lodged in the middle of my joy, the secret she doesn't know I'm keeping. She reaches out her hand and places something in my palm. It's a piece of string licorice, softened by her skin. Her lips move close to my ear and she tells me that everyone is talking about Chantal.

"They're saying mean things. They don't get it. I mean, they don't understand how bad it really is." I move my head an inch and see all the bewilderment in her eyes. "Do you think it's Roderick's fault?"

I shrug and mimic her solemnity as best I can, let her hook my arm and lead me up the rest of the steps.

We move through the hallway and into the lobby. There's chaos without ballet class, and the room teems with loose-haired girls with nothing to do but talk. They sit everywhere, bounce idle legs as though they're kicking in water, trying to keep afloat. Instead of piano music, I think I hear Chantal's name again and again. Someone calls out to Sixty. It's Veronica. She's perched on the railing with Anushka and a few older girls. She grabs Sixty's hand, and her wrist of bracelets clinks like wind chimes.

"Are her parents really suing?" Her eyes shift sideways to me. "She's totally nuts, huh?"

Sixty just shakes her head disapprovingly, pulls me away.

In math class, I let my eyes roll over the blackboard. I realize that I'm not paying attention and I try to force myself to absorb the chalk equations scribbled above eye level. I can't trace the moment when the negative exponent leads my thoughts to Pilar, but it keeps happening. I think of all the things I could have told her—that Roderick drove me home, that I sat on his lap and pushed his hand onto my boob, that I wrapped my photos with my thong and left them for him.

I forgot about the photographs.

The fear storms so quickly that it's dizzying and I grip the side of the desk to steady myself. Has Roderick taken them or are they still there, where I put them in his drawer? I twist in my seat, uncross and recross my legs. I need to go up to his office and check. If they're there, I need to remove them immediately. I eye the door and then Mrs. McGuinness's back. I could creep out right now like I was going to the bathroom. They're probably just as I left them, and all I'll have to do is slip by the other academic offices unnoticed, pray that his door is unlocked. Mrs. McGuinness pauses at the end of an equation and I start to get up. But my legs stop moving. What if Pilar called someone, the principal, told her what Isabel told her? The teachers could be watching me for suspicious behaviour. If I were seen prowling around the third floor, it would set off a hundred alarm bells. They would pounce on me instantly, probably ransack the office and find the photos themselves. The idea of strange eyes on the curves and gaps of my body makes me want to pierce my skin with my fingernails, tear through the evidence of myself.

Mrs. McGuinness looks at her watch and tells us to pack up. I follow Sixty out of the classroom and lean against a locker as she fills her Evian bottle at the drinking fountain.

"What's wrong?" she asks.

There are girls passing to our left and I signal with my finger to hold on a second, wait for them to go. I move in a little closer.

"I need you to do something for me. It's going to sound strange, but I need you to do it anyway."

She says nothing, but in her silence is a solemn pledge and she nods slowly.

"I need you to go to Roderick's office and take something from his desk."

"What?" she whispers.

"You'll know," I say. "It's in the top right drawer."

"How will I know?"

"You just—you *will*. It's all wrapped up together."

"And you want me to steal it?"

"No," I say. "It's mine."

Her face brightens. I know she wants to ask more but I witness a silent decision to suppress her curiosity, help me out regardless of the cause.

"Okay," she says. "Of course."

When I get home from school, there's a car I don't recognize in the driveway. It's wider than a car needs to be and the seats look oversized too, like they're executive class on an airplane. The exterior is that type of sickly beige that only exists on cars, and in the falling afternoon light, it looks deader than the sky. I walk around the car and peer in the window. There's a leather folder on the passenger seat and beneath it a canvas bag, the kind they give away at nice supermarkets. I try to see what's in the bag and make out the heels of running shoes, two puffy rubber soles like glazed meringues.

I'm careful putting my key into the front door. If there are visitors, they'll be seated in the living room, and any noise will tip them off that I've walked in. I unlock it slowly and slip inside. The first voice is my father's. It's only five in the afternoon and he shouldn't be home from work yet. I slip off my knapsack in the vestibule and step on the heels of my sneakers so that I can wriggle my feet out of them one by one. I take a single step into the hall, keeping my body close to the radiator so that I'm not visible, and listen.

Suddenly there's nothing to hear. The whole room has turned off and I can only imagine what it looks like on the inside, three or four bodies like marble sculptures. They've heard me, whoever they are. I rise onto *demi pointe* and take one tiptoe step towards the kitchen.

"Georgia?"

It's my dad's voice. He comes into the hallway.

"We'd like to talk to you." His voice is full of something terrible. He motions with his hand towards the living room.

I look at him and don't move. I recognize something in his expression, a displeasure that hangs from his eyebrows.

I've seen him look at my mom this way but there's a difference in it now, a disgust that makes it worse.

"We need to talk to you," he repeats.

Isabel and my mom are sitting on the sofa and Pilar is in the Morris chair with the worn leather seat. Pilar's hands are folded between her legs, fingers interlaced and elbows on her knees, just as she faced me this morning. I look at my mom. Her face is white, maybe as frightened as mine is, and her hands smooth the fabric of her skirt.

"I understand that something very serious has happened between you and your teacher, Georgia," my dad says.

My heart starts to drop. It's a long, numbing descent, like sinking in cold water.

"Can you please tell us what happened."

"*Larry.*" My mom's voice sounds stuck in her throat. Her eyes flick towards Pilar.

"Dad, maybe—" Isabel sits up a little straighter. "George, we know how . . . difficult this is. But let us help you. You're not in trouble, we just . . . we need to understand."

"Why don't you start with what you told Isabel on the phone?" Pilar says.

In front of me are the knees of my jeans, fibres of white, cobalt and navy weaved together so tightly that they swoosh into a single blue. They're the only thing I can look at; nothing else feels real.

"Georgia?" Pilar says.

"It's okay," my mom says to me. "If you're not ready to talk yet, that's okay."

Pilar inhales sharply, a sound that's almost an *um*, and my mom turns to her. It occurs to me that it's the first time I've ever seen them together. My mom fiddles with her pearl but she meets Pilar's stare, matches it.

"I think she's ready," my dad intervenes. "I think Georgia recognizes how serious this is, and she's going to pull herself together and explain."

Something about his tone, the anger tucked into its corners, makes me turn my head. I look at him, the heavy folds along his forehead, and have a feeling like the one I had staring at Isabel. Who is he now that I know new things about him? I look down at his hands, mottled with brown egg spots. They've touched his students.

"Okay?" he asks.

I'm barely listening. The story of what happened is a million miles away. When I don't say anything, Isabel sighs and Pilar moves forward in her chair.

"We're really trying to be gentle with you," Pilar says, "but maybe we're not being clear enough. If anything of a sexual nature happened between you and Roderick, we are dealing with something criminal. It means that it's vital you're honest with us so that we can protect you and all the other girls at school. You have a legal responsibility here."

"You're threatening her!" My mom stands up. "This is ludicrous."

"Lena, please sit down," my dad says. "Pilar's just trying to help."

"If Georgia isn't ready to talk about it, then we need

to give her time." My mom turns to me. "It's okay if you need time."

"I don't think that's the right way to deal with this," Pilar mutters.

My mom stares at her. Then she turns to Isabel. "I really wish you had come to me with this first, Isabel."

"I don't think we need to point fingers," Pilar says. "I'm not sure what that's going to accomplish."

"Do you want some time to yourself for a bit?" my mom asks me. "Would you prefer to go upstairs?"

"This is—" Pilar speaks to my dad. "Georgia needs guidance. You need to tell her what to do."

"Okay!" My mom's hands fly up. "Thanks for that suggestion, Pilar. I think we can just about take it from here now."

"Really?" Pilar's eyes jump around the room. "Well, I can't say you've made a very convincing case for yourself yet. You have a fourteen-year-old running around having . . . *sexual* relations with her teacher, and you're telling her that's fine by you."

My dad tries to interrupt, says, "Lena, Pilar. *Please*—"

"Shall I get your coat? Remind me what colour it is." My mom marches towards the alcove.

My dad mutters, "Jesus, Lena," and pinches the bridge of his nose as he shakes his head and stares at the floor. I look at all of them. My mom is motionless with rage and Pilar looks to my dad for a second, hoping he might defend her. When he doesn't, she gets up and storms out to the hall. Only Isabel is looking at me. I meet her eye, just for a moment, and it fills me with a deadness I can't handle. I run out of the room, past Pilar, and pick up my knapsack and parka from where I dropped them on the landing. I rush out the front door.

At first I don't know where I'm going. A February wind cuts my face, so I pull on my hood. I jog all the way to Avenue Road. It's past rush hour and the bus schedule will be erratic now. I keep moving to stop my toes from going numb and only then do I realize where I should go. Sixty will have found the photos by now and I'll feel so much better when they're mine again. Then I can just crash in Chantal's empty bunk. I hold on to the straps of my knapsack so that the whole thing doesn't thud against my lower back as I run. There's still a lot of traffic on the road and I wonder what I look like to all the drivers approaching me from behind. There's nothing very sexy about what I'm wearing, but I know some guys can find sexiness in anything. Maybe the tightness of my jeans over my bum makes them want to grab me. The thought sends a charge right up my groin. It's like I'm them, looking at me, and their desire becomes a desire I can share. I watch the sides of the cars as they whiz by. I imagine male eyes in the blur of black windows.

It takes me half an hour to get downtown. When I get to the Academy, I walk through the alley that leads straight to the residence. I press the buzzer beside the double glass door and speak into the plastic grate, give the supervisor my name. The door beeps and I go up to the second floor. I'm not in the mood to run into anyone right now, can't imagine dealing with

Anushka's giggling or Veronica's looks. I walk as quietly as possible, tiptoe almost, as if this will encourage people to stay in their dorms. I get to the end of the hall. On the wipeable board someone has used magnets to spell the names Laura and Chantal, in orange, yellow, purple and red. I knock on the door.

"It's me," I say.

Sixty opens it. It takes her a moment to say hi. I follow her into the room and we sit on the lower bunk.

"Did you find it?" I ask.

She hums as though she hasn't quite heard me. She gets up and moves to the mini-fridge by the closet. There's a bag of SunChips on top and she pinches the plastic and rips it open.

"Did you?" I repeat.

"Did I what?"

"Find the *thing*?"

She's facing the corkboard and doesn't do anything. Finally she nods a little. She turns around and there's a strange look on her face. Her lips harden into an awkward rose and her eyes dart sideways, like they're unsure where to go.

"Georgia—" She hesitates. "Who took those pictures?" Her voice is thin, a notch above a whisper.

"No one. You don't understand."

Sixty shakes her head. She comes over and sits beside me, her body skittish and compact. "Why did Roderick have pictures like that?"

"It's not like that. You're misunderstanding things."

"Did something . . . ? Did he do something to you?"

"Oh god!" I roll my eyes, try to laugh. "Of course not."

I wait for her expression to change. It doesn't. She brings her hands to her chin in a prayer shape. "What happened, Georgia? Are you okay?"

"Yes!" I stand up, let my hands slap my thighs. "I'm okay. Look, I'm okay. Can I just— Can I have the pictures now?"

"You have to tell someone about them. Someone who can help you."

"Can you please just give them to me?"

She looks down at her hands. "I don't have them."

I bolt up straight. "You said you found them!"

"I did. But I don't have them anymore."

"Where are they!"

Her head is down, eyes on her lap. "Please don't be mad at me. I was so worried when I saw them."

"You promised you'd give them to me!"

"I know. But when I saw them . . . I didn't know what to do." She looks up at me, her eyes huge, frightened. "What happened to you, Georgia?"

"Nothing! Nothing happened! Just tell me where they are."

She takes a deep breath. "I gave them to someone who can help."

"What!" The beat of my heart is crushing. "Who?"

She gets up and walks across the room to the door. She unzips the top compartment of her hanging toiletry bag. "Just someone. Someone who will really be able to help you."

I watch her pull out a tube of toothpaste and a soap case. My eyes burn with tears. "Tell me who you gave them to!"

She opens the door, steps into the hall, and before she

shuts it behind her, she says, "I gave them to a staff member. Someone trustworthy who'll do the right thing."

The door starts to close. I get my foot in the crack. I'll chase her down the hallway if I have to.

"Who?" I yell.

She doesn't flinch. I reach out to grab her shoulder and Sonya Grenwaldt steps out of the bathroom. I must look like a monster because I feel like one, oxygen cinching in my throat and my skin flaming red, purple. I go back into the room and let my body drop on the floor. I bring my forehead down, let it lie flat on the scrubby rug. I imagine all the blood going to my head, torrents the colour of ketchup. Even when Sixty steps back into the room, I don't move. She slinks around me, opens her set of drawers, and then her cell phone twitches diagonally on the corner of the desk, bursts into song.

"It's you." She's picked it up. "I mean, your number."

I ignore her. She answers and addresses my mom as Mrs. Slade, tells her that I'm here and that I've already gone to sleep. My mom must push further, maybe demand that I be woken up, because Sixty insists that I'm safe and exhausted and will call her first thing the next day. The phone claps shut in her palm, is discarded back on top of the desk.

"Are you just gonna sit there like that?" She looks funny upside down, her frown inverted. Then something gives a little, softens her sternness, and she adds, "I did the right thing."

This sets me off more than anything. "No, you didn't!" I yell. "You broke your promise. You have no idea what you've done!"

"You're not being normal, Georgia. Those pictures . . . it's not normal."

"You promised me. You're supposed to be my friend and you promised!"

"You're not thinking straight!" she yells back. "I don't know what's wrong with you but I'm just . . . I'm going to bed now."

And in an instant she's flicked off the light switch and my eyes press into darkness. I blink at the void, hear her climb up to the top bunk. I consider running out the door, maybe out of the building, but when my eyes have adjusted a bit, I just start to take off my clothes. I leave them in a pile beneath me and get under Chantal's blanket in my underwear. If I were someone else, someone stronger, I would take the sourness coursing through me and do something with it. I would get up and shove Sixty against a wall, pin her arms behind her body, punish her for what she's done. What staff member has she given my pictures to? The fear stabs the middle of my chest. I curl into Chantal's sheets and let the sourness stay in my body, let it feed on my heart while I try to sleep.

SEVENTEEN.

SIXTY AND I GET UP the next morning and move around the room without looking at each other. It's like a choreographed ballet, three metres of space wedged between our bodies as we pull on our clothes and gather our stuff for class. I wonder whether we'll make a point of leaving separately too, but we're ready at the same time and neither of us has the energy to be that childish. We go down the hall. I am like Manon, my face too tired to show resistance, moving through the desert to my death. There are lots of other girls in the stairwell. Ballet is still cancelled, so everyone has their hair down. I can smell it, fruity shampoo and fresh laundry, but something else too, girl smell, a tang of musk and citrus. In the lobby, people gather under the bulletin board. We cut across the room. There's a notice on the board that everyone's reading. Veronica and Anushka are directly beneath it. Anushka says something and Veronica slaps her lightly on the arm, throws her head back laughing.

Sixty gets up to the sign first. I read over her shoulder. It says that all grades are scheduled to participate in gym classes at Eastern Collegiate, the local high school, until ballet resumes. The grade nine class begins in an hour and the girls are to make their own way to the collegiate's backfield. Anushka tugs on Sixty's shoulder bag, then throws her arms around her neck in a languid hug. *This is so perfect*, I think I hear her whisper. Sixty smiles politely and disentangles herself like she's been caught in a net.

I take a step away from the crowd, rest my weight on the railing over the benches. Veronica is talking to Sixty too, looking as happy as a maniac. I see Sixty take a step away. I know she wants to come over to me, but I'm pretty sure she doesn't have the guts. I direct my gaze down the other hallway and hear footsteps, teacher footsteps, the click-clack of high heels. The shadow comes first, long and lithe like a dancer's, and then a woman steps into the lobby. It's Beatrice Turnbull.

The girls notice her immediately. They respond by dispersing a little, as though space between their bodies is a sign of respect. I've never seen the principal in the lobby before and I assume no one else has either. She stands on the landing as though she's on stage, watched by everyone but unbothered by it. Her head is a perfect oval and her clothing drapes in heavy folds, like a Greek statue come to life. She scours the group of us, looking for someone. The dread creeps through my body. I try to catch Sixty's eye so that she can see how upset I am and feel terrible about it, but she's the only one who's not watching.

"Hi, Georgia," Beatrice Turnbull says. "I'd like to speak to you in my office now. Will you follow me?"

I wonder if she expects me to be surprised or defiant, or to ask her what's going on. She walks back up the landing and I follow, keeping just a foot away. As we pass into the hallway, I look over my shoulder. Veronica and Anushka are frozen, staring. Sixty averts her gaze, eyes coasting over her own shoulder as though something more interesting is happening behind her.

The principal's office is off the reception area near the Academy's entrance, not on the third floor with the other faculty offices. Beatrice Turnbull walks without turning around, but even from the back she exudes something stern and foreboding. She's from a different era, which I know will make her hate me even more, see me the way they saw girls back then. We zigzag through the desks in the reception area and I walk with my nose in the air, refuse to check if any of the secretaries are looking at me. Beatrice Turnbull opens her office door and holds it. I step inside.

My dad is sitting at the far end of the room. He faces me and there's a coffee table between us with two piles of things on top of it. I force myself to look down at these things, even though a part of me knows what they are. I drop my eyes the way you shove yourself off a diving board. One pile is my zebra thong. It's been folded neatly, straps tucked inside the material so that you can't even tell it's a thong at all. The strangeness of this makes me feel off, almost dizzy, and I realize I'm rubbing my forehead back and forth with my whole palm. I picture unknown fingers on that little bit of fabric and it makes me want to throw the thong in someone's face. I try to breathe to calm myself, and I look at the other pile. It's computer paper, the images face down like they're too horrible for the light of day.

The numbness I felt the night before comes back, a gassy feeling like nothing around me is real. I take my seat where I'm instructed and Beatrice Turnbull sits down in the only other spot left. I look at my lap and wait for someone to start talking.

"We need to know what happened now, Georgia," my dad says. "Everything."

I might be shrinking, my organs shrivelling up a millimetre at a time. My face is hot and the heat eats at my neck, like a candle burning up its stem.

"Where's Mom?" I manage to ask.

"Your mother couldn't—" He starts to answer but stops himself, annoyed, jostles his head as though a fly has landed on the tip of his nose. He reaches out and lifts the top piece of computer paper. His hand turns in infinitesimal increments and it seems like it takes forever for him to flip the picture face up. It's the one of my bum pressing up into the camera so that the rest of me, spine, waist, shoulders, tapers away in the background. My dad pushes it towards me, as though making me look at it is a punishment in itself. His thumb is flat on the white of my thigh, and it's like I can almost feel it, the roughness of his hand on this impossible part of my body.

"Did Roderick take these photos?" he says. "Did he ask you to take them for him?"

I can't believe this is happening. My dad's voice, his words, the picture in his hand. I cover my face with my hands.

"Georgia," Beatrice Turnbull says, "you need to be honest with us."

I breathe into my hands. It makes a pocket of warm air. I squeeze them in tighter and shut my eyes. Why did they have to bring the pictures here? They could have just told me that they found them. It seems too cruel that they're right here in front of me, shoved in my face.

"That's enough." My dad's voice clenches. "Move your hands away and tell us exactly what happened!"

His anger scares me and my hands weaken, fall from my face. It's like I hear it in his body, the sizzle of rage as it fries his blood.

"Right now, Georgia. We're waiting."

The trademark wrinkle cuts his forehead, the one I believed was a fossil of great thought. Something is happening as I look at him. He's furious at me, but I think about my mom. I see that image of her again, as young as Isabel and dressed in her clothing. He thinks Roderick's a perv but what does that make him? *Can you tell me what happened, Dad?*

What you did to your own student? My hands tremble but I do something that surprises both of us. I shake my head.

He raises his eyebrows, holds them up. His face takes on an expression that's supposed to make me feel stupid. Normally my dad's disapproval would elicit unbearable shame in me, but not now.

"You won't tell us?"

"No."

He inhales very slowly and his chest expands. He scratches the back of his head as he exhales and looks across the room at Beatrice Turnbull.

"Well, we've already discussed what needs to happen, then. It's clear that this environment isn't helping you. We think, and Mrs. Turnbull agrees, that you need a break from ballet."

I stare into his eyes. My heart isn't racing. It's pounding at a regular pace, but the pounds are so fierce that they shake my whole body.

"No, I don't," I say.

"We aren't trying to be mean, Georgia. We're trying to protect you. Since we really don't have a clue what happened here, we have to take extra caution. If you were willing to co-operate a little more . . . well, that might change our approach."

"Talk to us, Georgia." Beatrice Turnbull's voice is dead flat, her eyes like dangling marbles.

I look down at my feet. I can't feel my heart at all now and I wonder if it's stopped. "I took them."

"You took these pictures?" she asks.

I nod.

"Why did you take them?"

"To give to Roderick."

There's a pause. "Why did you want to give them to Roderick?"

I shut my eyes for a second. I need to answer her but the difficulty is bigger than my embarrassment. "I thought he'd like them."

"What in Roderick's behaviour led you to believe that he would like them?"

There's a tickle in my eyes. I'd hate myself for crying. I could tell them all the things that happened between us, but I know they won't even make sense. How can I explain it? Fury twists inside me again, because it's not fair that I have to do this. No one talks about private things this way.

"Take your time," she says. "Start at the very beginning."

Even though I'm getting angrier, I try to do this. I try to think of the very first thing that Roderick did. I know he's the one who started it, but what was it? What was that first move? I clench my fists and try to sort through my thoughts. Every second makes me more desperate. I need to tell them or they'll take away ballet, and the hugeness of this, the unjustness, rises like steam in my body. And in a moment, it's swallowing me, burning my nostrils, my throat, the backs of my eyes. I turn away from them so they can't see me crying.

There's silence in the room. I must be sobbing but I can't hear it.

"Okay," Beatrice Turnbull whispers gently. "That's okay, Georgia." I hear her get up. She places her hand on my shoulder. "That's okay." Her voice is different now, nicer. "This is difficult for you. We know."

I keep my back to them. They tell me they're going to have a quick chat outside the office and ask if I mind waiting for a minute alone. I shrug. As soon as they've left the room, I stuff the photographs and my thong into my knapsack and zip it up. I hear the drone of voices outside but I don't even try to make out words. After a moment they return.

"We're going to arrange a couple of appointments for you," my dad says. "We're going to have you speak to a psychologist. There'll still be lots of questions to answer, but this should help."

Beatrice Turnbull glances at her watch, a wiry thing that looks a hundred years old. "If you hurry and go straight to Eastern Collegiate, you'll catch the end of the gym class."

They clear a space for me so that I can get to the door. But I don't move.

"What about ballet?" I direct the question at my dad, but when he doesn't answer I look at Beatrice Turnbull.

"We'll discuss it, Georgia," my dad says. "Ballet is still cancelled here, so we all have time to give it some thought."

"What does that mean!?"

"It means"—he rubs the back of his neck—"we'll see. It will depend on a lot of things and your co-operation with the psychologist will certainly help you."

I stare at his sea-sponge face and feel a loathing creep up from my bones. The sensation is unbearable, as if all nice things in me might explode. I reach for the doorknob, but

Beatrice Turnbull puts her hand out to stop me, her eyes on the coffee table.

"Where are the . . . ? Did you take those items?"

"They're mine," I say.

She frowns. "They're not yours anymore, Georgia. They're in our custody now."

I'm mad enough that I can imagine storming past the both of them, my things buried inside my bag. But pissing them off any more isn't going to help me. I unzip my backpack, take out the stuff and hand it to Beatrice Turnbull. My thong slips off the top photo and lands on the floor. I step on it as I walk out of the room.

I leave the Academy and turn right along the sidewalk. The sky is overcast, like the inside of a seashell, and the air smells like wet exhaust. I remember Beatrice Turnbull telling me to hurry, so I stop dead in my tracks and try to take the slowest step imaginable. I take another one exactly the same way. A car passes me and I can just imagine what I look like to the people inside, a weirdo impersonating an astronaut. I wonder if this is what it feels like to go crazy. I turn down Jarvis Street, tip my head back so that I can watch the clouds as I walk. Moving with your head like that distorts any sense of balance and I can feel myself zigzag but I don't care. The word *how* plays over and over again in my mind, like a CD that's all scratched and skipping. There's something about the repetition of the question that I like, how it evokes the vastness of my disaster. How has everything crumbled so quickly? The clouds shift into things, giant bugs and flattened hearts, and

I try to convince myself that I've forgotten what clouds are, what purpose they serve in the universe. I reach down and squeeze my thigh. I haven't danced for three days now. I haven't even stretched. It's the longest I've gone without stretching in two years, and the thought slows my heart.

Eastern Collegiate is just a few blocks south of Wellesley. Out front are clusters of kids. I pass three girls first, each holding a takeout coffee. They have long hair and deep side parts; two have leather purses that cross their bodies like camera cases, and they're wearing leggings that get swallowed into their snow boots. The one on the end brings the lid to her mouth, tilts it back hard and instantly buckles sideways, spitting. The other two bend over her and laugh. She wipes her chin with the back of her hand, yells at them, laughs too. I don't really know how I'm supposed to get to the backfield, so I figure I should just go in the main door. There are kids lining the railings. Some wear big headphones and others have cigarettes tucked like pencils behind their ears. I weave my way around a clump of them, squeeze by a girl with blonde hair and realize that it's Veronica. She's talking to a few guys. I see their heads over her shoulder and I notice Anushka beside her now. Then I see Sixty. She's on the edge of the clump and she's already spotted me. She hoists her shoulder bag out of the way and comes over.

"Hey," she says quietly. "Did everything . . . I mean, was it okay?"

I can't believe she has the nerve to ask this. Everything would have been okay if she'd kept her promise. I turn around and am walking back towards the curb when I think I hear my name. Then I hear it again. It's a male voice and I turn around. There's a guy looking down at me. He rubs his hand over his whole head and his hair doesn't move at all because it's thick as a rug and an inch from his scalp. He's pretty tall and he has smooth skin the colour of a coffee stain.

"Kareem?" I say it as a question even though it's not a question. A heat rises over my cheeks.

Kareem jerks his chin over his shoulder a little, something between a nod and a tic. "What are you doing here? Did you transfer?"

"No—"

"Didn't you go off to ballet school?"

"Yeah. I'm still there. I mean, not this very second, obviously—"

"We need a gym credit," Sixty interrupts, and I realize that she's followed me. "We're just here for gym."

"Oh. Cool." He shoves his hands deeper into his pockets. His arms are too long to stretch in this position, but he tries to straighten them anyway and this makes his shoulders pop forward, his chest retreat in a curve.

"Well, look, we're having a party. Oh man, is it gonna be good." He reaches for something in his back pocket and pulls out a stack of flyers. He gives one to me and one to Sixty. "It's a house thing. My buddy's trying to get into promotion."

I look down at the flyer. There's a black-and-white photo of two skinny guys in bomber jackets leaning against a wire fence. On the other side there's all the information: an address, directions and the date, which is tomorrow night. It also says "BYOB."

"I'll give you my number." Kareem pulls a pen out of something behind him; it's hard to tell whether it's his jean pocket or his bag. "You know—in case."

He looks around for something to write on. I push my sleeve up and thrust out my arm. He inscribes his number in big blue digits across the inside of my wrist. I watch his forehead as he writes. It seems crazy that I was ever scared of him.

"All right. Hope to see ya." He wanders back into the cluster of guys behind Veronica and Anushka.

I trace my finger over the ink to see if it will smudge.

"You don't want to go, do you?" Sixty says.

I just ignore her, turn and walk up Jarvis Street towards the subway. I suddenly couldn't care less about this gym class. I'm going to go home and run myself a scalding bath and soak in the ceramic drum until my muscles are warm as pizza dough, can be kneaded into anything. I have to make up for two days of not stretching and the house will be empty, so I can do it wherever I like.

I sit on the train and stare at my interlaced fingers while I concoct a ballet schedule in my head. I'll do *adage* and *grands battements* and *fouetté* turns. I picture myself not in my leotard but in something gossamer and filthy, dragged through swamps, like Manon's rags as she nears her death. When the subway reaches my stop, I don't bother waiting for the bus, climb the dirty staircase out of the station and move through the glass atrium to the street. The sky is still white, but there's sun burning beneath it now. It bleaches out detail, so that sidewalks and buildings and faces are coated in a colourless glare and I wish I had a pair of sunglasses. Even though it's cold out, I think of a desert instead of a city. This is the kind of starkness that Manon died in. I can picture her elegant body go slack in a beam of sunlight. Her throat is parched like overcooked bacon and her head lolls from side to side. Still, she points her toes. When her lover finally shows up to save her, it's too late. Her head falls backward and her body tenses in one last spasm, arching in an endless curve, arms unfurled by her ears. Then she goes limp. What does her lover do with her dead body in his arms? He probably cries. I see him grope for some life in the body he'd loved so dearly, his hands grabbing indiscriminately at waist, thighs, chest. The sun is still everywhere, like invisible peroxide gas. He rips open her dress. Her breasts glow in the light—in fact they're practically translucent—and he brings his lips to one of her pointy nipples for the last time.

I open the front door and my mom is in the living room. I stop dead in my tracks. Does she know about the photos? They'd make her imagine the most horrible things. I step through the alcove. She's surrounded by boxes and I hear the screech of packing tape as she pulls it over a flap of cardboard. There are giant gaps in the bookshelf.

We watch each other, unmoving, her body behind the mess of packing and my arms hanging at my sides. We're so quiet that I think inanimate objects are making noise instead.

Electricity tickles the glass jars on the mantel. My mom's expression doesn't change as she moves towards me, and in a moment she has her arms around my neck. My face goes into her hair as she hugs me. She smells like cigarettes but I don't care.

"Are you okay?" she asks.

Her voice is thin as a reed and I wonder if she's crying. It makes me feel terrible. I've caused this sadness when she was already so sad to start.

"Yeah. I'm . . . I'm all right."

"Poor sweetheart." She sniffs. "Poor baby. We'll get through this. I promise we will. You'll be fine."

She takes me by the shoulders and moves my body back so that she can look into my eyes.

"Do you want to talk?"

I shake my head.

"That's fine." She wraps her hand around my ponytail, leaves it there like another elastic. "We'll talk whenever you want to."

"Where are you going?"

She doesn't answer me. I feel her take a massive inhale that lifts her shoulders and widens her ribs beneath her sweater. "We're moving," she finally says.

"We are?"

"Yeah."

"Oh," I say, and I nod the way I imagine a lawyer would nod, a doctor would nod, like it's clinical information that can't show on my face. "Where?"

"Long term—I don't know. I've booked a hotel for a few nights. I know the timing couldn't be worse, but you'll like it. There's a spa and an indoor pool." She tries to smile. "It's walking distance from the Academy."

She waits for me to say something, probably show some sign of consent. But I feel like this isn't even my life, that nothing about it can bug me. And I like this indifference, love it maybe, because nothing matters if I just don't care. She goes back to the box she's been packing, places another pile of books inside. I watch her for a moment. There's something different about how she moves. Still smooth and dull, like an endless note on the piano, but in spite of everything, maybe today her body looks less sad. I move to the bookshelf.

"Are we taking them all?" I ask.

"Except those." She points to a clump at the end of the shelf.

There are unformed boxes on the carpet. I lift one and fold it into shape. I take books from the lower shelves and put them inside.

"Are you going to get divorced?"

"Yes," she says immediately, and then she looks at the ceiling, thinking, as though she's taken aback by her own speed.

We keep packing the books and we don't talk for a bit. I lift her old textbooks from the bottom shelf and lay them flat in a new box. When I'm holding her thesis, she reaches over and touches my hand.

"Do you want to ask me anything, George? You don't seem very surprised."

I rub my finger over the gold writing on the front, carved into the leather like a stream through rock. I think I might be the opposite of surprised. I look down at her thesis and think that this news, this divorce, explains things I've known for a while.

"I know the timing is awful, sweetie," she continues. "And when I find a place in a month or so, you can decide what you want to do. I'm sure your dad will tell you what his plans are."

"Won't he just stay here?"

"I don't know."

Her answer strikes me as strange, or maybe it's the way she's said it, each word spoken so slowly that it splits from the one beside it.

"Why wouldn't he stay here?"

She turns to me. Her eyes are still but there's so much happening inside them that they look extra dark now, black. "I don't know anything about this woman. I don't know what she wants."

"Who are you talking about?"

"I think you know, Georgia."

She goes back to packing books again, and I just stand there and watch the way her sleeves fall over her hands as she bends down.

"No, I don't," I say. "I have no idea."

I think it's my quietness that catches her. If I'd raised my voice, I don't think she'd be turning to me the way she is now. She stares into my eyes, first like she's trying to gauge my sincerity and then with something else. It's a merciful look, softening down her neck.

"Your dad has met someone. A woman. He's having a relationship with this woman."

"Oh."

"I kind of thought you had figured that out."

I nod as though I might have figured it out, then turn to the bookshelf so that she can't see my face. I wonder if this is what it feels like to get beat up, when all your bruises bleed into one bruise, and that combo of pain takes over your whole body. I bring my fingers to the corners of my eyes to push back tears.

"Is it Pilar?" I ask.

"What?" My mom sniggers. "Of course not. Where on earth did you get that idea?"

I can't answer. I'm not sure where I got any of my ideas anymore. Wherever it is, it's the wrong place, like someone gave me bad directions ages ago, maybe when I was just a baby, and never bothered to correct the mistake.

"So you're getting a divorce because dad's screwing around with some slut?"

She comes over to me and wraps her arms around me from behind. The tears flow freely now, like the hug has squeezed them out of me.

"Well, it definitely hasn't helped things," she says.

"So it has nothing to do with what happened *before?*"

"Before what?"

But I have no idea how to put my question into words, how to ask about bad things that happened years ago, when she was only Isabel's age.

"It has to do with a hundred things, George," she says while she hugs me tighter. "I think that's generally the way these things work."

We go back to packing the books, and when we've finished, she goes to the kitchen and pours us both glasses of juice. We sit at the dining room, drink.

"We'll leave in an hour, okay? You should get a bag together."

I feel like I can't move. I drill my elbow into an eye in the wood, fight the urge to climb onto the table and lie down, become a body on a stretcher. But I find my feet and drag them through the alcove. The living room looks undressed without books. Light slings over the mantel and my eyes are pulled to a border of reflective chrome, a knick-knack picture frame that must have been a gift. The photo wasn't taken all that long ago and I wonder who stuck it up there—my dad, who looks like he barely tolerated the moment, or my mom, who stares at the lens like she's begging it for help.

I go up to my room, where I take an overnight bag from my closet and start to fill it with the obvious things: socks, pyjamas, T-shirts. Inside the top drawer of my dresser is a neon garden of dots and stripes, all the things my mom bought me. I bundle the underwear into my arms and go to drop it in the bag, but my eyes latch on to another photo, my mom with a bundle of her own, a baby's head resting in her elbow. It was always her expression that struck me as embarrassing in this shot, her laugh-aloud smile and lolling summertime head, like a kid stuck in a grown-up's body. But now I think about the photographer, the much older man with the camera pointed at his new life. What had my dad been thinking? What was it like to step out of one life and move straight into another, as though the steps didn't go up or down but wound so snug to his body that they barely displaced him at all? I open the next drawer and pack a bunch of tights and the only two black leotards that aren't in the laundry. Maybe this is the true difference between my dad and me, the fact that a dancer's steps are constant, heartfelt, while he sits stiff in the front row, shadows of wives and daughters doing the moving instead. I place my ballet slippers on the pile, zip up my bag and pull my door shut tight, hear the latch click in its hollow.

"You ready?" My mom faces me from the bottom of the stairs, her expression squeezed into a happiness that neither of us believe.

I take my parka from where I left it on the banister and she points at my wrist.

"What's that?"

Scribbled, vein side up, is Kareem's smudged printing.

"Nothing." I ram my arm through my sleeve. "Is it okay if I go to a party tomorrow?"

"Oh, Georgia." She shakes her head and pouts. "Of course it is. Things will go on as they normally do. I promise you they will."

"Okay." I stuff my other arm into its sleeve. "Just checking."

We drive through the city without saying much, the greys and whites of winter dragging what's left of themselves beneath the car.

EIGHTEEN.

THE NEXT NIGHT, MY MOM drops me off at the Academy residence, and as I get out of the car she hands me a sealed envelope. I turn it around in my hand, press the pad of one finger into the needle-prick of its corner.

"What's this?"

"I've written down all the information you might need, the hotel address and phone number and my cell . . . I know, I know, you have it memorized. I've put a little money in there too. Just in case. Call me when you get up in the morning. I'll come pick you up."

I've told my mom that I'm sleeping here tonight, in

Chantal's empty bed, even though I haven't asked Sixty. I say thanks and try not to slam the car door.

The supervisor buzzes me into the building and I tear a zigzag into the envelope as I climb the stairs. A note ripped from my mom's day planner folds over five stiff twenties fresh from the bank machine. I tuck it all back in and knock on Sixty's door. She doesn't seem surprised to see me and still has that guilty look smudged into her features, every gesture a tiny apology. It only makes me madder. A door closes down the hallway and Veronica moves towards us in her bathrobe, two shampoo-type bottles balanced in the crook of one arm while she juggles a towel and her toiletry bag with the other one.

"You guys going to this thing?"

"What thing?" Sixty asks her.

"That party."

"I don't think so," Sixty says.

"Definitely!" I say. And when Veronica looks at me strangely, I add, "For sure!"

Veronica goes into the bathroom and Sixty tells me she's off to the cafeteria for dinner, says I can eat there as her guest. I tell her I'm not hungry and drop my overnight bag on Chantal's bed, lay the envelope on top of it. Then I go after Veronica to make sure it's okay that I go to the party with her. The water is already rushing full blast in the first shower stall, so I move to the mirror and pretend to fix my hair. Veronica screams that she's nicked her ankle and in a second she's pushed back the plastic curtain and hobbles to the counter. A crimson rivulet trails behind her on the tiles, thin as unravelled yarn. We fix our hair side by side in the mirror, her towel at her armpits and me still in my parka, the furry lining going steamy on the back of my neck. She pulls a mesh of blonde from the purple plastic teeth of her comb, leaves it balled beside the sink. I ask her if I can use her gel. She raises her eyebrows instead of saying yes and the goop is chilly on my fingers.

"Kareem says he went to school with you."

I shrug to say, *So what?*

"What are you wearing tonight?" she asks.

I'm in jeans and an ordinary sweater and haven't brought anything better. She twists the cap back on her gel and makes sure her towel is tucked tightly.

"You can borrow something. I have a million things."

I follow Veronica back to her dorm room. She reaches into the top drawer of the dresser and tosses a bundle of things onto the lower bunk. I'm struck by fabrics like stained glass, see-through clothes that suck at the light and make blinding colours on the mattress sheet. She starts rifling through them and I pick at the things she discards.

"Here."

She pushes something at me. It's electric blue and I can't tell whether it's a top or a bottom until I hold it out in front of me. Sparkles are scattered through the material, but the mechanics of how they stick are invisible, as though they're sewn with transparent thread. It's a halter dress that ties around the neck. I take off everything but my underwear and Veronica pulls it over my head. She moves behind me and ties it tight at the big vertebra at the top of my spine. I feel sandpaper crystals on my stomach. Veronica shoves me in front of the mirror so that she can analyze my whole reflection. Her hands clamp the crown of my head, like the teeth of a clip from the hairdresser's.

"You look older with your hair up. If you had your hair like this and I didn't know you, I'd think you were sixteen."

She opens a cosmetic bag with a design of cartoon flowers pressed inside rings of lattice and hands me an uncapped lipstick. I put it on. Nobody has lips this colour. The dress is cut low enough to show the tops of my boobs. I stare at my reflection and think I look better than I ever have.

I have to go back to Sixty's room to get my purse, and as I leave, Veronica tells me the dress is mine forever.

"There might be more occasions, now that there's no ballet."

"It will start again soon," I say.

"You know Roderick resigned, right? He put in his letter yesterday."

"Who told you that?"

"Mary in grade twelve."

I shut the door and walk down the hall. It could just be a stupid rumour but I can't control my panic. I try to remember the exact things I said to Isabel on the phone. Were they enough to get him in trouble? The possibility does something new to me. It fills me with a heaviness that twists and heaves, something I want to grab hold of and wring out.

Sixty is sitting on the lower bunk, already back from the cafeteria. Her back is pin straight, regal even. No one sits like that when they're alone and I know she must be waiting for me. I pull a pair of tights from my overnight bag and step into them, grip the waistband to hoist them up. I wish I had high heels, but I can't ask Sixty to wear hers, so I just shove my feet into my snow boots. I bring a tiny purse with just enough room for the flyer, take just one of the twenties my mom gave me because the money will be safer here.

"I've made a big decision," Sixty says, and it's not even clear she's talking to me because she's staring at her slippers.

Ignore her, I think. *Act like you haven't heard.* I take the list of information my mom scribbled and fold it into rectangles over and over until it's the size of a gum wrapper, and then I put it in the purse too.

"I'm leaving," she says.

"Leaving where?"

"The Academy. My dad got me into a private school."

We look at each other and I just say, "Are you stupid?"

She shakes her head at me and sighs like she's suddenly a decade older and it makes me mad enough to kick things. I send my boot into the closet door and even the handle rattles.

"What about ballet?" I demand.

"I don't know. I'm not sure I want to do it anymore."

"What are you talking about?"

"I might quit."

It catches in my throat, her answer, and my whole body wants to hiccup or shake or scream. I should say a thousand things but they all judder in my head and my lips become useless. Veronica and Anushka knock on the door and ask if I'm ready. I zip up my parka and just leave.

It's past eight and the night hangs limply from the sky, too lazy to rain or snow. I won't think about Sixty now. I'll follow these other girls and forget things. Veronica has put on high boots with heels like big fangs. She has to leap over puddles of slush, and after a few minutes her toes are capped with triangles of salt. Still, I wish I were wearing them. The party is in Cabbagetown, which means we have to walk east to Parliament Street, then jog a little north. The cold will eat through my gloves soon, so I ball my hands up inside of them and stick my fists in my pocket.

"If it's lame we should go to a club," says Anushka.

"It won't be," Veronica says. "Trust me, it will not be lame."

I see the party and hear it at the same time. There are kids clustered out front of the house, and we hear talk and shouts and laughter. We walk down the sidewalk towards it. No one notices us approach, but I still feel like everyone's watching. I try to seem busy and aloof. My parka covers my whole dress, so I'm just ballet tights and boots, and I hate myself for how stupid it must look. I open my purse and rifle for an imaginary cell phone. We move up the path to the front door and Veronica waves at someone and calls out *what's going on* like it's a lyric from a song and then we're pushing past the murk of cigarette smoke into the hallway.

Veronica and Anushka take their jackets off and drop them on the landing, where a hundred others have been left. I take mine off too, try to put it neatly in the corner by the wall so I'll be able to find it later. It feels like rush hour in the subway. People clog the hallway in tight clumps, leaning against walls with bottles in hand. There is music coming from the room on the right. When I turn my head, I see a few girls dancing in a group, four or five of them in the centre of the room making a kind of lopsided circle. A sofa's been pushed beneath the window so that it's out of the way and under it is a carpet rolled into a tight coil. The girls raise their arms above their heads, letting their bodies dangle and drift below. One begins to sing along with extra feeling, the way people sing national anthems in old movies, and then another girl does too, placing her head on the first girl's shoulder. Her eyes are closed and she moves her hips slowly from side to side. It's weird watching non-dancers dance. Their bodies have no purpose and they don't care, let them hang soft and shameless and lazy. I wonder what these girls do in the evenings, what they think about when they go to bed, because this will be Sixty now, just a boring person.

Anushka tugs on my arm to pull me through the hallway. It's jammed with people but I out-talk my nerves. This is what I want, to dive into everything and think only about things that are in front of me, things I can actually see, the boys and girls who lean against the wall, their brown-glass bottles and plaid shirts and easy swear words and all the things that are just so hilarious right this second that their heads jerk whiplash-back. In the kitchen, someone says hi to Veronica, and she and Anushka are absorbed into the crowd, leaving me with a fridge to lean against or maybe the counter, the knobs of drawers to rest my hands on. There's a gap between two girls I don't know, an entry point, and I edge my way towards it because maybe then I'll be sucked in too.

Then I hear my name. I turn in the direction of the voice. Kareem has stepped in from the backyard and he's standing on the doormat, kicking his sneakers into a bit of thatched rug. There's another guy with him too, as tall as Kareem and probably as broad. They move towards me, heavy in the arms, and it looks funny to me, this carelessness in both of their bodies, as though I'm being approached by two animals from the same herd.

"Where's your beer?" Kareem asks.

I shrug and laugh like I think this is a pretty crazy oversight too. The laughter comes easily and it actually feels good. The other guy ogles Veronica's back and I turn so I can see what he's seeing. Her blonde hair hooks eyes. Veronica must hear something behind her, or maybe she can even feel the guy's stare, because she looks over her shoulder. The guy waves—I guess he knows her—and in a moment they're talking, Veronica tracing the thin skin inside her elbow with her finger while she presses one hip out.

"Georgia?" Kareem's looking at me like I've missed something. "Do you wanna go grab a beer?"

"Sure."

I expect Kareem to move in towards the fridge, but he gestures with his head to the back door.

"Let's go downstairs. There's another fridge there."

I don't get what the difference is, but I won't ask. I worry about getting separated from the other girls, but if I stay here, I'll have no one to talk to. We leave the kitchen and go down some carpeted stairs. The music down here is different. It's boy music with heavy bass and angry lyrics. The lights are dimmed and the ceilings are low. I follow him from one room into another. I can feel the air between my thighs as I move and I press my hands down the sides of my dress. There's a couch where a girl and guy are sitting together. Her legs are stretched over his lap and I can't see his face because it's stuck between her neck and her long hair. I feel a hand in mine and Kareem pulls me towards a corner. The suddenness of us touching, the private fleshiness of his palm, makes me nervous. But I tell my brain to screw off. This is what I want, all this normal stuff.

He goes to get us beer and I stand by myself, look at the people scattered around the periphery of the room. Some are leaning against the walls and others sit on the carpet with their backs curved and their legs crossed. I'm standing in the middle of everything, like a buoy popping high in a harbour. Kareem pushes a beer into my hand. Its coldness is surprising and reverberates all the way down my spine to its root. He brings the neck of his bottle to his lips and drinks. His Adam's apple bobs with each gulp and I see it like a shadow, something bulging in the dark. I bring my bottle to my lips and force back a sip. The beer tastes flat and sharp at the same time. I take a second sip and try to brace myself for the flavour with the muscles around my mouth. The effort aches at the base of my jaw but I gulp it back for as long as I can. This is just the thing that will help me. I want to be drunk now, badly. I have no idea how much I'll need to drink.

Kareem takes my hand again and pulls me towards the couch. The girl is sitting on the guy's lap, facing him with her legs parted and tucked beneath her. Kareem sits at the end away from them. I don't want to sit so close to the other couple, so I move to Kareem's other side and sit on the armrest.

"Is that comfortable?" he asks.

"It's okay." I try to fit more of my bum on the armrest. The covering is threadbare and the frame digs into the back of my thigh.

He takes another sip of beer. "You've got Ms. Franks for gym, right?"

"Yeah," I say, even though I don't know.

"She's a total hard-ass."

"Yeah. Pretty much."

"I've never actually had her," he continues. "But I've heard."

"Oh."

I try to think of something better to say. Nothing comes and after a few seconds it's been too long to add anything else. We're quiet. I look down at the spout of my beer bottle. I can't see the liquid inside of it and it occurs to me that it could be any colour, that I could be drinking something violet or radioactive blue. I bring it to my lips anyway and force down another sip. Then I feel a weight on my thigh. I look down. Kareem has placed his hand there, his fingers a little splayed. I keep my leg very still, as though I haven't noticed that he's touching me, even though all I feel is skin and weight and warmth. My heart's beating fast but I tell myself not to be stupid. This is how it works.

"Do you—" he starts to mumble.

"What?"

I feel him shift his position, pressing into my thigh to hoist his body towards me. His face is there, next to mine. I hold my chin very still. He presses his mouth into my mouth. It feels hot and suffocating and I turn my head in the other direction, so that his mouth slips to my cheek. His hand starts to squeeze my leg, one squeeze, then a shift, then a squeeze in this slightly altered position. I watch it as though I'm watching something that has nothing to do with me, like a bug crawling slowly across the floor. Kareem mutters again under his breath.

"What?" I whisper.

"Come here," he says.

He places his other arm around my lower back and pulls me towards him. I lose my balance and totter sideways and my hand juts out into his lap. I think he laughs at this, or at least chuckles. The girl at the other end of the couch stops what she's doing and looks at us. I hoist my body over Kareem's, as though I'm moving towards the aisle on an airplane, and sit on the cushion beside him.

He's closer to me now, and I feel him register this in his body, adjust his position so that his thigh touches mine. He brings his mouth straight onto mine. We start kissing. His mouth is hard at first, but then it loosens and he lets his lips drag against mine. I imagine what it looks like, up close and in the light, the wet pink part of his mouth snagging on the dry pink part of mine. There's a weight on my breast. The abruptness makes my heart pound. He cups my breast and then squeezes it, as though testing a tomato. It rubs my dress into my skin. His mouth is pushing harder now and I have to open my own to breathe. I feel his other hand move down my lower back and slip up my dress. I wiggle farther into the couch so that he can't get into my tights.

"You are so pretty." His lips are right against my ear. "Do you wanna go somewhere private?"

"Sure."

He has to lift his hand out of my dress to stand up, which is a huge relief. We walk back out through the first room and up the stairs. I don't know where he's going and I realize that I don't care, that one place is as good as any. My bum feels so strange that I want to go to the bathroom and look at it in the mirror. I want to touch it the way he just did so that I'll know exactly what it felt like to him. We step back into the kitchen and it's like coming up for air, everything bright and ordinary. I look around for Veronica and Anushka, but I don't see either of them. Kareem lets go of my hand and talks to a few guys we pass. He hands me another beer and I wonder what I did with the first one. One of the guys, the one with fuzzy hair that hangs in his eyes, nods hello at me. I pull on a strand of my own hair and nod back. Kareem turns to me a little and cocks his head towards the hall. He wants me to follow him, expects that I will.

"You coming?"

He looks at his friends and I do too. Their eyes are on me, not antagonistic, but I see that they could slip that way, animals deciding who they can trust. Kareem reaches his hand out. It's awkward for him; I can tell by the wooden way he holds his head, tilting it back as though it's pulled by string. I have nothing to do, so I may as well do anything. I move towards him, slide my palm into his.

We move down the hall. It's this easy, I think, this easy to do things you don't want to. I look at the carpet and watch my feet. Each step is a tiny betrayal. There's almost something delicious in this, ridiculous even, a big *fuck you* to myself. Kareem is staring ahead of him. We're moving up the stairs. His haircut tapers into two shaved points. I wonder what he's thinking. I look down at the darker hand pulling mine. The tendons in his wrist are sharp as wires. I think what I'm feeling is envy. Imagine wanting something so badly from another person that it turns into an action, that you pull her up the stairs.

Kareem lets go of my hand and moves ahead of me, opens the door beside the bathroom. I follow him inside. There's a small bed under the window, lower and maybe narrower than an ordinary bed. It's a kid's room. The comforter on it is a faded green that reminds me of camping, a green of water canteens and army vests and more than that too, earth fresh enough to smell. It's a boy colour but something makes me think the room belongs to a little girl. A giant flower is painted on the closet door and even though there's a rug with the image of a steam engine alongside the bed, I see fluffy animals on the bookshelf, a shingled dollhouse on the floor. Kareem closes the door. He walks across the room and hesitates over the bed. He looks big next to it, funny big, and I wonder whether we'll have sex on it, whether both of our bodies will even fit. He sits down on the rug.

"Are you gonna sit?"

I sit beside him. My foot covers the chimney of the train. I take a giant gulp of beer and then another one immediately after. I stay absolutely still to judge if I'm drunk. I think I might detect a new feeling in my head, something close to tiredness. The closet opposite is half open and I see small girl shoes on the floor, sandals with pink straps and the shine of patent leather. I feel the heat of Kareem before I see it, his face approaching mine. There's a funny look in his eye, or maybe what's funny is that there's no look, like a runner blind to everything but the finish line. His mouth is on mine and it feels soft in a gross way. I think of furless animals, puppies in pink sludge. I keep my arms at my sides until he's lifting my dress. I raise my arms, let him pull it over my head. Everything goes blue and sparkly until the neck un-catches from my nose. He looks at my boobs. I want to reach for my dress and cover them, but I know that it's supposed to go this way, that I have to let him look. He lies down on top of me and brings his lips to one of my nipples. The shock of it sends a bolt through my body, but then I realize that it doesn't feel bad. His hands course down the sides of me to the top of my tights, but then he stops, looks at the door like he's heard something. He gets up and pushes the dollhouse in front of the door, adjusts it again with his foot.

"Privacy," he says.

He comes back and lies down on top of me. We start kissing again, but the weight of him makes it impossible for me to kiss back. Instead I feel like I'm controlling traffic with my lips, trying to keep an open channel to my lungs so that I don't gag or choke. He gets his pants off in one swift motion and then takes off my tights and thong. He grabs his shirt from the cuff of the neck and yanks it forward. I wonder why he does it. His shirt could just as easily stay on and it's all skin now, gummy, inescapable. He lowers his chest on top of mine and his body blocks the overhead light. I prefer the shadows anyway.

I think about a million things while we have sex. I think about the pain first, but it lessens every time he rocks into me. In my head, I see a rock dropped into a pond, the ripples slowly dissipating until everything calms down again, goes still and smooth and numb. Then I think about Chantal. I picture the starved knobbiness of her body and wonder if you can get so skinny that sex becomes dangerous. Kareem's hips knock against me, and if my bones were deprived of normal nutrients, I bet they could crack in half. Then I think about Roderick, how he probably has sex just like this with other people. I try to find more things to think about but

Kareem gets louder as he moves around on top of me. It sounds like he's breathing through his mouth and his nose at the same time, and this makes it impossible for me to do anything but let his sweaty exhales slap my cheeks. If I could lift my arm I would smother his face with my hand, smush all his features together. He's moving faster and I just want it to stop. I start saying things under my breath that I know he won't be able to hear and I realize that I could laugh or stick my tongue out and he wouldn't have any idea.

"Get off," I whisper. "Get off, you jerk."

Finally Kareem arches his back and his eyes cross towards the bridge of his nose. There's a pause, and then he stands up and pulls on his pants. I want to get out of the room as fast as possible. I pull on my clothes, too, and tell him I need to find my friends. I step into the hallway and rush down the stairs. I feel weird between my legs and wonder if other people will notice, if I'm hobbling like someone who's been hurt but doesn't want anyone to know. There are still tons of people on the main floor. Veronica and Anushka are nowhere. I bring my hand to my forehead to see if I'm sweating, but my fingers tweak dry. The indoor air is stagnant, slowed by the hordes of people and smoke wafting in every time the door opens. If someone talked to me, maybe even just glanced in my direction, I think it would knock something over inside me. I find my parka where I left it in the corner, and when I think no one's watching, I go out the front door.

I run straight down the walkway and up the sidewalk in the direction from which we came. My feet pound the cement and the temperature's dropped more now, or maybe it's just that the wind has picked up, swings knives to the tips of my ears. I have to keep running so that if anyone sees me they won't have a chance to laugh at me, make me feel like a freak. I run all the way to Parliament Street, and when I stop, I'm so out of breath that it feels like my heart could burst through all its valves and ventricles and sputter onto the pavement. I bend over and suck new air in as slowly as possible, dip my head into my chest to encourage the oxygen to flow. When I feel as normal as I'm going to feel, I drag my feet forward.

I don't know much about this part of the city, except that it's not the kind of area where I should be walking alone at night. I don't see anyone on the sidewalk, but I hear sounds of downtown mischief, screeching car brakes and a siren coiling like a nearing storm. Some of the buildings I pass look like they've been deserted for centuries and shadowy alleys split one from the next. I hear something across the street. A man in sloppy sweatpants stands on the step of a convenience store and hollers something at the street. His jacket is open and I think I see the gleam of his exposed belly and it might be the ugliest thing in the world. I worry he's talking to me and I walk faster. The label of my dress scratches my back inside my coat but I can't fix it, don't want to feel the skin of my spine and remember that the night has its tongue on me. This is exactly the kind of neighbourhood where cars slow down and beg women to climb inside, take them to fields near the highway. I lift my purse and cross it over the opposite shoulder, as if the white vinyl strap will cover more of my body.

I think I'm heading south, although that doesn't really help me since I have no idea where I plan to go. My fists are in my pockets, fingerless. This is the craziest I've ever felt, and as soon as I've acknowledged this, I dare myself to prove it. I stop stiff as a mannequin and stare at the sky. A swath of murky velvet. There's a stoop to my left, some kind of oily coffee shop, and I decide that I'm just going to sit there until I figure out what to do next. I move towards it, check whether the stoop is slushy, but it's just salt crystals and boot grime, so I pull on the back edge of my parka and drop down. I can't stay outside for much longer. I wonder what time it is. Probably after midnight. On any normal day, I'd be fast asleep so that my muscles would be rested for rehearsal. I have nothing to do tomorrow; nothing to do the next day either. Stopping ballet will make new time, hours of it, and maybe that's what makes its loss unbearable, the mess of pointless minutes.

I pull a red fist free of my pocket and move my fingertips under my parka and dress, slowly up my tights. I guess I'm not expecting to find any difference and maybe that's the real ache, the inconsequence of the whole thing, borrowing a body the way you'd borrow a book. Can this be all that ordinary people want out of their muscles and bones? I get up off the stoop and start walking again, but every step is a battle against what's dawning on me, the nothingness of normal life. It's such a waste when I know another way of moving, a real way. I wrap my arms around my middle and remember Roderick's hands there. His touch wasn't disgusting because it was more than just one body perving over another one.

We were creating a perfection that mattered to us both. I swallow and feel the hugeness of this vibrate in my chest and collarbones. It's like the feeling before you burst into tears, a lump at the back of my throat and then the truth burning up my face. What have I done? Roderick must be collapsing now, suffocating with rage. I bet he's so angry that he wants to hurt me, would take my neck and snap it the wrong way. I push my fingernails into my thighs and let the sting of it sharpen the guilt. I've ruined everything. Roderick was my biggest supporter and I've done something so horrible that it's made him resign. The tears start running now. One drips off my nostril, another off the edge of my jaw.

And then I have an idea. Maybe it's just that I've exhausted myself from crying, but I think, suddenly, that it may not be too late. I may still be able to fix things. I remember the twenty dollars in my purse, step to the curb and look for a taxi. I figure I'll have better luck on Carlton and I jog in the direction I hope is south. As I near the intersection, I see a cab heading towards me, about a block away. I step out to the curb and wave my hand. The taxi pulls a giant U-turn and stops beside me.

I listen to my voice as I tell the driver the address. I wonder how it must sound to him, a stranger, whether it sounds like an address I've given a hundred times before. I watch the driver in the rear-view mirror as he nods. We pull back into traffic and drive south. I slip my hand into my purse so that I can pinch the twenty between two fingers. I smooth the other hand over my hair and pull on my dress so an inch of electric blue borders my parka.

Eighty-three Richmond Street looks silver in the moonlight. I give the driver my twenty and he gives me back some coins. It's only when I'm out of the car that I realize I didn't check the meter. Two glass doors with S-shaped handles lead into the building. The vestibule is shallow, just a few steps from the front door to the lobby, but as wide as the width of the building. Mailboxes line the wall to the left, silver as the building's exterior, and beside them is the apartment buzzer, a keyboard with a flat microphone mounted into the wall above. I walk over to it and skim my finger over the keys. They're formatted three in row, like a normal telephone. It's probably a four-digit buzz code—I know they usually are—and if I ever paid attention in math I'd know the number of potential combinations, probably even the most likely ones to pick.

There's a click behind, the sound of an opening door. A woman steps in from the lobby. She's wearing high heels, toes that direct her like arrows. Her steps echo to the ceiling and her pale hair is piled high on her head.

"Are you looking for someone?"

"Yeah."

She points to the two arrows above the number key. "You can scroll to the right name. Then just enter the buzz code."

"Thanks."

She waits for me to do something. I move my fingertips down the seam of my dress. It's a senseless, childish fidget and I do it intentionally, play the part of a lost kid. If I ring Roderick from here, he won't let me in.

"Who are you looking for?" she asks gently.

I say his name just loud enough to be heard.

"Oh, *Roderick*?" She adjusts her shawl over her shoulder. "I know Roderick. The choreographer?"

"Yeah."

"He's just down the hall from me." She takes a step towards the lobby door but pauses. "He's expecting you?"

"Yeah."

I watch her calculate the risk of letting me into the building. At first her focus is internal, but then she scrutinizes my hair, my face, the blue fabric orbiting below my parka. She walks to the lobby door and fans her handbag over the sensor. There's a sound of a distant click and she pushes the door open.

"He's 507."

I walk past her, thank her with my eyes. I take the elevator to the fifth floor. The hallway is quiet and I calm myself by absorbing the details of the decor, the shiny oak panels along the wall with sheets of mirror between the wood, like sandwiches of glass. There's adrenalin in my bloodstream. I feel the mechanics of it, the thud of every pump. I stop outside his door. My fingers are more than skin and bones. They feel huge and weightless simultaneously, like the long balloons that clowns twist into animals for kids. I knock.

I listen for sounds on the other side. I watch the peephole beneath the number, look for a shadow or the contour of an eye. Then the thought of actually seeing these things scares me and I look down at my feet. The door clicks. I raise my head just as it's pulled open. Roderick is standing in front of me.

I fumble backward a step or two and it looks like he does too. His head retreats as though he needs a wider angle to credit what he sees.

"Hi."

My voice sounds quiet and he doesn't say anything. I see nothing on his face. He's wearing jeans and a short-sleeved rugby shirt. I have never seen him in jeans before and I see all his arm hair now, a tangle of darkness.

"What do you think you're doing here?" It takes effort for him to ask this. I can hear it in his throat. "How the hell did you even get in?"

His expression is terrible, eyes small with hate. I begin to say that I'm sorry, but he isn't listening. He starts to close the door.

"Please don't. I . . . I really need to talk to you."

"You need to go. Now."

"Please!" I cry. "I am so sorry. I'm going to tell the truth."

"Keep your goddamn voice down."

"Please don't shut the door."

He moves to shut it fully.

"Please!"

His eyes jog down the hallway and they're sharp with rage. I have seconds to get it all out, so I start talking as fast as I can.

"I'm going to fix everything. I'll tell everyone the truth and you don't have to worry. There's something wrong with me and they're going to know that, so they'll believe it had nothing to do with you."

His hand is on the edge of the door, but he pauses now. I've had a tiny impact; I see it in his face.

"How?" When I haven't understood, he goes on. "Tell me how they'll believe you, Georgia?"

"I'll go to Mrs. Turnbull's office first thing Monday. I'll swear that I made it up."

He shakes his head tightly.

"I won't leave her office till they believe me," I add.

He frowns. "That won't do it." His hand adjusts on the door.

"I'll swear up and down. I'll give them a thousand reasons to believe me."

He pauses, thinking. Then his eyes climb the door frame. When they drop back to me, they stab with a new grit. "You tell them that I walked out of my office immediately that day."

I nod.

"You tell them that you came up with all those ideas yourself, that they were your own . . . deranged imaginings."

"I'll do that. I promise."

He looks at me differently, silent for a moment. "You little twit. What in god's name were you thinking?"

"I'm sorry."

"Do you know what this has done? Do you have any understanding of what you've done?"

"I . . . I'm really sorry."

"I'll never understand girls like you. Students who think . . ." His face winds into a smirk. "It's a shame because you're actually pretty damn good." He shakes his head again. "Now get the hell out of here before anybody sees you."

I leave his glass lobby and step out into the night. The air swings through me and I imagine my lungs like the doors to a saloon. I start to walk but the feeling stays with me. I wonder if it could drag me through the cement. What is a girl like me anyway? The question is stupid but awful. I look around like the answer could be here, hanging next to me or in the slush of sidewalk under my boots. I've never seen hate like that before, the venom that swirled in Roderick's eyes. He'll despise me forever now and the truth is that I deserve it. I am a girl like that, a sex girl, a girl who has cheapened everything. I feel it on my shoulders as I walk, a shame that tires my whole body. Two high-rises make skinny checkerboards to my right and a parking lot floats low in between. This neighbourhood is safer than the last one. Noises are closer to me, traffic just around the corner and I hear people too, the faraway hum of chatter. I cross my arms over my chest so that I can feel the bulk of my parka as though it's actually mine, new mass protecting my body. Even if I'm a girl like that, at least I probably won't get attacked here.

I reach into my purse, feel lint and wrappers and coins, and I pull out the big ones, jangle three toonies in my palm. It's not enough to get home. It'll probably cover a taxi to the Academy, but there's no entry to the residences after midnight. I'm not sure whether pay phones exist anymore but I decide I'll walk until I find one. At the intersection, I see a hot dog stand and, beside it, a short grey shelter with a blue overhang. I pick up my pace, squint to be sure.

I put two quarters into the slot and dial my mom's cell. It goes straight to her voice-mail. Sausage smoke surfs the cold air, and when I cough, I'm sure the hot dog man glares at me. I wonder where I can catch a bus. I'd ask the man, but his fingers are black from the barbecue and his mood looks burnt too, his face dewlapped with grumpiness. I remember the paper in my purse. It's crumpled into a cauliflower, but I manage to smooth it out enough to read and dial the hotel's number. They ask me for the room number and I read it off the page. In a second, my mom exhales a slipshod hello.

"I need you to get me."

I try to explain to her where I am. Richmond Street and something. She tells me to ask the nearest woman, but the hot dog man is the only person around. I describe the grey building towering behind me, the empty patio across the street. The panic in her voice gets worse.

"I'm fine. I'll just—" I look around in every direction. "Someone will walk along soon."

"Hey," the hot dog man calls out to me. "You looking for something, kid?"

"Yeah," I say. "I need to know where we are."

"Richmond Street and Peter."

I repeat the intersection to my mom and hang up the phone. The hot dog man keeps looking at me.

"You got someone coming to get you?"

"Yeah. I do."

He sticks out his lower lip and nods like this is a decent answer.

I lean against the phone booth and wait. I wonder if I look like a hooker but then I think that hookers probably don't wear coats or snow boots. I know that I'll never wear this dress again.

My mom's white car pulls up. I look at her profile through the bluish gleam of the window tint and try to prepare myself. I get inside and we just hug.

"Roderick didn't do anything, Mom. I think it was my fault."

She's craning her neck over her shoulder, trying to merge into traffic, but she drops the steering wheel. I see the purest shock sweep through her features, leave a dark crescent between her lips. "Thank god," she whispers finally.

"Aren't you mad?"

All she does is shake her head.

Outside the window, a group of guys are staggering out of a bar. They look about Isabel's age and I bet she'd call them jocks. We drive past them and I see a tree growing out of the sidewalk. Even in the darkness the leaves seem unbelievably green, webbed with a floss of snow.

"I don't even understand what I was doing," I say.

She leans over and squeezes my leg. "I understand," she whispers. "It's okay."

"It is?"

She turns to me, smiles sadly. "Well, I'm sure you had your reasons. I mean, I bet it's more complicated than just that."

"Yeah." The tree with green leaves shrinks behind us. I turn and watch my mom drive. I always thought her emotions ruined her, but now I'm not so sure. "It is complicated."

NINETEEN.

THE SUN WAKES ME UP because my mom hasn't put up blinds yet. She lives south of King Street in a restored heritage building where they used to make farm equipment. Her apartment has two loft-style bedrooms that remind me of hammocks, cocoa floors that look tied to the ceiling beams. I moved in a month ago and I sleep on a futon beside a wall of exposed brick left over from the factory. If you stand in the kitchen, the bricks look red, but from my futon they are the colours of mud and archaeology, terracotta, orange and brown. Four bricks are completely black, scattered illogically as moles, and an ochre stripe cuts through the wall's belly.

I like to trace my finger along the zigzags of ancient putty and push, search for a brick that's loosened.

My mom brings me a mug of coffee while I make my bun. I started drinking coffee when I moved in with her and I'm not sure if I actually like the taste. Caffeine is an addictive drug, though, and I like thinking about that as the hot liquid curls down into my esophagus. She watches me in the mirror.

"You might see some people you know today."

I reach for another hairpin and bore it through the mesh net on the back of my head. The trick is to glide the metal right against the scalp, as close as possible without piercing the vellum of skin.

"So?"

"Well, I just— Don't let it upset you." She crosses her arms over her chest, leans her hip into the wall beside the towel rack. She bought clothes to celebrate the divorce, shirts that are dry-clean only, and the one she wears now gapes low on her chest. "People are little shits. They gossip."

"I know."

"And nobody blames you for Roderick's resignation. He made that mess himself."

I smile at my mom for her own sake. She's referring to the uproar around Chantal's eating disorder, but her reassurance isn't necessary. I know Roderick's resignation had nothing to do with me because I fixed things, told everyone the truth. And the truth I told was even better than the real one, edited of all its grey zones and uncertainties, so that not even the scent of responsibility could be found on him. I understand something at last, maybe what Roderick has always been trying to teach me: that the rules of the real world just aren't suited to ballet. I've tasted something of this real world now and it is the saddest flavour imaginable, dreary as a piece of gum that's been in your mouth too long, that's waiting to be spat against the sidewalk.

"We should go. I want to be early."

The audition is in the company buildings on the waterfront. The Montreal School of Ballet is doing one day of tryouts in Toronto. The school doesn't have the same reputation as the Academy, but my mom and I agree it's best that I have a change. The leadership of the Academy is in transition anyway and it's hard to be sure of its future.

From the car window the lake is a sheet of tinfoil stretched taut to the horizon, and there's a gummy smell of seagulls and algae. The sky has the pallor of morning, like a face that's not quite awake. We park underground and the wind cuts under my nose as we cross the street. I cover my bun as though it might blow away.

As we step into the building, my mom's phone rings and she fumbles through her purse to pull it out. She answers, says, "Oh hi, Isabel," and looks at me with a question in her eye. I can't imagine why Isabel is calling. She came to my mom's apartment two weeks ago, faced us on the sofa with her hands curved around a mug of tea, and asked whether ballet was making me happy anymore.

"Is it really the healthiest environment for you?" she said, her gaze level and lacking shame, as if her question were somehow acceptable. When I didn't answer she turned to my mom. "I just . . . I wonder if there's something not right about it."

"What exactly?" my mom asked.

Isabel sat unmoving, her eyes on the terracotta bricks.

"The stuff with Roderick is over," I told her.

"It's not that," Isabel said.

"Then what?"

After a moment, she just sighed and offered up an empty palm, claimed it was nothing she could put her finger on.

Now my mom pushes the phone at me. "I think Isabel just wants to wish you luck."

But there's no way I want to hear the falseness of this, the empty sound of Isabel saying things she doesn't mean. I take a step away and shake my head, hear my mom be sweetly obliging, invent something about my having already gone up to the studios.

I sign in at a desk in the lobby and climb the wide staircase to the change room. The junior school auditions aren't until the afternoon and the senior girls are scheduled to be seen one at a time. It's much harder to get into a ballet school when you're older. I'm trying out for grade ten and they're unlikely to accept more than a couple of girls. But I'm not worried. Even as I climb the stairs, the old feeling enlivens my muscles, like I've smoked drugs that make them supernatural. It's like sleeping in your own bed when you've been away for a week, a private warmth that you can't explain to anyone. I know now for sure that this is what my body was meant for, that

I have no interest in what normal bodies do. I'll be accepted. I close my eyes and feel the certainty swell in my heart.

A swinging door opens into the changing area. I get a smell memory like an ice-cream headache, hairspray and baby powder rushing up my nose. I pull on my bodysuit and tights and move to the mirror. A girl hunches over the far sink. Her spine pops out of her leotard, each vertebra big as a marble. She has her foot angled under the tap so that the water hits the heel of her pointe shoe. I wonder why she's prepping her pointe shoes now, whether she's been in for her audition yet. I'm about to ask her when she lifts her head. It's Chantal. I feel my eyes get as big as hers do. She unhitches her leg from the sink and in a second we're hugging. She squeezes tight and I match her grip, like we're both worried the other might slip away.

"I can't believe you're here," she says.

"Me neither."

She moves away from me and we look at each other. Her face is the same illuminated storm it used to be, and there's flesh on her cheeks again. Her curvy lips force them upward into bumps round as Christmas balls. We both realize we're listening to the tap run and we start to laugh at the same time. She goes to turn it off and I scan up and down her body. She's still brittle in her thinness, but her thighs widen at the tops. She might not look completely starved.

"I've been training privately." She starts telling me what she knows about the audition, who will be on the panel and how many girls they're likely to see. Her voice is the same breathy rush of passion, overwhelming her tongue and lips so that she almost can't keep up.

"It's Vaganova method. So keep your arms back. And aim for height above all else. They love dancers like us, gumby ones who can do anything. And look"—she holds out her arm—"I stayed really thin, huh?"

I feel a bit weird about this question, and at first I'm just going to shrug. But the shrug isn't truthful. She'll have to stay skinny if she wants to make it, and if they let her out of the hospital, she must be healthy enough.

"You did," I say. "That's good."

Her face goes bright. "We should be roommates," she says. "If we both get in."

"Yeah. That'd be nice."

Her big lips part and she takes my hand. "*Merde*, Georgia."

I grab my pointe shoes and we hug once more.

The company building is nothing like the Academy. It's only a year or two old and it has the uncluttered feel of a well-designed kitchen, spacious rooms unhampered by doorways, steely surfaces that reflect bodies and light. I walk slowly up the staircase to the third-floor studios. It feels funny that I ran into Chantal here, a coincidence that seems like a symbol. We've both travelled back from nether regions of the universe to find ourselves in exactly the same place.

There are arrows that mark the way to the studio entrance. I follow them and end up in a small foyer, with a metre of practice barre mounted to the wall and a young woman with a clipboard. She asks my name and ticks it off on her list. She tells me I have about ten minutes. I place my hand on the barre because it's there for me and go through the ritual of rolling up onto *relevé* and then rolling back down.

"They'll take a five-minute break when this girl's done." The woman points to the closed studio door. "Then you're in."

I wait for my nerves to ricochet. Nothing happens. I breathe in and marvel at the easy flow of my exhale. There's the sound of applause in the studio, then movement around the door. It opens towards me and a girl steps out. I've never seen her before but I recognize everything about her, the make of her pointe shoes, the cut of her leotard, the way she's pinned her bun. The assistant hands her a water bottle and the girl tears off the plastic cap and drinks.

"You're in," the assistant tells me.

I step into the studio. The audience is on my left. It comprises several rows of foldout chairs and it's bigger than I'd anticipated. I figure there may be a hundred people. My mom is in there somewhere, but I won't look. The impulse triggers a memory, though: Isabel in the audience the year before with a thumb stuck up in front of her nose, grinning. Then I picture her as she faced me last on the sofa, the limp sulk of her disapproval. I shake the image off and feel the grit of what I love charge up my middle, and I tighten my thoughts around what I'm about to do, and then, for a second, I think about Roderick.

The panel is set up in front of the first row. There are four people behind a long, collapsible table and the grand piano is to their left. The man at the end of the table stands up to greet me. He tells me they need a moment to get organized and I stand beside the mirror, covered with brown paper for the audition, and stretch through my feet one last time.

"All right, Miss Slade." The man waves his hand, as if to say *proceed*.

I move to the centre of the studio. The pianist plays the introductory chords of the variation. I step into the first pose.

Acknowledgements

My deepest thanks to my agent, Clare Alexander, and my editor, Lynn Henry, for their invaluable insight, expertise, and encouragement. I am also indebted to Kristin Cochrane, Nita Pronovost, Ruta Liormonas, and everyone at Doubleday Canada; Andrew Cowan and Anna Stein; and David Higham Literary Associates for their generous award. I am grateful, as ever, to my family and should mention particular help from Michael Schabas and Veronica Lam in London. A thousand last thanks to my dearest friends and readers: Divya Ghelani, Fadi Hakim, Katherine Orr, Natasha Negrea, Ariadne Siotis, Jessica Somerton, and Michael Wheeler.